NOVA

KINGS OF RETRIBUTION MC LOUISIANA

CRYSTAL DANIELS

SANDY ALVAREZ

TWO PENS-

CRYSTAL *Daniels*

Sandy ALVAREZ

-ONE STORY

1

NOVA

My eyes pop open at the sound of my phone vibrating against the surface of the nightstand. With my face still plastered against my pillow, I grab my phone, turn it over, and peer at the dimly lit screen. "Shit." Something or someone set off the security alarm at the clubhouse. Throwing the sheet to the side, I climb out of bed. Crossing my bedroom, I grab the pair of jeans I stripped out of a few hours ago, slide them on, and grab a shirt from the basket of folded clean clothes Piper left sitting on a chair nearby.

My phone rings. Swiping the screen, I answer the call. "Talk to me," I tell my brother, Riggs, as I shrug my cut on over my shoulders, then step into my loosely laced leather boots I toed off just outside the master bathroom.

"I need you to ride out and check on things. Momma and munchkin both have low-grade fevers. I'd go, but I've been up since we closed the bar, and need to be here."

I remember those days. Minus the wife part. "Already on it," I inform him and make my way down the hall, stopping long enough to open Piper's bedroom door, checking on her before heading out. "Have you heard from Everest?" I ask, knowing he is the only one at the clubhouse other than Payton and Josie. Usually, Fender would be there too, and I wouldn't have to worry about a walkthrough, but he's out of town. In Nashville, to be precise, handling some personal shit to do with his family.

"Yeah. He's got the place on lockdown until you arrive, just in case."

I nod. Safety first. With Everest being alone with the women, it's wise that he waits for backup. The club has gone through too much shit over the past year to risk him checking out the property alone. Wars between gangs have been brewing in the Crescent City over the past few months. Crime is at an all-time high. Gang violence is running rampant, polluting the streets with drugs and death. "Take care of your family, brother. I'll shoot you a text once I get there and check things out."

"Stay safe."

"Always," I respond before disconnecting the call and sliding my phone into my pocket.

Once downstairs, I walk into the kitchen, taking a moment to write a note for my daughter on the dry erase board hanging on the refrigerator door, letting her know I ran to the clubhouse and that I would be home soon. I smile as I write *I love you Bean* at the bottom. Sometimes I can't believe how much time has gone by, and think about how little she once was and the young woman she is growing up to be.

Disarming the security system, I open the door leading to the garage, then close it behind me after stepping out. Punching in the code, I secure my home and the single person of value, still asleep in her bed upstairs. As the garage door lifts open, I mount my bike. A custom black chopper, with kick-ass airbrushed blue flames fanning down the gas tank. It's just one of three bikes I own.

The horsepower of the engine thunders as I bring her to life and pull down the driveway. Rolling to a stop, I wait for the garage door to lower completely before taking off down the long road and watch my house disappear in my side mirror.

Out here, where I live, it's as dark as night can get. As loud as my bike's engine purrs, I can still hear the calming peaceful sounds of the bayou. Eventually, I pass my Pop's place, and the home my brother and I grew up in. Once Piper came into my life, I knew raising her out here, where my soul always feels at peace, was the best choice to make.

The muggy air whips at my face as I travel down the road, and memories of the years gone by invade my headspace. My brother was always the driven one. He knew what he wanted in life from an early age and excelled at everything he set out to do, including following in my Pop's footsteps and joining the military. For me, it wasn't always that black and white. I was restless and a little unfocused. I had no idea what I wanted to do with my life, never satisfied, or wanting to settle. That was, until Piper came into my life, and I became the Enforcer for The Kings of Retribution MC. My grandmother once told me I had a little touch of my mother in me. A gypsy soul. That I was born a free spirit. I'd like to say that not having my mother in my life didn't bother me, but that would be a lie. A part of me is broken from her abandoning my brother and me. Not to take away from my grandparents, they did the best they could, and until this day, I'm still amazed by the strength, love, and devotion they gave us. They helped shape me into the man I am today.

Increasing my speed, the early morning air hits my skin a little harder, and I breathe it deep into my lungs, reenergizing my system.

Before long, I'm taking the exit to downtown, winding through the city as she sleeps, slowing as I turn onto the frontage road near the clubhouse. In the distance, I catch two dim lights near the fence line closest to the river on the far side of our property.

Bringing my bike to a stop, I pull my phone from the inside of my cut, swipe the screen, and pull up Everest's number.

"Hey, brother."

"We have ourselves a couple of trespassers by the shed near the river."

"Where are you now?"

Cutting my bike's engine, I throw the kickstand down. "Down the road. I don't want these assholes to get away." Dismounting my bike, I take a look around before squatting and opening a concealed compartment, retrieving a loaded Glock. "You come up on them from the front side and I'll come in from the back. I don't want them to have anywhere to run beside the mighty Mississippi." Ending the call I stand, tuck my phone away, and slide my weapon into the back waistband of my jeans.

It takes only a few moments to get to the edge of our property, then I proceed to follow the fence line until happening upon the spot our visitors entered, along with fence cutters laying on the ground. Instead of going further, I wiggle my large frame through the barely big enough opening, covering my ass in mud, and ripping a hole in my jeans along the way. "Dammit." I get to my feet.

Reaching behind my back, I grab my gun and stealthily make my way toward the dumb fucks who decided it would be a good idea to enter Kings property. It's not long before I catch sight of Everest's massive frame moving along the side of the clubhouse, staying in the shadows.

Peering around the corner of the shed, I find two dipshits trying to gain entrance into the building, with one guy standing on the other's shoulders, trying to crawl through the high narrow window. Still in the shadows, with only the moonlight shining on my face, I raise my arm. "You are some dumbass motherfuckers." The sound of my voice startles the guy holding his friend, and he bolts, leaving his accomplice hanging with only his ass and legs exposed. Unfortunately for him, he smacks right into Everest, bouncing off his solid chest.

"What the fuck dude?" the guy dangling from the window harshly whispers. Taking a few steps forward, I reach up, grab the scrawny shit by the back of his pants, and yank him from the window. His sorry ass falls to the muddy ground like a sack of potatoes. The moment he looks up and sees me hovering above him, with the barrel of my gun pointing at his face, his eyes widen with fear.

"Get the fuck up," I order, and he slowly stands on wobbly legs. I look to Everest who has the other guy by the nape of his neck, and the barrel of his weapon pressed firmly against his ribcage. "What do you say we show these two what they were after?" I do nothing to hide my smirk. Nodding, Everest leads the way, keeping his hold of one guy as I plant my palm between the shoulder blades of his friend, shoving him forward. "Move it."

The rusty hinges on the heavy metal door squeak as it swings open. Flipping the switch on the wall, the fluorescent overhead lights flicker on, illuminating the inside of the shed. The two punks take a good look around. Everest and I push them into the center of the room, finally getting a good look at their faces. "Fuckin' hell." They're just kids. "You two look young enough to have your mommas still wipin' your asses."

"Fuck you," the older looking of the two spits, his voice cracking.

"Do you even realize whose property you broke into?" I ask them.

"We know who you are, and we don't give two shits." The little asshole juts out his chin, balling his fists at his sides. I take in his attire, noticing the gang colors he's wearing, and his friend standing beside him, mute, is wearing the same.

"Don't try my patience, kid. You don't have enough hair on your balls to bow up to me like that." I circle them, their eyes following my every move. Breaks my fucking heart seeing kids caught up in the gang lifestyle, guided by the wrong people, idolizing thugs as if they were gods. Both out here on the streets trying to play the part of a man before their balls have even dropped. "Look around you." I spread my arms wide. "Since you two want to act like men, maybe we should show you what we do to men who trespass on our property and attempt to steal from The Kings." I choose my words carefully, trying to strike enough fear in them to do some good. The youngest of the two finally finds his voice. "Trent, man. I don't want to die." His voice trembles.

They don't know it, but I have no intention of harming either one of them. They are just kids for Christ's sake.

"We won't come back here again. I swear," Trent's buddy adds, looking at me with pleading eyes.

"Where do you live?" I question them, my arms crossed over my chest. They look at each other for a moment before Trent himself speaks up.

"Bellview apartments over on 34th Street."

"Is he your brother?" I question, seeing a little resemblance. The kid nods. "I'm going to assume your parents have no idea where you two are?" I raise my brow, and Trent lowers his eyes to the ground, giving me the answer I was looking for. "They know you go around sporting gang colors?"

"No," Trent says.

"I'm going to take a guess here that you aren't even a part of a gang." Again, their faces prove that I hit the nail on the head. "Not smart kids. Wearing those colors will get you killed by not only rival gangs but the gang you are falsely representing." I breathe slowly through my nose. "Everest."

"Yeah?"

"See to it these two get back home," I tell him.

"You got it." I stay rooted in my spot and watch Everest lead them out of the shed, then follow as we cross the property.

While the two kids climb into the cab of Everest's truck, I stop him.

"Do a little investigating. Find out if their family needs assistance in any way. Prevention starts at home." I clap him on the shoulder. Everest does a lot of volunteer work with inner-city youth. If they want it, he can help them seek resources and hopefully get these two off the streets before something happens and they end up altering their lives forever. "I'll stick around until you get back."

Forty minutes later, Everest returns, and Riggs has been filled in on what went down. Leaving the clubhouse on foot, I walk back to my bike parked down the street. I'm running on two hours of sleep, and two cups of coffee Josie brewed for me while I waited at the clubhouse. Throwing my leg over my bike, I fire up the engine. With the sun rising at my back, I head home.

My ass is dragging by the time I get home. The smell of freshly brewed coffee and bacon frying puts a little pep in my step as I enter the kitchen, finding Piper at the stove cooking breakfast while she bobs her head to the music playing from her phone sitting on the countertop.

How did it go from me taking care of my daughter to her taking such good care of me? I toe my boots off, sit them on the rug near the patio door, and listen to her hum to the music. I watch her, taking in how happy she is this morning, almost afraid to blink because if I do, she'll be a grown woman. And I don't think my heart is ready for that yet.

Piper looks at me. "Hey, Daddy."

I smile at her. "Mornin', Bean."

Piper looks so much like her mother. Tall, slender, long dark hair. The resemblance stops there. My blood turns cold at the mere thought of Madison. She was the one woman I tried having an actual relationship with. She seemed to be okay with my way of living and didn't mind the weeks I spent away working on offshore rigs. I worked on a 14/14 rotation. I was gone two weeks then off two weeks. In my twenties, it suited my lifestyle. I wasn't tied down to anyone and had no responsibilities aside from myself and making sure my grandparents were doing well.

Three months into our relationship, I came home to find her screwing some piece of shit in my bed. I decide to commit to one woman, and she screws the shithead in the apartment next to mine. Within a week, she had disappeared. I heard she left town with a stranger passing through. I'd all but forgotten about her until she showed up months later, with a crying baby in a car seat. That very day changed the course of my life. Of course, I allowed her to stay with me, but two days later, I woke up to find her gone, leaving my daughter behind. I had no idea what to do. No clue about taking care of a baby. Funny how things work out. My daughter has been the best thing to ever happen in my life. She gave me purpose and direction. Piper keeps me grounded.

Walking past her, I pause, kissing the top of her head.

"I hope you're hungry." She flips the bacon, then cracks an egg in the same skillet. "Everything okay?"

"Starving," I admit, then add, "I'm good, baby girl. Just tired is all. It's been a long mornin'." Striding across the kitchen, I grab the mug sitting beside the coffee maker, filling it to the rim. "So." I take my coffee to the kitchen table and relax. "Semester tests start today, right?" I slump down on the chair, stretching my legs out in front of me.

Piper retrieves two plates from the cabinet. "Yeah. I'm exempt from all of my exams except biology." She rolls her eyes and begins to plate the food. "One lousy point. That's all I needed to get out of that one." She crosses the kitchen, placing breakfast on the table, sitting across from me. The two of us fall silent for a moment. As I lift a bite of food to my mouth, I glance across the table. I can tell my daughter wants to ask something by the way she's poking at her food and biting her lower lip.

"Spit it out, Bean." I grin, popping a piece of bacon into my mouth.

"A few of my friends are going to Grand Isle this weekend, and I was wondering if I could go?"

"Piper, we've talked about this before."

"It's only for the day. Come on, Daddy. Please."

Shit. I don't know how other fathers do it, but I'm finding it very hard to let go and let my little girl, who is not so little anymore, spread her wings. I pinch the bridge of my nose and lean back in my chair. I'm not sure if it is delirium from the lack of sleep or the fact that I don't want to stifle her spirit that has me considering her request, but I am. Piper is a good kid. A straight-A student, and never gets into trouble. "Which friends do you want to go with?" I ask and her eyes light up, hopeful that my inquiry will lead to the answer she is looking for.

"Sara, Heather, Dylan, Troy." There is a short pause. I know she's going to say his name, and my insides cringe. "And Colton."

Her boyfriend of almost a year. I hate boys. Loath them. I know what they are thinking, and I know he's thinking about those things with my beautiful daughter. If I could have it my way, she wouldn't have a boyfriend or start dating until she is at least thirty. "If I say yes to this little adventure, you have to promise that you will keep in touch with me. Every hour on the hour. No texting either. You call me. Got it?"

Piper leaps from her chair, throwing her arms around my neck.

"Oh my God! Thank you!" She squeezes me tighter, and I hug her back. She pulls away, and I notice how happy she is, but tears fill her eyes.

"What's wrong?"

Her smile lights up her face. "I'm just happy, dad. You're trusting me to travel on my own, without you, or one of the guys tagging along to chaperone. It's a huge step." She embraces me again. "I'm so proud of you." I hear the playfulness in her voice, and I poke her side, causing her to laugh.

"Who's the parent here, smartass?" I grin, looking up at her.

Piper shrugs. "That's debatable sometimes." She laughs again. "I need to get ready for school. Finish your breakfast then get some sleep," she throws over her shoulder as she turns to leave.

"Don't make me change my mind, Bean. Oh, and one more thing. No sex," I throw the last part out before her foot hits the stairs.

"Dad, we've had this talk, like a million times."

"And what have I always told you?" I ask with a mouth full of food.

"Ugh, come on," Piper whines.

"Piper," I say in a stern voice, and her arms fold across her chest with a huff.

"The right one is worth waiting for," she grumbles under her breath as she bounds up the stairs to her room.

2

PROMISE

The courtroom falls silent as the only eyewitness in the Velasco case makes his way to the stand. My client, Leon Velasco, is on trial for the murder of Eddie Melba, a sixty-three-year-old man who was the owner of a gas station where he was shot to death while working the graveyard shift. Ever since a guy named Kostas disappeared from New Orleans months ago, Leon Velasco has taken over running drugs in the city. It appears whenever one dealer is taken down, another one quickly takes their place. Although rumor is Velasco is the top boss, whatever that means. All I know is the cycle never stops, which brings us to today. Mr. Melba was simply in the wrong place at the wrong time when a stray bullet pierced through the window of his convenient store, striking him in the chest. Eddie Melba was dead before he made it to the hospital. He leaves behind a wife of thirty-five years and a son. Both of them are in the courtroom today. I can't bring myself to look over my shoulder to where they are seated. Because the truth is, I'm no better than the man sitting to my left, the one currently sending death glares to the young man on the stand. Robby Hunter is a twenty-two-year-old who spends his life on the streets. The young man spent his teen years in and out of juvie and has been arrested half a dozen times in the last two years, all drug-related charges. These things are what I'm going to use against him today. I will use his past and his criminal record to discredit him on the stand. As much as I hate to do so, it is my job. I'm a defense attorney. I spend countless hours helping men like Leon Velasco. The rats of society, the scum of the criminal underground. With each case I win, I find myself questioning my choice to keep doing what I do.

"Miss Bailey," the judge calls my name, bringing me out of my wandering thoughts.

"Do you wish to cross-examine the witness?"

I stand from my chair, smooth out my skirt, and put my usual game face on. The cold one I have adopted since becoming a lawyer. "Yes, your honor."

My face stays expressionless as I approach the stand where Robby Hunter's eyes shift from the judge to me and then over my left shoulder to where my client sits. I note the way his pupils constrict and his bloodshot eyes. Mr. Hunter has a history of heroin abuse, and it is clear he's on something now. "How are you today, Mr. Hunter?"

"Fine." Mr. Hunter fidgets in his seat.

"Are you okay? Would you like a glass of water before we begin?"

"No."

"Alright, then. I'll begin by asking you where you were on the night of June sixth, at approximately one o'clock in the morning?"

"Um...was that the night the old dude was shot?" Mr. Hunter asks, his voice shaking.

"Yes, Mr. Hunter. The night in question is when Mr. Melba was shot and killed."

"I uh... I was sitting under the bridge across the street from Mr. Melba's gas station."

"What were you doing under the bridge at one o'clock in the morning, Mr. Hunter?"

"Objection, your honor. Relevance?" the state's attorney jumps in.

"Withdrawn, your honor." I turn my attention back to the witness. "Can you tell the court what you saw that night, Mr. Hunter?"

"I saw that man over there," he points to Leon Velasco, "pull up and park in the empty parking lot next to the gas station. Another car pulled up, and two men got out, then Velasco climbed from his car."

"Then what happened?"

"They looked to be talking and were there for a few minutes before I heard gunshots."

"What did you do when you heard the gunshots, Mr. Hunter?"

"I ran and ducked behind the bridge pillar."

"If you were hiding, how did you see my client allegedly fire a weapon?"

"When I heard tires squealing, I peeked and saw Leon Velasco shooting a gun at the car that was driving away."

"And you're positive it was Mr. Velasco you saw in the parking lot that night? How many yards would you say the bridge is from the empty lot?"

"I don't know."

"Well let me enlighten you then, Mr. Hunter. It is twenty yards. Not only were you sixty feet away, but it was the middle of the night. Are you positive it was my client you saw that night when you were twenty yards away in the dark hiding behind a pillar?"

"Look. I saw what I saw, lady."

I ignore Robby Hunter's frustrated remark and keep going. "Is it also true you were under the bridge that night to buy drugs? And were you, in fact, high at the time of the incident, Mr. Hunter?"

"Objection, your honor!" The state's attorney flies out of her seat.

"Sustained. Please continue, Miss Bailey."

Given the go-ahead by the judge, I continue my line of questioning. "Were you high the night of the incident, Mr. Hunter?"

The witness begins squirming in his seat, his eyes darting around the courtroom. He shrugs. "I may have had a hit of something. I don't know."

"So you're telling us, with it being dark outside, and you being roughly twenty yards away from the scene of the crime, plus you were high as well, you can positively identify Mr. Velasco as the shooter?"

"I...I," Robby Hunter stammers. "I don't know. I could have made a mistake. Maybe it wasn't him I saw."

"You made a mistake? It might not have been Mr. Velasco you saw that night? Is that what you are telling the court?"

"Yeah. I guess so."

"You guess so?" I take another step closer to the stand. "Are you high now, Mr. Hunter?"

"I may have had a little something earlier," Robby Hunter confesses under pressure, and the courtroom fills with murmured voices.

I turn to the judge. "Your honor. Clearly the state's only witness holds no credibility. Not only is he under the influence now, but he admits to his drug use the night he allegedly saw my client."

The judge addresses the state attorney. "Mrs. Williams, do you have anything to add?"

"No, your honor. We have no other witnesses."

The judge slams the gavel. "Court will adjourn while the jury reaches a verdict."

"All rise," the deputy orders as the judge steps down from the bench and exits the courtroom.

An hour later, I'm at a deli across the street from the courthouse grabbing lunch when I get the call the jury is back with a verdict. When I arrive back in court, I can feel the tension in the room. The victim's family is visibly nervous while my client oozes confidence and looks almost bored.

"Will the jury foreperson please stand?" the judge asks.

A middle-aged man at the end of the jury panel stands.

The judge speaks again, "Has the jury reached a unanimous verdict?"

"Yes, your honor, we have."

"Please pass it to the deputy."

The jury foreperson passes a piece of paper to the deputy, who hands it to the judge. I try to read the judge's face as he opens the paper but his features reveal nothing. The whole courtroom watches nervously and patiently for the verdict to be read.

"For the crime of murder the jury finds the defendant, Leon Velasco not guilty. Mr. Velasco, you are free to go." The judge bangs the gavel.

As soon as the judge makes his ruling, the victim's wife breaks down in sobs as her son consoles her. I chance a glance in their direction, finding the victim's wife and son distraught. I then look back at my client who is smirking. I follow his line of sight to see he too is looking at the victim's family. The victim's son looks at me, and I don't like what I see—sorrow and defeat. My stomach sinks. I want nothing more than to run out of the courtroom. Instead, I keep my usual stone expression plastered on my face and turn my attention to Leon Velasco. "Congratulations, Mr. Velasco." Then I gather my files, stuffing them into my briefcase.

"Thank you, Miss Bailey." Mr. Velasco stands and buttons his suit coat.

I don't bother making conversation with the man. The three months I have been working this case I have rebuffed countless inappropriate passes from him. I even get weekly flower deliveries to the office. All from Leon Velasco. His attention toward me is borderline creepy. It makes me uncomfortable and what I want is to get as far away from him as possible. Once I have my things, I turn on my heel and walk out of the courtroom. The moment I step outside, I release the breath I was holding and tip my head back, allowing the Louisiana sun to warm my face. I stand in place while taking several deep cleansing breaths.

Hearing the doors to the courthouse open behind me, followed by a commotion, I look over my shoulder to see Mr. Velasco exit the building along with several of his men flanking him. He makes eye contact with me and smirks. He's slimy and knows he is guilty. Men like Velasco don't care about right or wrong. They have no remorse. As for me, it eats me up inside. It's cases like this one that keep me up at night. On the outside, I'm good at coming off as cold and ruthless as the criminals I defend, but on the inside, I hate what I do. I do it to please my stepfather. But lately, I find myself wondering if my family is worth sacrificing my conscience and my heart. I have spent more than half of my existence trying to please Thomas Collins, doing whatever it takes to gain his acceptance.

Ever since my mother married Thomas when I was a little girl, I craved his fatherly affection. Since losing my biological dad to war when my mother was pregnant with me, a father figure is something I missed and desperately wanted. The day I gained a new dad, a sister, and a brother, I was ecstatic. Only I soon learned their feelings were not mutual. Thomas wasn't always cold and distant toward me. Back when my mother was still alive, he at least tolerated my existence. But something in him changed when we lost her. To Thomas Collins, I will forever be the stepdaughter he was stuck with when my mother died.

My phone rings, knocking me from my daze, and I tear my eyes from Velasco. Digging my phone from my bag, I see London, my best friend's name flash across the screen. "Hello?"

"Hey. How was court?" I let out an audible sigh. My best friend, who knows me better than anyone, doesn't have to ask another question. She knows. "Want to come over to my place? I have a bottle of wine with your name on it."

I smile. "Have I told you lately how much I love you?"

"I love you too. Now, what time are you coming? I'm leaving the office now. I should be home in twenty minutes."

I look down at my watch. "Maybe an hour. I need to stop by the office before heading your way."

"Alright, girl. See you then."

I hang up with London and make my way to my car. Unlocking it with my key fob, I open the door and toss my bag and briefcase onto the passenger seat, but before I get the chance to slide in, a hand grips my arm, stopping me. My breath catches in my throat when I come face to face with Leon Velasco.

"Miss Bailey, you walked away before I could ask you to dinner. A celebration of sorts."

I swallow the lump in my throat. "I'm sorry, Mr. Velasco but I'm going to decline your invitation to dinner. I have to get back to the office."

Leon Velasco studies me, his face hard. I can tell he doesn't like my turning him down. Just like he didn't like the numerous times I confronted him on his sending me flowers. His grip on my arm tightens briefly. "Perhaps some other time, Miss Bailey." He lets me go and I breathe a sigh of relief.

Mr. Velasco steps away and starts making his way back across the parking lot to where his men are waiting for him next to a black SUV. He gets about ten feet from me when he stops and turns. "I'll be seeing you around, Miss Bailey."

Five minutes later I'm sitting in traffic and my phone rings again. This time it's Thomas.

"Where are you?"

Typical Thomas. He can't so much as say hi. "I just left. I'm on my way back to the office now."

"How'd it go?" he asks.

"Mr. Velasco is a free man." Thomas's only response is a grunt. Again, not surprised.

"I'll be out of the office by the time you arrive. I'm taking Avery to dinner." I roll my eyes and don't get a chance to say another word before the line goes dead.

Avery is my stepsister and three years younger than me—twenty-nine to my thirty-two. Avery is also spoiled to no end, and the biggest bitch I know. What's worse is she's a daddy's girl and has Thomas wrapped around her finger. She is lazy and has no ambition. Her biggest worry in life is deciding what color her nail polish should be. And her only goal in life seems to be spending her dad's money until she finds some rich, spineless loser to marry and do the same to him. Growing up, Avery made it her mission to make my life a living hell. I'm the orphan her dad was stuck with raising and she never lets me forget it.

Then there is Jackson, my stepbrother. He, on the other hand, is a great brother and nothing like his sister. Jackson is a couple of years older than me and is also a lawyer. He knows how difficult my life has been with Thomas and Avery and has always been an ally of mine. Jackson resents the way his father treats his sister. Jackson and I busted our butts in law school to make Thomas proud while Avery skirts through life as a freeloader. Jackson has voiced his opinion on several occasions, telling his father he needs to make Avery grow up, but Thomas sees nothing wrong with his precious daughter. Hell, I'm not even blood, yet I followed in Thomas's footsteps right alongside Jackson, and I still get treated like an outcast. I sometimes wonder why Thomas offered me a job at his firm in the first place when I passed the bar. I think it's because he still feels he owes it to my mother. My mom has been gone for years, and the one good thing I can say about my stepfather is he adored her.

Just after my sixteenth birthday, we lost my mom in a skiing accident. Me, my mother, Thomas, Jackson, and Avery were on a trip to the mountains. Our second day there I decided to try my hand at skiing and begged my mom to take me. Once we were out on the slope, I realized I forgot my helmet. Mom gave me hers. Neither one of us thought there was any real danger to not wearing one. We were wrong. Twenty minutes into our adventure mom lost her footing and fell backward, hitting her head on the snow-covered ground. She insisted she was fine and was back on her feet within minutes. She even had a good laugh at how clumsy she had been. We skied and goofed around for another hour until mom started complaining of a headache. We went back to the cabin where everyone else was and watched a movie while lounging in front of the fire. Mom seemed fine by the time I went to bed. She even said her headache was getting better. But the next morning, we found out mom was not fine. She had died in her sleep. The doctors said the cause of death was a hematoma caused by a blow to the head. It was a freak accident. That day will go down in history as the worst day of my life. And though Thomas has never come out and said the words, I know he blames me for my mother's death. Had I not forgotten my helmet, mom wouldn't have given me hers, and she would still be here today. I don't need Thomas or anyone to blame me. I blame myself.

By the time I arrive at the office, I realize I practically drove all the way here on autopilot. Peering around the parking lot, I spot Avery's BMW, but I don't see Thomas's car. I also note the familiar Jaguar belonging to Brad, parked in its usual spot. Brad is my fiancé and works for Thomas too. He was hired about four years ago, and we started seeing each other not long after that.

Brad proposed two years ago, and I accepted. An engagement and moving in together is as far as our relationship has progressed. He keeps nagging me about finally setting a date and planning our wedding. Only I'm dragging my feet. Something has me holding back. I care for Brad, but I can't say I'm in love with him. I'm in love with the idea of him; of having someone care about me. Also, Thomas treats Brad like a second son. That alone is another reason I have stayed with him as long as I have. Every decision I make is based on whether or not I think Thomas will approve. I'm beyond messed up.

I'm standing behind my desk, putting away some files, still lost in thought when Brad's voice causes me to jump. "Hey."

I look up, and he takes a step forward. Brad stands at 5 feet 11 inches, is lean, and has sandy blond hair. His looks are nothing to write home about, and he doesn't make my tummy flutter. He's a tad on the dull side, but he's a decent guy. "Hi," I return.

"How'd court go? I heard you won."

I give him a small smile. "Court was fine. What about you? How was your day?"

"Good. I just wrapped up a meeting with a new client. I saw you come in and wanted to let you know I have another meeting in an hour so I'll probably be home late."

I wave him off. "That's fine. I'm going to London's for drinks anyway." Brad rolls his eyes at my statement. He doesn't like London, and to be fair, she hates him too. They only tolerate each other for my sake.

"You've been spending a lot of time together lately. You're at her place more than ours," Brad accuses. "We hardly spend time together anymore. And it's a wonder you haven't been mugged yet going to that side of town."

I ignore his last comment and go straight for his first accusation. "Really? Says the man who has been having a lot of late evening meetings the past couple of months. Look, Brad. You're busy with work, and I get that, but don't pin the fact that we don't see each other as much on just me. There are two people in this relationship. If you are off at a meeting, there is no reason for me to stay home bored to tears when I can be having a few drinks with a friend."

Brad and I have drifted apart these last few months. Hell, it's been weeks since we've had sex. And in the last year, he's gotten lazy about it. More times than not, when he's finished, I go into the bathroom with my vibrator to finish myself off. Sex with Brad has never been mind-blowing, but he used to make sure I was taken care of.

Brad sighs. "You're right, sweetheart. I'm just stressed and taking it out on you." He kisses my cheek. "See you at home tonight?" he questions.

I look at him for a moment and nod. "Yeah. I'll see you tonight."

Thirty minutes later, I'm knocking on the door to London's apartment. A second later, the door opens, and a glass of wine is shoved into my hand. "Now this is what best friends are for."

"You know it. Now get your ass in here before the creepy dude across from me sees us." London lives in a crap part of town and an even crappier apartment building. And she's right, her neighbor is creepy.

London and I met at law school and have been joined at the hip since. She's my soul sister, and we'd do anything for one another. London currently works for the state and doesn't make a whole lot of money. But she loves what she does. I admire my best friend for it. I do worry about her living here though. She is a beautiful, single woman living alone. Pair that with where she lives, and you better believe I worry often.

Taking a hefty swallow of my wine, I stroll across the living room. "I'm going to change into something more comfortable."

"Help yourself," London sing songs as she plops down onto the sofa.

When I walk into her bedroom, I set the glass down on the dresser and walk into the closet to where several articles of clothing I keep here hang. I spend as much time at London's as I do mine and Brad's apartment, so some of my things have accumulated here. Once I've kicked my heels off and stripped out of my pencil skirt and blouse, I pull on a pair of black leggings and a t-shirt.

When I walk back out in the living room, London is getting off the phone. "Pizza will be here in twenty minutes."

"Great, I'm starved." I sit in the chair across from her.

"So, where is Brad? You two didn't have any plans tonight?"

"No. He's meeting a client for dinner and drinks," I wave my hand. "Or whatever."

"Still trouble in paradise, I see," London says drily.

"Yeah. Honestly, I don't know what's up with Brad and me. We're just off lately. Neither of us makes much of an effort anymore. Plus, we haven't touched each other in weeks."

"Have the two of you talked about it?"

"Not really. Honestly, Lon, I think mine and Brad's relationship has run its course. I care about Brad, but..."

"You don't love him," London finishes for me. I don't answer but my silence speaks for itself.

Two bottles of wine and a couple of hours later, I've unloaded my entire day and concerns about Brad onto my best friend.

"For the life of me, I don't understand you sometimes, Promise. I get it, I do, but you are making yourself unhappy, and for what?"

"I know, Lon," I sigh.

"Those people don't deserve you, Promise. You think you're not good enough for them, but the truth is, they're not good enough for you."

London refers to Thomas and Avery as 'those people.' She can't stand either one. Especially Avery.

"They're the only family I have, Lon."

"Thomas and Avery Collins are not your family, Promise. I'm your family. Sadie and Ruby are your family," she says with conviction. "A family is people who care about you and want you to do what makes you happy, not what makes them happy. A family doesn't treat you like your less than, Promise. A real family are people who go out of their way to make you feel special, who make you feel appreciated."

London sets her glass down and scoots to the edge of the sofa, making sure she has my full attention. "One day, Promise you are going to realize those people are toxic. One day you are going to open those pretty eyes of yours and see that you would be better without them."

3

NOVA

The next day, I wake before Piper. Since my daughter doesn't have school today, I got the chance to sleep in a few more hours. Getting out of bed, I pull on a pair of joggers, run my fingers through my unbrushed hair, and make my way downstairs. Piper passed her only exam yesterday, with an A+. Since she's always taking care of me this morning, it's my turn to make her feel special. Once I have the coffee brewing, I retrieve all the ingredients I need to make her favorite, chocolate chip waffles. Do I spoil the shit out of my daughter? Hell yeah, I do. She deserves everything her family and I give her, and more. Just as I have everything set out on the kitchen island, the rumble of an engine grabs my attention. Glancing to the counter near the pantry, I look at the security feed streaming on the computer screen and see Kiwi pulling around the circular driveway at the front of my house. Last night he asked if he could borrow my trailer to haul some of the supplies the club needs to pick up for the biker rally we'll be attending in a couple of days in Jefferson, the next town over. I wasn't expecting him so early.

I meet him at the front door. "Hey, brother."

Kiwi's window rolls down. "You look like you just rolled out of bed, mate." He cuts the truck's engine. "Want me to come back later?"

"Naw. Come on in," I tell him. Climbing from his truck, Kiwi follows me inside. "Coffee?" I ask as I pour myself a cup.

"You got some of that sweet shit Piper put in mine the last time I was here?" Kiwi sits at the kitchen island.

I raise my brow. "You like that girly shit?" Pouring another, I sit the steaming mug in front of him and walk to the refrigerator. Opening the door, I grab what he's asking for off the shelf.

I set it next to his cup, and he pours the buttered pecan flavored creamer in his coffee. "Hell, yeah. It reminds me of Hokey Pokey." Kiwi looks up, taking in my expression, and chuckles. "It's a type of ice cream from back home. Good shit."

"The biker rally is turning into a bigger event than expected," I mention as I go about whisking the batter, then pour some into the hot waffle iron, sprinkling some chocolate morsels on top before closing the lid.

"I had to pick up extra raffle tickets yesterday. I think it will be twice the turnout as last year," Kiwi tells me.

The event is to help raise funds for some of the nonprofit organizations in the area that support our local veterans. This year, a local bike shop donated a Harley, sporting a custom paint job. It will be auctioned off to the highest bidder. It's the largest prize up for grabs since the event has been held and it's bringing in a buttload of local and out of state clubs. Most of society won't look past our rough exteriors and loud bikes, but you'd better believe your sweet ass that bikers care about their communities and the people in them.

After shooting the shit over breakfast, I head out to my shop, while Kiwi drives around back for us to hitch the trailer to his truck. Waiting, I open the shop doors, letting the light and fresh air in. Gravel crunches beneath Kiwi's truck tires as he backs up alongside the building then climbs out. I grab the soft fabric sheet covering my current project. "You still workin' on her, mate?" Kiwi walks up beside the fabric, pooled on the concrete floor. He whistles. "I've known you for years now, and you still fuckin' amaze me with your talent, brother." His compliment fills me with pride as he strolls around the glass statue. The sunbeams hitting the backside of the sculpture, filter through the half-finished wings made up of many individual pieces of blue and green blown glass.

"Haven't had time to work on her lately." Walking around her, I inspect it for any weak spots or stress fractures. I started working on this massive project about six months ago. She stands about three feet, without the completion of her outspread wings. Her colors are green and blue. A feminine angel with soft curves— every smooth slope carefully sculpted to match the natural feel of a woman. She's meant to stand up on a pedestal, looking down. Art is very personal. What one person sees another interprets something entirely different. This one represents one of our brothers from the Montana chapter, Logan and his woman, Bella. It's a symbol of the love that they share.

"What do you plan on callin' this one?" Kiwi asks, knowing I give all my art and identity.

"It's not mine to name."

"This is your best one to date, brother," he tells me. "My mum still brags about the piece you were nice enough to make for her birthday last year."

Kneeling, I lift the fabric. "Grab the other side." I usher to Kiwi, who then helps me cover the statue up again. "Let's get the trailer hitched." The two of us exit the shop, and I close the doors. "Piper will be heading out soon. Why don't you hang for a few more minutes? I'll ride with you, and give you an extra hand settin' shit up."

Later that night, I'm behind the bar. It's busy tonight. Within the last four hours, we've had at least three bachelorette groups stroll in. The bar tends to get a little rowdy when we have a bunch of ladies in here helping their girlfriend celebrate their last night of being single—the last fling before the ring. And the regulars, mainly bikers, love the hell out of all the eye candy. As I wipe the bar top down for the hundredth time, I watch Everest escort a trio of frat boys out the door. That's another thing we won't tolerate here—unwanted advances—male or female. Don't put your hands on someone unless they agree to you doing so. Fucking hate people like that. Typically it's men we have to knock down a peg or two, but every so often, women get a little too handsy themselves. Another thing is that, unfortunately, we've seen an influx of drugs. Shit's getting out of control.

A good looking blonde sidles up to the bar. The pink sparkly headband on her head is the best damn thing I've seen all night. Hanging my head, I try to hide my amusement, then look her way again once I've gotten myself under control. She's eye fucking me so damn hard I almost feel violated—almost. I shoot her my signature grin, making her wait for a beat before stalking toward her. I stare at the tiny pink dicks wobbling on the ends of the spring antennas attached to her headband. Laughter bubbles up again, and I chuckle. "Nice cocks." The busty blonde flicks her hair over her shoulder, leaning her forearms on the bar top. She smiles, and I can tell she's already a little lit.

"Thanks."

"What can I get you, sweetheart?" A young man steps beside her and orders a long neck. I slide him his beer and take his money while he checks the woman out before walking away.

She licks her baby pink lips. "A round of tequila shots for me and my girlfriends over there." She twists her body, pointing to the table near the stage, where Fender is gearing up for another set. I take in the rest of her group, all wearing the same accessories as her, except for the one getting hitched who is wearing a sash, along with a tiara on her head.

"You got it." Setting five shot glasses in front of her, I grab the bottle of liquor, and fill the glasses to the rim. "Anything else?" I ask knowing what her response will be as her eyes continue to take me in.

"Take me home tonight?" The blonde gets straight to the point.

"You with someone—married?" I ask this of every woman I bed. Though I'm sure I've been lied to before, I don't set out to wreck someone's life by sticking my dick where it doesn't belong.

"Not married." She cocks her head. "Would it matter?" she asks, and I let my look do the talking for me. "Ok," she adds.

"I don't do relationships," I tell her upfront. "I'll show you a good time, but afterward, that's it." My words seem harsh, but my intentions need to be clear and no reason to sugarcoat them for anyone.

"I can live with that." I place her shots on a small plastic tray, making it easier for her to travel across the busy bar without spilling them. Lifting the plate, she turns to leave but stops. "When is your shift over?"

"Don't worry, sweetheart. I'll find you before the night is over," I assure her. She smiles, and I watch her round ass jiggle a little as she retreats.

Music fills the air, as Fender starts playing a tune on his guitar while Josie walks around with a jar, stick-it notes, and a pen in her hand, taking song requests from bar patrons. He started doing this months ago, and people love it. He'll sing just about anything— rock 'n' roll, country, blues. Fender loves the club and being a part of something bigger than himself—the brotherhood—but his passion is music. Girls scream and start dancing as he belts out a little Whitesnake.

The rest of the night passes by without much incident. To my surprise, the group of women my blonde bombshell arrived with stuck around. It's about two hours until we give the last call and close the doors, and we have about half the occupancy of people still going strong and having a good time. That's until a woman shouting for help breaks out over the noise. It draws almost everyone's attention, as heads shift toward the bathroom area. Flying from behind the bar, I reach the hysterical woman, before anyone else does. She's had way too much to drink, and her words aren't forming coherent sentences. "Calm down." She's half-ass hyperventilating but manages to suck in a deep breath of air before speaking."

"My friend. She passed out in the bathroom, and I can't get her to wake up."

Kiwi is suddenly at my side, as a crowd begins to form around the frantic woman and me. "Shit. Kiwi, keep her here." He nods, and I burst into the bathroom, not giving two shits if there's anyone else in there. I go stall to stall until I reach the third, finding it locked. "Are you okay?" I knock on the stall door, getting no response." Listen, sweetheart, if you don't speak up, I'm coming in after you." I give it a second before squatting, seeing nothing but heels and legs, before deciding to peer into the stall. I'm not prepared to see the same young blonde I flirted with earlier in the night, currently slumped over, with a needle in her arm. "Motherfuck!"

Laying on the dirty floor, I manage to slide my big ass under the stall. Unlocking the door, I hoist the woman off the toilet, thankful she's fully clothed. I hate having to lay her down in here, but I have no other options. Once I have her on the floor, the bluish tint to her once pink lips kicks my ass into high gear and I press two fingers to her neck, feeling for a pulse. "Fuck." I don't feel one. Goddammit. I call for Kiwi, at the same time I tilt her chin back, pinch her nose, giving two slow breaths into her mouth.

"Holy shit!" Kiwi skids to a halt.

"Call 911 and bring me the Narcan," I bark my orders before

repeating the same process, trying to bring the woman back from death. Kiwi disappears. "Come on," I keep trying for a response.

"Move back," Riggs shows up. In his right hand, the life-saving medicine this young woman needs. I just hope it's not too late. My brother notices the needle that had fallen from her arm nearby, then checks her pupils, before spraying the medicine into each nostril.

We wait. Watching for signs of life. Her chest begins to rise and fall, so we roll her onto her side. That's when the paramedics arrive and take over. One of them thanks us as they load her into the back of the ambulance, her friend climbing in, sitting beside her. She mouths a thank you to us just before the ambulance doors close. It goes to show that you never know a person. She didn't look like an addict, but, apparently, from what her girlfriends said, their friend had been sober for the past three months. It's sad. I hope she gets the help she needs because her relapse tonight could have killed her. What's worse is that we usually keep the medicine on hand, often stowed away in Riggs' office for scenarios like this one, due to the fact we found a young man in the same situation months ago. The only difference is it was too late to save him.

"Let's shut it down for the night." Riggs claps my back as the ambulance tail lights disappear. "I need to hold my woman and kiss my daughter."

Thank fuck. It's nights like tonight that make me want to go home to my daughter and count my fucking blessings.

4

PROMISE

Waking before the alarm, I look over my shoulder and find Brad's side of the bed empty. When I got back from London's last night, he was already home. The two of us went about our nightly routine and when it came time for bed, Brad was giving me his usual 'I'm in the mood' signals, only I wasn't feeling it. He didn't take my rejection well and ended up sleeping in the living room on the sofa.

Turning over on my back, I stare up at the ceiling and sigh. As much as I don't want to deal with mine and Brad's situation, I know the conversation needs to happen. We both have to commit to fixing our relationship or it needs to end. Sadly, I'm not upset at the second scenario.

Climbing out of bed, I pad into the bathroom and take care of business. After washing my face and brushing my teeth, I snag the robe from the back of the bathroom door, slip it on, and tie it at my waist. I then prepare myself to face Brad. When I open the bedroom door, the smell of coffee lets me know he is already awake. Walking into the kitchen, I find him already dressed, sitting at the dining room table with his coffee and his laptop open in front of him.

"Morning," I murmur as I go about pulling a mug down from the cabinet and fixing myself some coffee.

"Morning," Brad returns but doesn't look at me.

"You're ready early," I point out.

"Yeah. Figured I head to the office and get a jump start on my day."

"That's good."

I'm silent for a moment before I speak again. "Listen. I have court again this morning, but I thought we could grab lunch together and talk."

Brad finally tears his gaze from his computer and looks at me. "Lunch sounds good. I agree we should talk." Brad closes his laptop, stands, slides it into his briefcase and strides up to me as he hitches it over his shoulder. "I know things have been off between us and I'd like to work on making things better." I don't say anything, only nod.

He kisses my cheek. "I'll see you later."

Once Brad has left, I head back into the bedroom to get ready for my day, which I'm anxious to get through so I can mentally prepare myself to talk with him. He says he wants us to work out the rut we're in, but I haven't entirely made up my mind what I want.

Tossing those thoughts away, I go into the bathroom, where I put on a touch of makeup and tie my long hair back into a bun at the nape of my neck. Finished with that task, I move to the closet I share with Brad and pull a pair of black slacks from the hanger along with a grey button-down blouse, then pair my outfit with some black four-inch heels. Making my way back into the kitchen, I fix myself a cup of coffee to go.

An hour later, I'm sitting in the courtroom gathering my things along with the state's attorney. Court was supposed to begin an hour and a half ago, but word has just gotten back that my client was in a fight earlier this morning. Now the hearing has been postponed until next week. The stunt my client pulled will not bode well for him. Word is, he was the one who instigated the fight in which two other prisoners and a bailiff were injured. He'll be facing more charges now.

Leaving the courthouse, I note the time and decide to call Brad to find out if he wants to make an early lunch. I place the phone to my ear and listen to it ring several times before it goes to voicemail. I try one more time only for the call to go to voicemail a second time. Knowing he's probably with a client, I decide to head to the office in hopes he'll be finished by the time I get there.

Pulling into the parking lot at work, I notice Brad and Jackson are here. I also see Avery has decided to grace everyone with her presence.

The sweltering New Orleans heat assaults me as I climb from my car. It's not even 10:00 am and it's like a furnace outside. I breathe a sigh of relief the second I step inside and a gust of cold air hits my face making me feel like I can breathe again. The humidity in the south is damn near unbearable. I don't bother addressing the receptionist as I pass by her desk because she's a bitch who is chummy with my step-sister. She sucks at her job and the only reason she got it was because of Avery.

Stepping off the elevator, I make my way down the hall and notice Thomas's office door wide open. I take a peek inside but don't spot Avery waiting in there for him. Maybe she's visiting with her brother. Passing my office, I walk to the end of the hall to Brad's. His door is closed, so I lift my hand to knock but think better of it since he must still be in a meeting or on the phone. Just as I go to turn and leave, I hear a throaty moan come from behind his door, followed by a grunt. I stand rooted in place with a sickening feeling settling in my gut. Knowing I probably won't like what I will find when I open the door, I twist the handle anyway.

There in front of me is Avery, on her back, on the top of Brad's desk. And between her boney legs is my fiancé, with his pants down around his ankles as he moans and thrusts into my stepsister.

I take in every detail before me. Avery's heels digging into Brad's ass. Brad's hand over the top of Avery's exposed fake breast. The way his head is thrown back in pleasure. Lastly, I note the way my bitch of a stepsister is peering over at me with a smirk on her face.

Finding my voice, I finally speak, sounding eerily calm, considering I just found my fiancé fucking my sister. "Apparently you have a different definition of 'working it out' than I do. Thanks for making my decision to dump you an easy one."

My voice and words cause Brad to startle. He peers over his shoulder at me. His face pales and his eyes go big. "Promise!"

My name is the only thing he has a chance to say before I turn on my heel and walk away. Jackson hearing the commotion appears from his office. He looks at me and then his attention diverts to Brad who bursts down the hall toward me, calling out my name.

"Avery," Jackson growls. "What the fuck have you done now?"

I don't bother looking at the scene behind me, and I sure as hell don't bother sticking around to wait for an excuse. Avery is a vile bitch, so her doing something like this doesn't surprise me, but Brad is a whole other story. I never once thought he would be capable of doing something so cruel, especially since he knows how I feel about my so-called family and how I feel about Avery.

"Promise, wait!" I hear Brad shout as I bustle down the hall to the elevator. The ride down feels painstakingly slow until finally the doors open. My body is in a heated daze as I fly out of the office building and dash across the parking lot to my car. I ignore Brad calling out my name as I jump into my car and peel out of the parking lot on to the road. Immediately my phone starts ringing. A few seconds later, it stops and starts again. Stopping at a red light, my phone rings for the third time. This time it's London calling. I answer. "Yeah."

"Jackson just called." I seriously love my stepbrother. He knew I'd need my best friend and she's the only person I'd answer right now. "I'm going to kill that stupid son of a bitch. And don't get me started on that cunt!" London shouts into the phone. "Where are you now?"

"In my car."

"I'm leaving work. I told my boss I wasn't feeling well. Meet me at my place in ten minutes. Wait! Make that twenty minutes. This calls for the hard stuff, and I'm out."

"I'll see you in twenty," I mutter, my voice sounding small.

"Promise?" London calls out just as I'm about to hang up.

"Yeah?"

"I'm sorry, babe."

"Thanks for being here, Lon."

"Always," she declares, and we hang up.

Apparently, London thought we needed not only copious amounts of alcohol, but she also called the other half of our squad, Sadie and Ruby. My best friend was right; ex-boyfriend bashing is a lot more fun with Sadie and Ruby joining in.

"Sadie!" London jumps from the sofa where she is sitting next to me. The liquor in the tumbler she's holding sloshes out onto the carpet. "Doesn't that bitch Avery get her hair done in your salon?" She asks.

"Yes," Sadie answers, looking at London with slanted eyes.

Sadie, in fact, owns the salon in question. Not just any salon either. It's the best salon in the city, which is why Avery is a frequent customer.

"I don't do the bitch's hair, though. I do however take her money. That's why Karmen handles all of Avery's appointments. That and I don't trust myself not to do something I'll regret. Like having my scissors 'slip' or 'miscalculate' the amount of developer I put in her bleach."

"Fuck yeah!" London shouts. "That's what I'm talking about."

I reach up and pull on London's arm. "Sit your crazy ass down, Lon. We're not going to make Sadie do any of that. No matter how awesome it would be."

London huffs. "I suppose you're right."

"Karma is a bitch," Ruby adds. "Avery will get hers—Brad too."

The room goes quiet as I pour myself another shot, bringing it to my lips, and down it. I close my eyes, welcoming the burn, and the warm haze that settles over my body, helping me numb the pain of Brad's betrayal.

"You know what hurts more than the cheating?" My friends look at me. "It's the fact that Brad knows how I feel about Avery. How she likes to throw in my face she's the real daughter. How I will never measure up when it comes to Thomas." I shake my head. "Out of all the women he could cheat with, he had to pick her. This is just another thing for her to rub in my face. Another way for her to prove she is better than me."

"I don't ever want to hear you say some bullshit like that again, do you hear me, Promise?" London gets in my face. "She is not better than you. Avery is nothing but a spoiled, vindictive brat who has been jealous of you her whole life."

I look at my best friend, stunned. "Jealous?"

"That's right, Avery has always been jealous of you. Hell, everyone can see that shit but you."

I look at Sadie and Ruby, who are both nodding in agreement.

"You're a smart, beautiful and successful woman. You are everything that Avery wished she was. People like her will spend their lives being hateful and nasty because it's the only way they know how to make themselves feel good."

"London is right, Promise," Ruby says. "At least you found out

Brad wasn't the right man for you instead of something like this happening after you two were married."

"You're right. I mean Brad and I have had some problems lately, but I didn't think they were bad enough for him to cheat. I don't even know if today was the first time. God, what if it's been going on for longer? I'm such a fool." I close my eyes and let out a shuttered breath. "This morning Brad said he knew we were having problems and wanted to work them out. How can he go from wanting to make things work with me to banging Avery on his desk?"

"I'm not saying Brad is not to blame, because he sure as fuck is, but I'd bet anything it was Avery who instigated it," London says. "The bitch can't stand to see you happy. She doesn't want Brad. She only used him to hurt you. It's just like that shit she pulled on you in college. That shit-show with that guy."

As soon as the words leave London's mouth, I know them to be true. I close my eyes and force myself not to think about the past. But it's not like it matters because the present is pretty damn painful too.

The next morning, I wake to the sunlight peeking through the curtains in London's bedroom, my head pounding. I hear London snoring next to me, and for a split second, I wonder how I got here. Then it all comes flooding back. Walking into the office, catching Brad and Avery and then me getting piss drunk with the girls yesterday. Stumbling out of bed, I don't worry about waking London since she sleeps like the dead. I slowly make my way across the hall to the bathroom and grimace when I flip the light on and get a glimpse of my reflection in the mirror. "Holy hell," I mutter.

After I've brushed my teeth and washed the day-old makeup

from my face, I grab some pain reliever from the medicine cabinet and chase two of them down with a glass of water. Once finished, I head to the kitchen, where I left my purse. Sifting through my bag, I find what I'm looking for—my phone. Twenty-six missed calls from Brad and three from Jackson. The latest one was an hour ago. I also see I have dozens of texts from Brad. I ignore those and open the one I have from my stepbrother.

Jackson: Hey. I just wanted to let you know I told Thomas you were sick and wouldn't make it into the office. Call me if you want to talk. I'm sorry Avery pulled this shit. Love you.

I text him back.

Me: Thanks for covering for me. Love you too.

No way in hell was I going to work today. Thank God it's Friday. That gives me a few days to figure out how I'm going to face Brad on Monday.

"Hey," London's groggy voices call out. I turn to see her step into the kitchen and go straight for the coffee maker.

"Morning."

Several minutes pass in silence as London, and I make some coffee, then we sit down at her small dining table.

"How are you holding up this morning?"

I ponder my emotions before I answer. "I'm feeling okay."

"Really?"

"Yeah. When I think about it, Lon, I'm more hurt by the betrayal than the loss of a fiancé."

"Good." London smiles.

I quirk a brow. "Good?"

"Yeah. Good. I know you, Promise. Brad was not meant to be your forever. You're not in love with him. If you were, you'd be an absolute mess right now. And to me, that is a good thing."

"You're right, Lon. I've never come out and admitted it, but I'm not in love with Brad. I was in love with the idea of him. Of being with someone and starting my own family." Closing my eyes, I take a sip of my coffee and finally allow the tears to fall. I'm not crying because what I had with Brad is over. I'm crying for the loss of a dream. I want the husband, the kids, a house, and summer vacations. When I open my eyes, London is staring back at me with understanding. "I just want to belong to someone, Lon."

"I know you do, sweetie. And one day, you will."

Later that night, London declares we've had enough heavy shit and it's time to go out and let loose. Part two of Operation Break-Up was about to begin, which leads us to this moment. Me, London, Sadie, and Ruby are in London's bedroom getting ready to go to a bar called Twisted Throttle.

"So," Ruby hedges as she shimmies into a little red dress. "Have you thought about where you are going to live? Since the apartment is Brad's?

"No," I sigh from where I'm perched on the bed as London does my makeup. She insisted she would pick out my clothes and fix my hair and makeup. London knows I would have thrown on a t-shirt and jeans then tossed my hair up in a ponytail. "I'll probably get a hotel for a couple of weeks until I find a place."

"No, you won't. You'll be staying with me until you find a place," my best friend informs me.

"Lon..." I go to protest only to have her cut me off.

"Zip it, Promise. I know my place isn't much, but it's better than a damn hotel."

I smile. "Thanks, Lon."

Finished with my makeup and hair, which is left down in loose curls that hang down my back, I take in the scrap of material London is holding out in front of me. "I can't wear that."

"Yes, you can, Promise. And you will."

Blowing out a breath, I take the skirt and top from London and put them on.

"Lose the bra, Promise. You can't wear one with that top."

"Seriously, Lon?"

"Do it. You'll thank me later."

"Somehow, I doubt that."

Ten minutes later, I stare at myself in the floor-length mirror in London's bedroom. "Okay, I stand corrected."

"Told you." She smirks.

"Damn, Promise. You look fucking hot," Sadie declares with a big smile.

"We all look fucking hot," I tell them. And we do. Ruby is wearing a skintight red dress that ends a couple of inches above the knees with spaghetti straps. She looks nothing like the kindergarten teacher she is. The skirt complements her beautiful curly blonde hair and big blue eyes.

Then there's Sadie. She's my height with red hair, olive skin and green eyes. She is wearing a gold sequin short jumpsuit with black booties.

London is wearing a short wrap dress with a cinched belt at the waist, plunging neckline, and her black hair tied up in a high ponytail which makes her golden-brown eyes pop.

As for me, I'm in a black leather skirt that sits a few inches below my butt and my top is a black lace bustier that leaves my midriff bare and makes my breasts look fantastic. I don't have much up top but the bustier accentuates what I do have. I look good and I feel good. I haven't felt this great in a long time. London's idea for a girl's night is precisely what I need.

As the four of us stroll up the sidewalk to the entrance of Twisted Throttle, I take in the bikes parked directly in front of the bar and turn to my best friend. "Is this a biker bar?"

London shrugs. "Bikers own it, but I wouldn't call it a biker bar. I've been here a couple of times and seen all walks of life come through, not just bikers." I look at her wearily.

"Come on, Promise. You'll see. The place is pretty kick-ass and they have live music." London tugs on my arm, leading me inside. The moment I step through the open door, I take in the place. Off in the far corner of the bar is a small stage. On the stage is a man sitting on a stool, strumming a guitar while he sings. His voice is beautiful, raspy, and full of soul. I let my gaze drift around the bar, taking in all the people—some obvious bikers, but also some college-age kids and a few run of the mill regular folk.

"Look!" Sadie shouts over the music, pointing to a table on the other side of the bar room. "Let's grab that one."

5

NOVA

It's Friday night, and the bar is packed with bikers who have come into town for tomorrow's event. Needing a breather, I step outside for a bit of fresh air. Looking around, I take in all the people strolling Bourbon Street. Across from the bar, a man plays Use Me on his saxophone. He has his case splayed open on the ground at his feet, for those dropping dollars and coins as they walk by. On the balcony above him, partygoers take in the spirit of the city, throwing beads to passersby on the street below as they drink from their solo cups. Pulling a small packet of matches from the front pocket of my jeans, I rip one of the matchsticks out, and slide the tip across the black strip, sparking the flame. Cupping my hands, I light the cigarette I bummed from Everest before walking out here. Leaning against the brick wall behind me, I continue to listen to the sounds of New Orleans.

"Hey, brother." Fender appears, lifting a beer to his lips, taking a long pull from the bottle. "Fuckin' hot as balls in there. We haven't had a full house like this in a few weeks." I nod a few times, agreeing.

"How's your momma doin'?" I ask, knowing her being sick is the reason he went back home for a few days.

Fender's face falls. "Her cancer is back."

"Shit, man. I'm sorry." I can tell Fender is wound a little tight, so, instead of asking a shit ton of questions, we stand together in silence for a number of minutes. Dropping what's left of my cigarette to the ground, I snub it out with the toe of my boot. "She's beat it once before," I remind him.

"This time is different. I see past her brave smiles and optimism. She's tired, brother." Fender downs the rest of his beer then tosses the empty bottle into the trash can near the front door.

Before this conversation goes any further, some dipshit stumbles into Fender. "Watch where you're fuckin' going asshole," the young man, clearly drunk off his ass shouts.

Fender, who is already in the wrong headspace for someone to give him a reason to brawl, squares off with the dumbass. "You'd better mind who the hell you're talkin' to, you little pussy ass motherfucker." Fender's fists tighten at his sides.

"You gonna let that piece of shit biker talk to you like that?" one of his muscled-up friends, who is just as intoxicated, goads.

"You're not so bright, are you, motherfucker?" I zero in on the dumb fuck, and take a step forward, standing beside Fender. The two friends share a look between each other, then glance behind them at a couple of good looking ladies. The moment the redhead smiles my way, I know these two knuckleheads won't walk away. I know the type. They'd just as well tote an ass-whooping than get shown up and look like a bunch of pussies in front of their women.

"Fuck you, old man. I bench press more than you weigh." The one doing most of the smack talking steps up to me and takes a swing. Stepping to the side, his punch misses its mark, and I land a solid blow to his ribcage. He falls to his knees, trying to catch his breath.

"I'm done fuckin' around," I warn him.

His friend makes a slight move, causing Fender to grab him by his throat, shoving his back against the brick wall of the bar. His hands go up, pleading. "Shit, man. We don't want no trouble."

"Collect your friend there and get your drunk asses out of here." Fender's fingers flex around the guy's thick neck before cutting him loose. I can tell it takes every bit of restraint he has to not pummel the guy just for the hell of it.

"Shit. Come on, bro, let's go." The guy reaches for his buddy, who catches me off guard by rearing up, punching me in the nuts.

"Goddamn, motherfucker!" I roar, and bring my knee up, catching the sack of shit in his nose.

His hand covers his face, blood dripping onto the sidewalk at my feet. "You broke my fucking nose."

"You punched my fuckin' dick, you piece of shit!" I want to plant my boot on the side of his head, but instead allow his friend to pull him to his feet, completely forgetting the two females they were with as they disappear into the crowd of people passing us by as if nothing ever happened.

"You good?" Fender asks, his shoulders relaxing, as some of the tension leaves his body.

"Yeah, brother. Not like I haven't been nut punched before." I turn to the two ladies, who were left behind, with shocked expressions on their faces. "You two with those dumbasses?" I ask them.

"Not anymore," the redhead grumbles, her irritation evident.

"Why don't you two go inside and take a seat at the bar. Order whatever you want." They share a look, giggling as they whisper amongst themselves before sashaying past Fender and me. "Hey," I call out. The girls turn their heads in my direction before they step through the front door, "Tell the bartender Nova's payin'."

Fender laughs. "You're the only man I know who can get nut

punched by some random dude then buy his woman a drink afterward."

"I'm hospitable, brother." I laugh along with him as we stroll inside. "I gotta hit the head. Make sure the ladies get what they want." I take my leave, heading toward the back of the bar where the restrooms are located, taking wider strides than usual. Not gonna lie, the guy had a damn decent uppercut and my balls are still hurting like a motherfucker from his sucker-punch.

Once I'm done, I make my way across the room to join Fender, who I notice has already made his way to the stage and started his set. "Goddamn, would you take a look at the legs on her!" A burly biker seated at a table to my right yells over the noise as he elbows his brother sitting beside him. Curiosity getting the better of me, I follow his line of sight, catching a group of women, who look more like they should be in an upscale club, strolling in. To say they look out of place in a sea of leather and ripped jeans is an understatement. Except for one. Immediately my attention shifts to the sexy as fuck brunette amongst the three, who looks less confident to be here than her friends. I stand rooted in place as her friends lead her across the bar, her eyes cast down, avoiding any eye contact with those around her, which only makes me more curious. The closer she gets, the more I take her in. She's wearing a tight leather skirt, with the hint of black lace hiding beneath her leather jacket. The moment she brushes by me, the intoxicating scent of sweet caramel, mixed with the smallest hint of roses, invades my senses, and I find myself drawn to her like a bear to honey. Does she taste as sweet as she smells? Then her chin lifts, and her eyes lock with mine. All the air leaves my body as I find myself drowning in the bluest eyes I have ever seen. All too fast, she tears her gaze from mine, breaking the spell she held on me.

What the fuck was that?

I run my hand down my face and through my beard, utterly

perplexed, as I weave around a few tables and sidle up to the bar, keeping my eyes on the bewitching brunette with eyes like the ocean.

"Nova," Payton's voice pierces my concentration or lack thereof.

Turning my head, I regard her standing behind the bar.

"Yeah?"

She laughs. "I said, what would you like? Your usual?" I shift my attention elsewhere, then look back at her. "Just a beer, babe. I can't keep the peace here if I lose myself in the bottle." Payton's eyes cut in the direction I was fixed on and grins. "Which one?" she inquires.

"What?"

"Come on, Nova." Payton leans forward on her elbows. "The group of women sitting at the table in the corner. Which one? You managed to make your way clear across the bar and take a seat without taking your eyes off of them."

I like Payton. She is easy to talk to, straightforward, doesn't bullshit, and always gets to the point. I like that about her. "The brunette," I finally confess.

"The one currently throwing back vodka shots?" Payton observes as she fills a glass with tap beer, then sets it down in front of me, which I lift to my lips, downing more than half. "She's beautiful, but not exactly your type."

Payton is right. I usually go for more extroverted women. The ones you know are looking for nothing but a good time. The ones not looking to marry you or stake their claim. Which is why I'm throwing myself off with the intense attraction I have for a woman I don't even know, who appears to be the opposite of what I want.

"She seems to be just as intrigued by you, my friend. And, from the looks of it, her friends are doing their damndest to encourage her curiosity." Payton smiles at me before walking to the other end of the bar, tending to Everest and the two women from earlier, who look to have forgotten all about me. Which is just as well, because the interest I had in the little redhead before no longer exists.

Finally, after thirty minutes of flirtatious glances, the brunette stands. Her blonde friend looks across the bar, her eyes landing on me, before looking back at her friend, whose blue eyes lock on mine once more. I can see now, I'll need to dial back my usual game and let my blue-eyed vixen take the lead.

My stare stays locked on hers as she crosses the room, confidence oozing from the way her hips sway, but her eyes telling a different story. She slides onto the seat beside me at the bar, her bare leg brushing against my knee as she skillfully crosses her long legs in the leather mini skirt she is wearing. Again, her sweet scent engulfs me. "Can I buy you a drink?" she asks, and the softness of her voice goes straight to my cock. I play along and nod. She waves Payton over, who hides her amusement with a welcoming smile

"What can I get for you, doll?

"Can I get an old fashioned?" She glances at my almost empty glass. "And another beer for..." She waits for me to offer my name.

"Name's, Nova." I grin, letting my eyes fall from her face to her breasts, and don't fail to notice her breathing has picked up. Payton fills another glass, sitting my beer on the bar top, then places an old fashioned for my blue-eyed stranger in front of her.

"You got a name, Sugar?" I ask her.

Lifting her glass to her lips, she sips her whiskey. "Nova." The airy way she whispers my name to herself causes my cock to twitch. "That's an unusual name." She plucks the cherry from her drink, slowly sucking it past her plump red lips into her mouth, and I damn near lose my shit. "I don't think names are necessary." She lifts her eyes to mine again, fucking devouring my soul with her fuck me stare.

"What are you lookin' for, Sugar?" I press her a little, wanting to hear her sweet voice some more.

"Just one night to forget about everything. To completely lose myself. Think you can handle that?" She places her hand on my thigh, her fingertips dangerously close to my swollen cock pressing against the zipper of my jeans. Shifting, she uncrosses her legs and downs her drink.

Can I handle it? She's got fire in her.

I lean in, bringing my lips close to hers. My body shifting forward has her hand sliding a fraction further up my thigh, brushing against my cock. Her eyes widen at my erection. I want to kiss her, but I don't. Not yet. "Slow down, Sugar. I can give you what you need." I pull her a little closer, and place my hand on her knee. "I won't bite. Not unless you ask me to." Her breath hitches. I'm loving her forwardness, and the effect I'm having on her, but realize she's probably never done anything like this before. "Breathe, babe." She pulls in a breath, slowly letting it out.

I motion for Payton to bring two bottles of water. "Here." I hand her the bottle. "Pace yourself. I want you to remember everything you allow me to do to you tonight." She bites her lower lip. I can tell she's tipsy. She then runs her palm the length of my cock. Seated at the end of the bar gives us a bit of privacy, keeping her actions hidden from prying eyes. Enjoying her boldness, I shift in my seat, placing my knee between her thighs, and she strokes me once more as she sips on her water.

Feeling pretty damned turned on, I run my hand up her bare leg, skimming the hem of her skirt. She leans into me, as my hand falls between her thighs. I make lazy circles with my fingertips against her soft skin. "You ready to get out of here?" I can feel the heat from her sex as I move my palm further up her inner thigh.

"Yes." She drags her palm the length of my erection again, and the tip of my finger lightly skims over the thin scrap of fabric covering her pussy. "Just one night?" she says on an exhale.

"One night."

"No names?" she reiterates, wanting to keep her identity to herself.

"No names, Sugar."

"Let's go," my blue-eyed vixen says, giving me all the incentive I need. Slowly sliding my hand from beneath her skirt, I stand and help her from her barstool. Without a word, she lets me take her hand in mine, leading her to the opposite side of the bar, taking her right past her friends. The two of us slip through the backdoor and into the darkness of the alleyway behind the building where my bike is parked. Taking my helmet, hanging from my handlebar, I turn to her and brush her long hair from her shoulder.

"Where do you live, babe?" I slip the helmet on her head, securing the strap beneath her chin.

"We can't go back to my place," she says in a rush. "I mean, I live with a roommate, and well..."

Knowing my daughter is staying with a friend tonight, my reaction is quick. "You're coming home with me." The words I thought I would never hear myself say fall from my mouth with ease. What the fuck am I saying? Then I notice her hesitation as her expression changes. Hell, I don't blame her. She is agreeing to go home with a complete stranger. She should be apprehensive. "Give me your phone." I hold out my hand.

"What—why?"

"Phone, babe," I say once more, and she retrieves her phone from the small purse dangling on a gold chain at her side.

Swiping the screen, I notice her last text is to someone named London and look at her. "London. Is she one of your friends inside the bar?"

"Yes."

I type out my address, then press send. "London now has my address." I hand her phone back, catching the small smile she gives as she places it back in her purse. Grabbing her hand, I help her straddle the back of my bike. Doing the same, I look over my shoulder. "Wrap those arms around me, Sugar." Sliding forward, she does as I say, encasing me with her long legs. "You ever rode before?"

"You're my first." Her warm breath caresses my ear, tempting me to fuck her right here on the back of my bike. I start the engine, giving her a few twists of the throttle.

"Oh my God." My vixen's grip tightens, letting me know the vibration between her legs is turning her on, and I grin. Her hands slide down my abs, lacing her fingers together, pressing her breasts against my back. Her body fits seamlessly against mine as if she was made for me.

6

PROMISE

I'll admit, I wasn't only apprehensive about riding on the back of a motorcycle, I was scared shitless. Not only have I never been on a bike, but for a split second when I climbed on behind Nova, I wanted to change my mind about this whole crazy night. But now, I don't want the night or the ride to end. That tiny voice inside my head is like *So what he's a member of the local MC, live a little, Promise.* So here I am, living a little. Even if just for one night.

Leaning further into Nova, I can't help but take in the smell of his cologne paired with the scent of his leather cut and motor oil. He's intoxicating, and it's making the space between my thighs tingle. Almost as if he knows how my body is reacting to him, Nova peers over his shoulder at me and gives me that look. The same look he gave me at the bar, one that says he's got the skills to back up his cockiness.

Smiling, I loosen the grip I have on Nova's waist and unglue myself from his form, lean back a bit, close my eyes, and enjoy the warm night air as it dances across my face. When my eyes open, I take in the scenery around me. Nova turns off onto an unpaved road where nothing surrounds us but trees and darkness. We ride for at least a mile with no sight of the living. Nerves settle into my stomach, and I have a brief moment where I second-guess my decision to go home with a stranger.

Not just any stranger, but a man who is a member of the New Orleans motorcycle club, The Kings of Retribution. Nova's cut is one of the first things I took in when I approached him earlier. I don't know what came over me. Liquid courage, perhaps? Maybe it was my intuition paired with the fact he willingly gave his address to London so I would feel safe. I can't explain it, but something tells me I can trust him.

Before long, Nova takes a left turn, and I tighten my hold on him as a house comes into view. I continue to appraise his home as he pulls up in front of the house and parks. Aside from the porch light, I can't see much, but I can see Nova has a beautiful place. Not a home I expected him to have. My eyes go from the house to Nova when he cuts the engine to his motorcycle and holds his hand out for me to climb off. Not two seconds later, he swings his leg over his bike and rips the helmet from my hand, tossing it to the ground. The next thing I know, his mouth is on mine, swallowing my shocked gasp. He takes the opportunity to slip his tongue inside my mouth. He tastes like whiskey and sin and it's so damn good. I don't waste any time giving as good as I'm getting.

"Fuck. I knew you'd taste sweet," Nova growls, tearing his mouth from mine.

I don't let him get another word in because a fire I never knew I had, breaks free, and I tangle my hand in his thick hair and pull his mouth back down on mine. This aggressiveness is a new side to me. One I'm not sure of. All I know is, I need his taste and I'm desperate to have his lips back on mine. So much so, my panties are soaked. And when Nova brings his palms down, reaches under my skirt, and cups my ass, he slips his finger down between my legs, feeling how wet I am for him. "Fuck, babe."

This time when our connection breaks, we're both left panting.

"Wrap your legs around me, Sugar," Nova orders as he hauls me up. I do as I'm told and wrap my legs around his waist then proceed to pepper kisses along his neck while my fingers explore his beard. I never considered myself a beard woman, but now, I see what the fuss is about. I barely register him, carrying me up the steps of the porch and the front door swinging open before my back is pressed against a wall. With his right hand under my ass helping hold me up, Nova brings his left hand up and yanks down the front of my top exposing both breasts the same time I tear his t-shirt off over his head, displaying a hard chest full of colorful ink that also runs the length of his arm. I don't have time to take in his tattoos because my brain turns to mush and my body to molten when he dips his head down and takes one of my nipples into his mouth.

I moan. "Oh, God." His hot wet mouth on my body causes my pussy to clench and I start grinding against his abs. "Nova."

Releasing my nipple, he looks into my eyes, his chest heaving. "Take my cock out."

Oh, hell. He doesn't have to ask me twice. Reaching between our bodies, I go to work unbuckling his belt. I then unsnap his jeans, slide the zipper down and reach inside, finding him commando. My hand then comes into contact with Nova's long and very thick cock, so thick my fingers are unable to wrap around it fully. Once his cock is free from its confines, I waste no time guiding it to where I desperately need it. In a daze, I barely register Nova ripping my panties from my body. And the moment the head of his cock kisses my opening, he grabs my hand that's between us and pins it to the wall above my head. Next, he surges his hips forward, burying himself inside me, knocking the breath from my lungs. I gasp, "Oh."

"I knew this would be the sweetest fuckin' pussy I'd bury my cock in." Nova starts to fuck me against the wall as he grunts his dirty words into my ear. And the only thing I can do is hold on for the ride. I hold onto him so hard my nails leave marks across his back.

"Fuck yeah, babe. Mark me. Put your mark all over me while my cock marks your pussy like no man before me has and like no man after me will." The moment the words leave his mouth, my pussy spasms. "That's it, Sugar. Come all over my cock."

At Nova's command, my pussy clamps down around his length, and I come. I come like I have never come before as flashes of light dance behind my eyelids. With one final thrust, Nova plants himself inside me to the hilt and buries his face in the crook of my neck as he rides out his own release.

During my post-orgasm haze, I register Nova carrying me up a set of stairs and down a hallway.

"What are you doing?"

"Taking you to my bed where I can fuck you properly." Fuck me properly? I thought that's what he just did.

"But, we just..." My words are cut short as I'm tossed onto a king-size bed.

"What happened downstairs was just a preshow, Sugar. I haven't even begun to worship you yet."

I fall speechless and all I can do is stare up at him from where I'm lying and watch as he kicks off his boots and strips out of his jeans completely. Nova is taller than I first imagined. He has to be at least 6 feet 3 inches tall. He also has the most beautiful hazel eyes. And let's not forget the sexy as sin beard. A beard I have decided I'm obsessed with. He looks sexy as hell standing at the foot of the bed with only the moonlight shining through the window. The brown hair on his head is short on the sides but long on top. And right now, it's a disheveled mess. It only adds to his sexiness. I wonder what his beard would feel like between my thighs.

"Don't worry, babe. We have all night for you to find out." Nova smirks.

Wait. Did I say that out loud?

Stepping to the foot of the bed, Nova grabs hold of my ankles and hauls me toward him. Next, he takes my hand and urges me to sit up. When I do, I come face to face with his cock, which is still at attention. I lick my lips. Reaching behind my back, Nova slides the zipper of my top down, removing it, then tosses it to the floor. Taking advantage of what's in front of me, I take his cock in my hand and bring my mouth down over the head. A moan escapes my mouth as his musky flavor mixed with mine assaults my taste buds. He sucks in a sharp breath and lets out a string of curse words. "Shit, fuck."

His pleasure only intensifies my urge to take more of him in my mouth. I suck and lick the length of him like I'm starved for his taste. Too soon for my liking, Nova grips my hair and pulls me off. I release his cock with a pop.

"That mouth of yours feels so fuckin' good, babe, but it's your pussy I want."

At his declaration, I don't have time to protest because the next thing I know, I'm pushed back onto the bed and my skirt pulled from my body, then my heels tossed somewhere on the floor. Next, Nova dips one knee to the bed between my legs, snakes his arm around my middle, and hauls me closer to the headboard. I'm then flipped over onto my stomach and just as quickly brought up on my hands and knees, where Nova settles in behind me. "Hands on the headboard," he demands on a grunt.

I brace my palms against the headboard and peer over my shoulder at him. We're both still for a moment and my body begins to shake with anticipation. Nova's lips lift in a smile that does funny things to my tummy just before he grabs hold of my long hair and wraps it around his fist. He then pulls my head back until my hands come off the headboard and my back is to his front. "This is fuckin'," he rasps into my ear just before he slams inside me, knocking me forward. My palms hit the headboard once again to keep from falling on my face and I scream, "Fuck!"

Nova's cock stretches me so perfectly. The feel of him moving in and out of me is exquisite torture, and soon, I start meeting him thrust for thrust.

"That's right. Fuck yourself on my cock."

Rocking my hips, I grind down on his length. "Nova," I whimper.

"Jesus fuckin' Christ," he growls. "So damn sweet and so fuckin' wet. Knew you'd be wild for me. Innocent to the core but a greedy pussy."

I don't know how he knew, because I sure didn't. Sex has never been like this for me. I've never been so turned on and desperate.

Soon, I feel my orgasm start to build once again.

"Fuck, your pussy is squeezing the hell out of my cock."

"I'm coming, Nova," I pant.

"Yeah, you are. Come with me, Sugar." Nova lets go of my hair, palms both of my breasts and forces my body back against his. And for a second time tonight, I come with a strangled cry taking Nova with me. My pussy convulses around his cock as he fills me with his release.

I wake sometime later with a warm body pressed against my back. Turning my head, I see Nova sound asleep next to me. Careful not to wake him, I lift his arm and slide out of bed. The first thing I notice is the delicious soreness between my thighs. When I take another peek at the man lying on the bed, flashes of what took place tonight cause my belly to dip. It's also then my eyes travel south to Nova's impressive cock which is on full display. It also hits me that we didn't use protection. Fuck!

How could I have been so careless? At least I'm on the pill. Only the pill doesn't protect me from other things. I mean, look at the man. He's probably got a different woman in his bed every night.

Shaking those thoughts away, I turn my back to the bed, quietly gather my clothes and get dressed. Once my skirt and top are in place, I grab my shoes and start looking around the bedroom for my phone. Shit, where is it? It must be downstairs.

Tiptoeing across the bedroom, I take one last look over my shoulder. Something inside me wants to crawl back into bed with Nova, but then I remember our agreement. One night. So, with a heavy sigh, I walk out of the room and make my way downstairs, where I find my phone on the floor by the front door next to my discarded underwear. I snatch my panties up and my phone. Then as quiet as I can, I slip out the door and close it behind me. Next, I call London who answers on the second ring. Luckily, she must have been waiting for me because she sounds alert.

"Hello."

"Hey, Lon," I whisper. "Are you okay to come get me?"

"What? You're not staying the night with that hunk of man you left with?" There is a beat of silence before she is more alert with asking her next question. "Is everything okay?"

"Yeah, yeah. I'm good. I just want to avoid the whole awkward next morning thing. Can you drive out? If not, I can call someone else."

"Girl, no way are you calling anyone else. I need all the deets. I'll be there in twenty."

"Thanks, Lon."

Twenty minutes later, London pulls up in front of Nova's house and I breathe a sigh of relief, thankful he didn't wake up and catch me sneaking away.

When I climb into the passenger seat of the car, my best friend is giving me a cheeky smile. "Damn. That man laid it on you, girl."

I tried to play it off. "It was okay."

London shifts the car into drive and pulls away from Nova's

house. She shakes her head. "You're such a liar. I know that the man gave it to you good because your ass was walking funny to my car."

At her statement, I can't help but bust out laughing. "Fine. You're right." I lean my head back against the headrest, close my eyes and sigh. "I'm ruined."

"That good?" she asks.

"Yes. It was that good."

"Who knows, maybe you'll see him again. Did you leave him your number?"

I shake my head. "No. We agreed to one night, and that's what we both got."

"Hmm," is all London says and then goes silent for a few beats.

Only that doesn't last long.

"So, how big is his..."

"London!" I screech, cutting off the rest of her sentence.

"Okay, okay. No more questions. Geesh. Can't blame a girl for trying."

As the car falls silent on the way back to London's apartment I can't help the feeling of sadness that washes over me at the thought of never seeing Nova again.

7

NOVA

I felt my mystery woman slip from the bed more than twenty minutes ago. Knowing she was more than likely calling for a cab or her friend to pick her up, I lay on my back, staring up at the ceiling until finally hearing a vehicle pull into my driveway.

Climbing from my bed, with nothing more on than what God gave me, I cross the room. Parting the window blinds, I look outside, watching my brunette beauty lower herself into the passenger seat of a small car, then follow the taillights until they disappear in the darkness of the night. A sting foreign to me lingers. I'm not familiar with what I'm feeling at the moment. Earlier I was perfectly fine with being used as a one-night stand. One-night flings are all I do. But suddenly, just one night with her isn't sitting well with me.

I hate to admit it, but part of me wanted to stop her. I wanted her to stay. Like a caveman, I wanted to toss her over my shoulder and haul her sweet ass back into my bed. Bringing a woman home was already out of character for me but finding myself wanting her to remain in my bed...I want more. More than one night? I run my palm down my face. "Get your shit together." I try to force myself from the discomfort of my thoughts. This new feeling and revelation have my head all fucked up.

Not at all ready to crawl back in my empty bed, I decide to shower. As I step over the strewn articles of clothing on the floor, it dawns on me my woman left the house without tripping the security system, then quickly realize I never reset it when we arrived hours earlier. Another thought hits me like a ton of bricks. Motherfuckin' shit. We didn't use protection. My heart begins to thump against my ribcage as a bit of panic sets in. I always wrap it up. How could I have been so reckless? My focus was solely on giving my woman what she was asking for, and quite frankly, what she'd clearly been lacking for a long time. Sounds like a damn good excuse, but it's not.

Calm your shit.

I need a shower. Maybe that will calm my wracked nerves. It will be fine. I keep repeating that to myself

Plucking my jeans from the floor, I dig my phone from the pocket and pull up my home security app. With a few taps on the screen, the house is secure once more.

Tossing my jeans aside, then setting my phone on top of the dresser, I walk into the bathroom, dimming the lights throughout the room. Using the touchpad on the wall near the shower stall, I turn the water on, setting the temperature to 98 degrees. Having a set up like this happens to be a little over the top, but it's one of my favorite features in my house. Once my art started selling, and I decided to build a home for my daughter and me from the ground up, I knew there would be some things I wouldn't skimp on. After taking shit showers in tiny as fuck spaces for years while working offshore, I splurged on this top of the line steam shower.

As soon as steam fogs up the glass, I pull open the glass door, and step inside. Sprays of water hit me from every angle. My head lolls back as the heat from the water seeps into my skin. The tension leaves my body, my shoulders relax, and soon my thoughts drift back to my vixen and those hypnotic blue eyes. She walked into the bar looking like sin, but everything else about her said she was out of her element. Everything about her is perfect: the way her long waves of hair cascaded over her shoulders, the wispy ends barely kissing the small of her back, and long legs that seem to never end—the smoothness of her cream-colored skin. I grin at the next image to enter my mind; the dimples just above her ass where her back dips. Water soaks my hair as thoughts of her continue to flood my imagination. The way her small perky breasts fit perfectly in the palms of my hands. My cock begins to swell as my fingertips remember the curves of her hips—my name on her lips.

Before I know it, my hand is wrapped around my thick cock, stroking myself as I playback the night's events. Lost in need, my speed increases until I explode, and with my release, all reasoning as to why this woman is having this effect on me. Just one night of easily the best sex of my life, and I'm reduced to getting off in the shower because I haven't begun to have my fill of her. Not by a long shot. As I finish soaking in the warmth from the water, my entire way of thinking shifts. Determination sets in. I'm going to find my mystery woman.

Later that day, the club has our tent set up, and there's charcoal burning in the grill. Wick announced he and Tequila were walking to the other side of the park to check out the custom Harley to be auctioned later on today, while Everest went to meet my brother in the parking lot nearby to help carry a few items.

The smells from the nearby crawfish boil drift on the slight breeze blowing in our direction, causing my mouth to water. The afternoon's festivities are about to pick up and will be tame, and more suited for everyone to attend with families. Local businesses even pitched in and rented several carnival rides, along with a few game booths for all the kids to enjoy. Then as the sun sets, the place will turn into an adult-only party, with live music and a cash only bar. Again, all proceeds earned will go to charity.

Fender joins me at the grill, holding a box filled with multiple packs of hotdogs. "How's it goin', brother?"

"Feelin' pretty damn good." Spreading the hot coals evenly across the bottom of the barrel, I put the rack in place. "So, how'd it go with the blonde and the redhead from last night? I saw Everest hittin' them up," I ask. Pulling a small knife from my pocket, I start slicing open hotdog packets, then throwing them on the grill. Fender check's the second grill, before throwing frozen burger patties on to cook.

"I'm not kissin' and tellin', brother." The way his lips turn up into a mischievous grin tells me all I need to know.

I laugh. "That good, huh?"

"Brother. You have no idea." It doesn't take but a minute for him to ask questions of his own. "So...the brunette I saw you leavin' with last night."

I throw the last hotdog on the grill, then close the lid. What the fuck do I say? Nothing. Like Fender, I don't share the details of my adventures. The heat of the day is already nearing ninety degrees. I reach down to the cooler on the ground at my feet, lift the lid, and pluck two cold beers from the ice. With the backside of the skull ring that I wear on my right ring finger, I pop the tops off the long neck bottles, handing one to Fender. He eyes me for a beat, his brow lifting as he lifts his beer, taking a pull from the bottle.

"I can't believe it," Fender finally says.

Downing a swallow of my drink, I set it aside, grab the cooking tongs, and lift the grill lid. "What?" I turn the hotdogs.

"The brunette did a number on you, didn't she?" Fender states, his intuitive nature hitting the nail on the head. "I knew somethin' was off about you this mornin'."

I can't even be mad at Fender for calling me out. The fucker is right. I can't get my woman out of my head. My woman? Fuck, where did that come from? I've got a lot to do and be present for today, and she is all I can think about.

"Hey," my brother, Riggs calls out. Fender and I turn our heads to see him walking toward us with his baby girl in his arms and Luna at his side. Everest is bringing up the rear, carrying a stroller and a bag of toys. Riggs peers around. "Looks like everything is ready to go." Taking a few steps away from the heat of the grill, I lean in, kissing my niece on top of her head, her blonde curls tickling my nose and her tiny fingers grab at my beard as she giggles. I chuckle and run my finger along her chubby little cheek. I then sign to Luna. "Hey, sweetheart. You feelin' better?" knowing she and Aria have been sick for a few days.

Luna smiles. "Much better," she voices as she moves her hand, and I smile. Luna has been working hard on her speech. It gets better with each day that passes. Her confidence shows as she beams at her husband. As I stare at the three of them, the tiny family that they are, I find myself suddenly wanting a woman to look at me the same way Luna looks at my brother.

Luna looks around. "Where's Piper?"

"We realized we forgot buns for the hamburgers and hotdogs, so she offered to run to the store with Kiwi. They should be here soon." As I speak, I notice my daughter and Kiwi weaving through the crowd that is beginning to filter in, carrying grocery bags in their arms, and following behind them is Wick and his woman Tequila along with Sydney.

"People are starting to roll in." Kiwi sits the bags on the fold-out table, then helps Piper with the load she is carrying. "We bought what they had left on their shelves, but I don't think it will be enough." The thunderous roars of motorcycle engines can be heard in the distance as the first of many clubs roll into the venue, parking their bikes in the designated areas.

"Hey, Uncle Abe, and Aunt Luna." Piper hugs them both, then immediately reaches for her cousin, plucking her from my brother's arms. I watch the two of them for a moment, before tending to the food cooking again.

"Heard you and Fender had a little run-in with a couple of drunks last night," my brother mentions as he reaches into the cooler, grabbing a cold beer for himself and water for his woman, passing it to her. "Also saw you leavin' with a pretty little brunette." Wick and Tequila join us.

"Just a typical Friday night." I keep my voice even, even though it was far from typical, at least for me.

"I'm callin' bullshit."

"And why is that?" I start plucking hotdogs off the grill, placing them into the foil pans nearby. My brother kisses his woman, pats her ass, and nods for her to join Piper and their daughter on the other side of the tent. Standing beside Wick, Tequila laughs.

"And, on that note, I'm going to grab myself a beer." Once she has her beer in hand, Tequila kisses Wick and joins the girls.

"You forget I live above the bar, brother? I saw the two of you outside, getting ready to leave."

"So?" Now I'm curious. How much did he see?

"You took this chick home," Riggs clarifies.

"No fuckin' shit?" Wick blurts. My brother's statement grabs not only Fender's attention but Kiwi's as well. The next thing I know, I'm surrounded by all my brothers.

"It won't happen again." The words taste sour as I speak them.

"He's got the look." Riggs snickers to Wick, and he nods.

"What the hell is this? Gossip time with my girlfriends? Next thing you know we'll be paintin' each other's fuckin' toenails and talkin' about tampons."

Riggs ignores my sarcastic statement. "Look, man. Just call her up and tell her you'd like to see her again."

"No can do, brother," I tell him.

"Why the fuck not? You took this woman to your home and into your bed. Something I haven't seen you do since Piper came into your life. Clearly, there is something different about this one, or you wouldn't have gone against your cardinal rule." Riggs is quick to point out, and my eyes cut over to Piper, who is still occupied by her niece and the other women. "It's been a long time, Cain. You can't let one bad relationship dictate the rest of your life."

Nothing more is said after Riggs makes his last statement. Now is not the time or the place to get any deeper into my personal life and the choices I've made over the years. For the rest of the day, I push aside my thoughts and fully immerse myself amongst family and friends.

It's nearing sundown, and Riggs has already packed up his family, sending them home for the evening. With the last of our shit loaded on the trailer, Kiwi and I wait for Piper to come back from the restroom, while the other men are already having a drink at the bar. "Thanks for taking her back home, brother."

"No worries, mate." Kiwi tightens the strap, keeping the grills in place.

"I'm going to hit the head," I tell Kiwi, leaving him standing by his truck as I cross the park in the direction of the restrooms.

"No." I hear my daughter's distraught voice and suddenly I'm on high alert. "Let go of me!"

I take off in a dead heat, running faster than I have ever run before. Not seeing a soul standing outside the small brick building, I burst into the women's bathroom, the heavy metal door slamming against the concrete wall. A sea of red floods my vision when I take in the scene in front of me. A soon to be dead man has my daughter pinned against the wall, with a blade pressed against her throat. Rage fueling me, I grab a fist full of the motherfucker's greasy black hair, pull him off Piper, then slam his unsuspecting face into the wall, blood splattering across the cold concrete. At the same time, a searing pain rips through my forearm. Looking down, I notice the blade he had to my daughter's neck stuck into my flesh.

"Daddy," Piper moves toward me.

"Piper, get out of here." I hold the guy struggling against my hold, as tears stream down my daughter's face. I take in her shirt that's ripped open. The realization this guy was about to rape my daughter rips at my insides. It only causes my anger to grow. "Piper, go. Find. Kiwi. Now." My words are harsh but necessary to get her to do as I say. Finally, she rushes out of the bathroom.

I toss the guy to the floor, the knife once in his hand still sunk in my arm. I look down at the fucker getting to his feet. It's then that I notice the Hell's Punishers patch on his cut. "What the fuck?" He lifts his head, his beady eyes glaring at me as he wipes the blood flowing from the gash above his right eye. "You'll pay for this."

"I don't think so, motherfucker. You picked the wrong girl to put your filthy hands on." My fist comes down against the side of his head before he makes it to a standing position.

Shaking off the blow, the biker gets hold of the knife handle, ripping the blade from my arm, the jagged edges doing more damage on the way out. "I didn't see no property patch on the bitch. It seems to me she's fair game." He cocks his head. "Oh, I see. You like them young, do you?" he sneers. "That's okay. I like 'em young too." We circle one another. "I bet she's got a tight pussy." He taunts, and I charge him, slamming his body against the wall, knocking his weapon from his grasp in our struggle.

I lay into the guy. One blow after another. I don't stop until I feel hands grabbing me, pulling me off the guy. "He's out, brother. Stop before you kill him." Wick's voice breaks through my hazy rage. My breathing is hard and heavy as I watch the biker's body slump to the floor, his face a bloody mess, and his breaths ragged.

My brother enters the bathroom, taking in the scene. "Shit. Get him out of here," he orders Wick.

"Where is my daughter?" I let Wick walk me outside.

"She's with Kiwi," Wick informs me, and I finally feel like I can breathe again.

"The fucker was gonna rape her, man." I say the words, and my knees start to buckle. Wick sits me down on a bench nearby. A crowd begins to gather, and police sirens can be heard off in the distance.

"You've got a knife wound." Wick examines my arm that's still bleeding profusely.

"I don't give a fuck," I tell him and watch a group of bikers advancing. As they rush by, I take in their cuts—the same as the sorry fucker I just beat. "He's one of them." I lift my chin in their direction and Wick takes notice. Within a second, a commotion has me back on my feet, and us running back toward the restrooms. My brother, and one of the other bikers, spill out of the door, taking swings at each other. Riggs takes a blow to his side before clocking the massive biker in the chin with a right hook. Fender and Everest are suddenly at mine and Wick's sides. Us, along with three of the Hell's Punishers club members, are about to square off just as two cop cars arrive. Slowly we back away, both clubs standing down.

An officer climbs out of his cruiser, his hand at his side, ready to defend himself if necessary. He zones in on Riggs, while his other officers keep their eyes on the rest of us. "What the hell is going on here?"

"Just defending myself, and my family, officer." Riggs keeps his hands where they can be seen, showing he poses no threat. "Before we get into the what's of the situation, you mind getting my brother there patched up?" The officer looks in my direction, noticing the blood running down my forearm.

One of the officers enters the restroom, then reappears. "We have an assaulted male in the women's restroom." The officer looks around the crowd for answers, not getting any.

"Someone better start talking before I arrest all of you," he demands.

Typically, we don't take our shit to the cops. This time is different. As long as the motherfucker is still breathing, I'll make sure he pays for hurting my baby girl. I lift my chin. "I found that piece of shit assaulting my daughter." My eyes flash with anger.

I listen to him call for a female officer to come in and get Piper's statement. He then directs his attention toward me. "We're not done here. I don't take kindly to out of towners causing trouble."

"How about you carry your patronizing ass over there," I point toward the bathrooms, where the fucker I beat the hell out of is limping from, "and arrest that son of a bitch before I finish what I started." It takes everything I have to stand still. The cocky officer gives me a go-to-hell look.

"You're already facing charges. I suggest you keep your mouth shut before I add more," the officer warns.

Fuckin' perfect. A cop with a complex. That's just what I need right now. Not heading his warning, I smart off. "Fuck you. How about you do your fuckin' job, instead of trying to prove who has the bigger dick because I can assure you, you'll lose."

"Shit," Wick says beside me. "Quit poking the bear, Nova."

Maybe I should have left well enough alone, but right is right and wrong is wrong. For the most part, I respect what law enforcement does, but when they let their egos trump doing their job, it rubs me the wrong fucking way. Now, an hour later, Riggs is sitting with me in the hospital room as the ER doctor stitches me up, knowing my ass probably won't be going home tonight. The only thing putting my mind at ease is the fact Piper is home safe with Luna. "Alright. You're good to go. Keep it dry for a couple of days and take the prescribed antibiotics to prevent infection." The doctor places a clean bandage over my wound.

"Thanks, Doc." As my brother and I walk through the double doors into the ER waiting room, we notice the officer from earlier standing in wait.

"LeBlanc."

Looking past him, I catch sight of my daughter's assailant and blow past Riggs, and the officer getting to him, but a hand darts out, stopping me. "Remove your fuckin' hand," I warn the cop.

"Can't do that." My attention moves from his hand, gripping my wrist to his face, and my eyes narrow to slits. "The guy you attached is on his way to jail. He's also pressing charges. I'm arresting you for assault."

"You have got to be shittin' me!" My voice rises and garners attention from the few people sitting in the waiting area. "The motherfucker almost rapes my daughter, and I'm the bad guy?"

"The whole situation is beyond my control now. Charges have been filed. I have to do my job." He looks at me, his face becoming more serious.

My eyes shift to Riggs. "You hearin' this shit?"

"Yeah, brother."

"Take care of Piper," I tell my brother as the officer places the cuffs on my wrist and reads me my Miranda rights. Riggs follows us out the ER doors, where night has fallen.

"Don't worry about Piper, Cain. And don't say another word until I get you a lawyer," Riggs orders me as I slide into the back seat of the cruiser.

The gravity of today's events sinks in as the cruiser pulls away from the hospital.

8

PROMISE

As I pull up to work this morning, my stomach is in knots.

My life has been turned upside down the past few days. Not only did I catch my fiancé fucking my stepsister on his desk, but I immediately went out and celebrated my newly single status by jumping into bed with a sexy as sin, yet possibly dangerous biker —a member of The Kings of Retribution. God, I didn't even recognize the woman I was in that bar or the woman I had become when he took me back to his house. Even now, just thinking about Nova makes my tummy flutter and my sex clench. I ended up spending the remainder of the weekend thinking about Nova and whether I should have given him my name or at least left my number at his house. We agreed to one night, but the truth is I want to see him again.

Deep down, I know it's not possible. Nova isn't the type of man who settles down with one woman. I get the feeling going home with random women is something he often does. I'm sure he had a new body warming his bed the next night and I'm nothing more than an afterthought.

Sighing, I cut the engine to my car, lean my head back on the headrest, and rub my temples. My fantasy weekend is over and it's time to face the real world again, and that includes dealing with Brad. I'm a big girl. I can walk in that office and do my job without letting mine and Brad's drama affect it.

"We need to talk," Brad, who is waiting for me in my office, urges the second I step foot through the door. I sidestep him and ignore his demand as I set my briefcase down on my desk and fire up the computer. "Promise, I said we need to talk. I have been calling and texting you for days."

"Yes, Brad, I know," I say, not bothering to look at him. "I have been ignoring you for a reason. You should take the hint."

"Promise, you can't throw away three years over a little mistake." His words hit a nerve and my gaze slowly meets his.

"A little mistake?" I clench my teeth. "You fucking Avery is not something I'd refer to as a little mistake, Brad. Forgetting a birthday or an anniversary is a little mistake. Repeatedly buying whole milk instead of soy because after three years together you still can't remember I'm lactose intolerant, is a little mistake. But fucking my stepsister on your desk at a place where I work is not a little fucking mistake!" I nearly shout.

"Will you keep your voice down for Christ's sake, Promise?" Brad looks over his shoulder toward the hallway.

"Why? It's not like Jackson doesn't already know, and Thomas is bound to find out anyway since we are no longer together. Not that he will care."

"That's what we need to talk about, Promise. We can get past this, sweetheart."

I hold my hand up. "I'm not your sweetheart, and there is no working it out. We are done, Brad. You fucked up and there is no way I can or even want to forgive what you did." I look at him for a second, allowing my words to sink in before I continue. "You know what Avery put me through and how much she has hurt me, yet you still did what you did." I shake my head. Brad's shoulders slump and remorse crosses his face. The damage is done, and he knows it. "You can leave the same way you came in," I dismiss him and sit down at my desk.

Just as Brad gives up the fight and turns to leave, Thomas comes strolling into my office. "I'm glad I caught you two together. We have a new client, and I want both of you to head down to the police station over in Jefferson to talk with him and make sure he bonds out."

I stand from my chair. "What's his name, and what has he been charged with?"

"Cain LeBlanc. He was involved in an altercation and charged with battery, disorderly conduct, and disturbing the peace. His brother was here first thing this morning. Mr. LeBlanc is due to see the judge in an hour."

"Do we know the judge we are seeing?" I question as I grab my bag and start to make my way out of the office.

"Judge Brickman," Thomas answers.

I nod. Judge Brickman is a decent man. "Alright. I'll let you know how it goes." As I walk down the hall, Brad calls out from behind me.

"Why don't we ride together?"

"No," I answer and continue walking toward the elevator. I don't bother holding the door for him either.

I pull up to the police station ten minutes later, and Brad parks his car beside mine. To my left, I notice two motorcycles. Shaking off the memories of a particular biker, I make my way inside the station with Brad on my heels. A receptionist greets us. "Can I help you?"

"Yes. My name is Promise Bailey, and this is Brad Davis. We're here to speak with our client, Cain LeBlanc."

"Sure. Let me notify the Chief." The receptionist stands and disappears down the hallway. A minute later, she returns with the Chief of police in tow.

"Miss Bailey, Mr. Davis, if you'll follow me, I will take you to a room so you can talk with your client."

After Brad and I are led into a room with a table and four chairs, the Chief addresses us again. "Hang tight while I get him."

"Thank you." The door closes while Brad and I take a seat on one side of the table.

Five minutes later, I hear the door open. I stand alongside Brad and go to introduce myself to our client when suddenly all the air around me turns electric and I'm rendered speechless at sight before me. That's because walking into the room with handcuffs on his wrist, accompanied by Jefferson's Chief of police is Nova.

Nova stops in his tracks, carrying the same stunned look as mine before his face breaks out in a huge grin.

"Well, hey there, Sugar." Nova continues to saunter into the room and sits down at the table across from us. The whole time his eyes never leave mine. I also don't miss the confused look on Brad's face as his eyes dart back forth between me and Nova.

The sound of Brad's voice greeting Nova is what finally snaps me out of my stupor, and I quickly dive into the role of attorney. "Mr. LeBlanc, my name is Brad Davis and this is Promise Bailey."

At our introductions, Nova, who is still staring at me, smiles that smile, the one that once again makes my knees weak.

"Promise Bailey." Nova lets my name roll off his tongue. "I have to say I like it, but I think I like Sugar better."

My face heats, and I have a hard time hiding the effect Nova has on me. Brad starts looking back and forth between Nova and me again. "I'm sorry but do you two know each other?"

I ignore his question and decide it's time to get down to business. I clear my throat and take a seat. Unfortunately, Brad doesn't follow my lead and continues to dig. "Promise, do you know this man?"

I peer up at Brad. "Now is not the time or place," I say dismissing him. I don't miss the way Nova tilts his head to the side and studies Brad and me. It is not lost on me how Brad is acting a tad jealous and it looks as though Nova has picked up on it too.

"You could say Promise, and I know each other pretty well." Nova smirks and I close my eyes.

"That's enough," I snap at both men—Nova doesn't waver, but Brad's face has turned red. "Can we get on with what we came here for?" I look down at my watch. "We only have thirty minutes before we go before the judge, and I'd like to cover as much ground as possible before then." I go to move on but suddenly the sight of a bandage on Nova's arm causes me to gasp and on instinct, I lean over the table and gently touch his hand. "Oh my, God. What happened?"

"Just a little stab wound," Nova shrugs. "Nothin' to worry your beautiful head about. But I have to say. I like your concern, Sugar."

Nova's words hit me hard and I realize how inappropriate I'm acting. Composing myself I clear my throat and lean back in my seat. To say this situation is uncomfortable would be an understatement. Nevertheless, I still have a job to do. "As you know, Mr. LeBlanc, you have been charged with battery, disorderly conduct and disturbing the peace."

"He got what he deserved. The rest of those are trumped-up charges." Nova's harsh words and the venom in his tone shocks me.

"I will advise you not to admit that in front of the judge this morning. Our goal is to get you out of here, not keep you in."

Nova's back goes straight, and his tone turns deadly. "The motherfucker put his hands on my seventeen-year-old daughter and was going to rape her had I not stepped in. Fuck what the judge thinks. He should be worried about releasing the other asshole."

My eyes snap away from my note-taking and I look at Nova. He has a daughter. "Are you saying your daughter was assaulted?" Why in the hell wasn't I informed of these details before I arrived?

At Nova's nod my gut clenches. He was defending his child. I can't say I blame him for what he did. "I'm going to present this information to the judge and claim self-defense. Judge Brickman is not only a fair man, but he has three daughters himself." I look Nova in the eyes when I make my last statement.

Forty minutes later, Nova's bond was set, paid, and he was free to go. Just like I imagined, Judge Brickman sided with Nova when I laid out what happened to his daughter. And once the judge exits the courtroom, I turn to Nova who is standing between Brad and me. "We want you to come down to the office first thing in the morning so we can get to work on getting these charges taken care of."

Nova peers over his shoulder, and I follow his gaze. Sitting in the courtroom are three men. All are wearing the same leather vest Nova had on the other night. One of the men is a guy who looks to be in his twenties with blond hair, another is a man with brown hair and the third is a big black man and sitting next to him is a strikingly beautiful black woman who has a look on her face that says *don't fuck with me*. These are the same men who followed Brad and me from the police station to the courthouse. And though introductions have yet to be made, I'm assuming they belong to the same club as Nova, The Kings of Retribution.

A few minutes later, we exit the courthouse. Nova's blond friend whistles, gaining his attention. Nova touches my arm. "Hang back. I want to talk to you." I don't say anything as Nova jogs down the courthouse steps to his friends. I watch as he speaks to them and then watch as four sets of eyes land on me.

"Are you going to tell me what the deal is between you and that man?" Brad asks with an annoyed bite to his tone, stepping in front of me blocking my sight of them.

"Seeing as you no longer have a right to know jack shit about me, no, I'm not going to tell you a damn thing." Deciding that waiting on Nova is probably a bad idea and having enough of being in the same vicinity as Brad, I take my leave and head toward my car. Just as I go to open the door a large hand appears in front of me, stopping it from opening and Nova's gruff voice fills my ear, making me shiver.

"I told you to wait." Nova is standing so close; I can feel his heat on my back. Slowly I turn to face him.

"I didn't think it was a good idea."

"And why is that, babe?"

I swallow. "I'm your attorney now, Nov...I mean Mr. LeBlanc," I correct myself.

Nova steps closer into my space, his nose nearly touching mine. It takes all my strength not to close my eyes and take in his scent. Did I just whimper?

"Call me Cain. Not Nova and not Mr. LeBlanc. Cain," he growls, his nostrils flaring.

"Cain, I...I don't..." Oh, God. This man has my tongue tied in knots.

"Who's the fuckwit that came with you today?"

My brow scrunches at his rapid change of topic. "You mean Brad?" I debate whether to answer him, then cave. "Brad is an attorney that was assigned to help with your case."

"You two have a history?"

"Yes," I answer truthfully. "But it's just that; history."

"He know that?"

"Look, Cain," I sigh. "Brad and I are a long story. One I don't feel like getting into. The fact is, though, we are over. He's just having a hard time accepting it." I purposely leave out the part where it hasn't even been a week since the split happened and that Cain was my rebound.

"Maybe he needs some help understanding that shit," he clips.

I shake my head. Cain, acting jealous right now is confusing me. "I need to get back to the office," I say, trying to wiggle past him so he will move, only he doesn't budge. Instead, he runs his nose along the side of my face. I close my eyes and shiver at the contact.

"I'm going to let you run now. Just know this, Sugar. You and I, we're happenin'."

"Cain, there is no we. You and I both agreed to one night. Now that I'm your attorney. Let's pretend as if nothing happened." My voice shakes and the words taste sour as they tumble out of my mouth.

Cain shakes his head. "That's not possible. I haven't been able to stop thinkin' about you. You've gotten under my skin, and I can see in your eyes I've gotten under yours too. You might be good at winning in the courtroom, babe, but know this; you don't stand a chance when going head to head with me."

With those parting words, Cain steps back, taking his heat and scent with him. He then gives me a wink before he turns on his heel and makes his way back to his friends who are looking in my direction and all four of them are smiling. And I'm left with my head spinning.

Twenty minutes later, I'm back at the office. I'm still in a daze when I ride the elevator to the third floor and past Thomas's office and he calls out my name.

"Promise. A word, please."

Stopping in my tracks, I spin around and step into his office. My eyes immediately land on Avery, who is sitting on the sofa in front of the window. I toss a sneer in her direction and the bitch throws me a smug look. I want nothing more than to wipe the smirk right off her face with my fist. Next, I take in Brad who is sitting on a chair in front of Thomas's desk and he refuses to meet my eyes.

"You wanted to see me?" I address Thomas.

"Yeah. I'm taking you off the LeBlanc case."

"What—why?" I ask.

"It's been brought to my attention that you are involved with

Mr. LeBlanc. That's something I can't have; therefore, you're off the case."

I stand shocked for a second before I look from my stepdad back to Brad. Then I become pissed. "You asshole," I spit.

"Watch your language, Promise," Thomas warns.

"I will not watch my goddamn language. Yes, Mr. LeBlanc and I have met before and are only friends but that will not affect my ability in his case."

"I saw you two standing by your car after court, Promise. You looked like more than just friends," Brad says with disgust.

"That's enough," Thomas cuts in. "Promise, you're off the case —end of story. I can't have you making this firm look bad by associating with the criminals we defend. I won't stand for that sort of inappropriate behavior. I will not have you making a mockery of my family."

My anger turns to full-on rage. "You don't want me making you look bad?" I fume. "Let's talk about what's inappropriate here, shall we? How about your daughter fucking my fiancé in his office? How's that for inappropriate, Thomas?" I watch as Thomas's face turns red as I continue my tirade. "Oh, and while we are on the subject of reputation and how you are so worried about mine and how it affects you, let's shift our focus to your real daughters' reputation, shall we? Not only did she fuck my fiancé in this office, but she also goes around New Orleans opening her legs to married men. Do you know your golf friend, Kenneth Perkins? The same Kenneth who is married and has three kids? Your sweet daughter over there is sleeping with him. Well, she's not sleeping with him anymore. He cut her loose six months ago when she insisted he leave his wife. Now Avery is blackmailing him. He gives her money so that she won't snitch about their affair."

Avery flies off the sofa. "You better shut your lying mouth." Avery goes to stand next to Thomas. "You're just mad because Brad came running to me, a real woman, because you couldn't give him what he needed."

"I'm not jealous, and as far as I'm concerned, you two can have each other." I turn to Brad. "Be warned. You can't turn a whore into a housewife."

"You, bitch!" Avery screeches the same time Thomas slams his palm down on his desk. "That's enough! How dare you come in here and badmouth my daughter. You have been nothing but a thorn in my side ever since your mother died."

My heart drops at the mention of my mom. I always knew how Thomas felt about me, but it's different hearing the words said out loud.

"You know what? I'm done. I'm done with you and your spoiled bitch of a daughter, and I'm done with this job. I quit." Not giving my stepfather, Avery, or Brad a second thought, I turn and walk away, something I should have done a long damn time ago.

"I am so damn proud of you." London engulfs me in a hug later that same evening as we sit on her sofa drinking wine while I give her the rundown of the crazy turn of events that transpired today. I told her all about Cain and about what went down with Thomas. London especially liked the part about me outing Avery.

"Thanks, Lon. I have to say I'm pretty damn proud of myself.

It's like a weight has been lifted off my shoulders."

"So, what are you going to do about Nova?"

"There's nothing I can do. He'll learn tomorrow that I'm no longer his attorney. What's done is done."

"I don't know, Promise. I have a feeling you haven't seen the last of your biker."

I roll my eyes. "He's not my anything."

"Don't kid yourself, girl. Mark my words, that man is coming for you."

Standing, I grab my empty glass from the coffee table and make my way into the kitchen, where I pour myself some more wine.

"The real question here is, what am I going to do next? I need to find a job. I think it's safe to say Thomas won't be giving me a letter of recommendation." I snicker.

"That's an easy one. I say we start up our own firm."

My hand freezes mid-pour, and I stare at my friend. "What?"

London jumps from the sofa and walks into the kitchen. "I have been wanting to broach the idea of you and me becoming partners for a while now, Promise. Come on. You can't tell me you haven't at least thought about the idea before."

"I mean, I have, but..."

"No buts. We can do this, Promise."

We are both quiet for a moment as I mull over the idea.

"Look, you love being a lawyer, but you hated the side you worked on. Now is your chance to do what you love while making your own rules. Come on, Promise. Say yes. I can't think of a better person to be my partner than you."

I'll admit London's idea fills me with hope and excitement. With a big smile on my face, I lift my glass in the air and London does the same. "I say we do it."

"Partners?" London questions.

"Partners," I answer, tapping my glass against hers.

London and I take a sip of our wine just as the doorbell rings. "That must be the pizza," I announce making my way to the door. Only when I open it, it's not the pizza, it's a man holding a large bouquet of roses.

"Are you Promise Bailey?"

"Yes, " I answer.

The man passes me the flowers. "Have a good evening."

Shutting the door, I walk the flowers over to the kitchen table.

"Wow." London walks up behind me. "Are they from your biker?"

I pluck the card from the arrangement and read who they are from. My stomach knots when I read who they are from. I shake my head. "No, They are from Leon Velasco."

"Damn, Promise. That guy is still at it. I think if he continues you should consider going to the police. The guy is creepy."

"You're right. If this continues I'll talk to the police."

9

NOVA

I left a couple of hours earlier than necessary this morning before driving downtown to see my lawyer. I increase my speed. I need time to think—time to clear my head before seeing her again, so I hopped on my bike for a little therapy. Nothing feeds the soul better than the open road, wind in your hair, and sun on your face. Strike that. Maybe one thing—or someone I can think of—that trumps all that.

Promise.

My thoughts are a jumbled mess, as I take in the familiar scenery around me. After spending the night in a cold cell room with three other men, all I wanted was to get home and take a hot shower. I still can't believe those pussy ass cops charged me with battery, and a few other shit charges they could tack on. Regardless, if I end up doing time, one thing is certain; I would do it over again—do whatever it takes to protect my daughter.

I take the exit toward downtown, still replaying yesterday in my head. Riggs said he'd find me a lawyer, but never in my wildest dreams did I expect my mystery woman to walk through the door. Her scent gave her away before my eyes ever landed on her face.

And Lord forgive me for all the sinful thoughts I was having as I drank her in. The way her skirt hugged her hips, and her button-down blouse pulled taught across her breasts. But her confidence and the way she carried herself went straight to my cock. It was sexy as hell. All I wanted was to bend her sweet ass over the table, hike up her skirt, bury myself balls deep in her sweet pussy, and feel her walls convulse around my cock. I found myself wanting to do it all in front of that pansy-ass pretty boy she had brought with her. I wanted him to know. Promise is mine.

The only problem there is, Promise wants to keep things between us strictly professional. Not gonna happen. I've tasted her, and I'm hungry for more. Promise Bailey has something I want. My future. And I won't stop until she's mine.

As I pull into the parking lot of Promise's law firm, I glance around, looking for the car she climbed into yesterday, not spotting it anywhere. Nevertheless, I park and walk inside. Everything about the inside décor screams money, which doesn't surprise me. My brother mentioned they are supposed to be some of the best defense attorneys in our area. As I approach the front desk, the young woman on the phone locks eyes on me, the phone dropping from her ear. "May I help you?" Her eyes appraise me as she leans forward, pushing her breasts together. A flirtatious move I know all too well but has little effect on me.

"I have a 12:30 pm appointment with Miss Bailey." I give her my usual smile, and her face flushes.

The young woman tears her eyes away long enough to peer at her computer screen. "Mr. LeBlanc?" She looks up, and I nod. "Third floor. Would you like me to show you the way?" She continues to flirt with me. A couple of days ago, I would have taken her up on the offer, and maybe have shown her my gratitude, but I only have one woman on my mind these days.

"I'll find my way." I rap my knuckles against the counter. "You have a good day," I tell her before making my way to the elevator.

The moment the elevator doors slide open, I hear yelling coming from down the hall. A man rushes out an open office door, his face morphed in anger. Lifting his head, he notices me standing here, and comes to a dead stop.

"Can I help you?" he asks, then steps around me, throwing a folder in his hand down on a desk.

"I'm here for Promise Bailey," I tell him, and he stares for a beat before answering.

"She's not here."

"What do you mean, she's not here? I have an appointment with her today." I start to get a little irritated that she may be avoiding me.

"She quit, and no longer works here." The guy crosses his arms over his chest, still accessing me. "Are you the biker she was representing?"

"Is representing," I correct him.

"Your case has been taken over by Brad Davis." The way he says the prick's name lets me know he's not fond of pretty boy either.

"Where can I find her?" I ask, hoping he may give me a bread crumb.

"Name's Jackson." He sticks out his hand, and I shake it. He then looks down the empty hall. Stepping behind his desk, Jackson opens a drawer, pulling out a notepad and a pen. He scribbles on the yellow paper, then rips it from the notepad. "She's a good person. Don't hurt her." He narrows his eyes.

"What is she to you?" I harden my stare.

"She's my step-sister."

"She's in good hands," I assure him.

"Good. She's been through enough shit the past few days, hell, her entire life. She doesn't need someone else to come along, knocking her down again." I listen to what he says and approve of the fact he cares.

"By the way. Tell your boss I no longer require his services."

Jackson doesn't reply, and I don't wait for him to.

Without saying another word, I turn on my heel, ride the elevator down the way I arrived, and exit the building. Once I straddle my bike, I peer down at the piece of paper fisted in my hand and read the address. I know the neighborhood, and it's a real shit hole—just another part of the city that hasn't had enough invested back into it since Katrina. Pulling my phone from my pocket, I call my brother. I don't need anything from him, except for him to know I'm heading for a seedy part of town. "What's going on, brother. How'd the meeting go?"

"Meeting never happened," I inform him.

"Why the fuck not? I paid a hefty retainer fee already." I hear the irritation in his voice.

"My lawyer quit."

"Goddamnit," Riggs seethes.

"Don't worry. I'm on my way to find her, which is why I'm callin'. I'm going to text you the address her stepbrother gave me. It's in a seedy area."

"Somethin' you need to tell me, Cain?" I hear the smirk in his voice and know what he's hinting at, but I don't cave into his prying.

"Everyone still showing up at the bar later?" I ask with a plan.

"As far as I know."

"Good. I'm sending Kiwi with Piper to hang with you guys. I want her around the family as much as possible for now. I'll catch up with you later."

"Watch your back and stay safe."

"Always." Disconnecting the call, I shove my phone back into my pocket, then start my bike.

Twenty minutes later, I'm pulling up to the address Jackson wrote down. Rolling to a stop, I throw my kickstand down and cut the engine. It's not the worst place to live but it damn sure could be better. I sure as shit don't like the fact Promise is staying here.

After climbing a couple of flights of stairs, I stop outside her apartment door and knock. It takes a few minutes before the door swings open, with a pretty looking woman with black hair looking back at me.

"Holy shit!" Her eyes travel the length of my body before settling on my face once more. She grins, her eyes twinkling with mischief. "I know who you are." She pauses, before calling over her shoulder. "Promise!" the woman shouts before her head swings back toward me, still smiling like the Cheshire cat. "Someone's here to see you." She leans against the doorframe, crossing her arms over her chest.

"If that's Brad, you can tell him to fuck off." The last part of Promise's words fall silent as she appears, shocked to see me standing at her door. "Cain." She says my name in a way that goes straight to my cock. Her eyes cut to her friend, then back to me. "Why are you here?" She pauses, putting her hand on her hip. "Better yet, how in the hell did you find me?"

"You really shouldn't be answering your door before asking who is standing outside of it. I could have been anyone."

Her friend holds her hand up. "First of all, this is my apartment. Second, all I know about you is that you showed my bestie what it really means to get laid, which gives you zero, " she forms a circle with her fingers, "rights to tell anyone living here what they should or shouldn't be doing. Even if you do have a magic dick."

Promise gasps, her face flushing. "London," she says low through clench teeth. "Shut up."

"What?" London, now that I know her name looks to her friend as if she did nothing wrong. "Your words, babe, not mine." I do my best to hold in a chuckle.

"London," Promise pleads.

"Fine. I'll be in the kitchen, where the wine is, if you need me,"

London faces me. "You hurt her, I'll cut off your balls." She winks before walking away.

"Your friend is brutal." I laugh as Promise steps outside, closing the apartment door behind her.

"She has no filter," Promise says, unamused. "Seriously, Cain. How did you find me?"

"We had an appointment today. I showed, and you weren't there." I finally realize how tired she looks.

"Yeah, well, I quit yesterday," she admits to what I already know.

"Because of me?"

Her eyes lock on mine. "Oh, God, no. Well, I mean, seeing you yesterday was a bit of a shock, but no, you were not the reason. I quit for my own sanity. I couldn't take working beside someone I loathed anymore."

"You talkin' about the prick you were with yesterday?"

"His name is Brad. And that is none of your business, Cain." Promise crosses her arms beneath her breast, and my eyes fall for a moment. She clears her throat, causing me to look up. "Who told you?"

"Your stepbrother."

Promise growls. "I'm going to strangle him. Look, Cain. I'm sorry, but I can't represent you." Her eyes soften.

"I don't want anyone else." The words have much more meaning behind them, and by the look on her face, Promise reads me like an open book.

"Cain."

Reaching out, I pull her to me, and run my fingers through her hair, brushing her loose locks over her shoulder. "I meant what I said yesterday. And I want you to continue to be my attorney." As I play with her hair, Promise closes her eyes.

"Okay." She opens her eyes and looks at me.

"Yeah?"

"Yeah."

Stomping down the urge to kiss her lips so hard her knees buckle, I kiss her on the forehead instead. "Take a ride with me."

"Where?"

"Does it matter?" I watch her lips turn up in a smile.

"No."

"Go tell your friend you're leavin' with me, and that I'll bring you home later." I swat her on the ass.

"I need to change," Promise looks down at her leggings and oversized shirt.

"The hell you do. You look perfect just the way you are. Throw on some shoes, and let's go," I tell her. Hesitating briefly, she turns and opens the door, walking inside. I stand in the doorway, waiting for her.

"London, I'll be back later," I hear her call her friend from somewhere inside the apartment.

"Get you some more of that magic D, girl," London fires back at Promise.

"For fuck's sake, Lon. He's standing at the door and hears everything you are saying!" Promise yells.

"Good." There's a short pause. "Hey, Nova?"

"Yeah," I call from where I'm standing just as Promise appears, pulling her hair back and securing it in a high ponytail.

"I meant what I said about your balls." Promise rolls her eyes as she steps out the door. She waits to leave until she hears the locks engage from inside. "Have fun," London sing songs from the other side of the door, and I can't hide my laughter.

With Promise at my side, we make our way outside. Straddling my bike, I hold out my hand, helping her settle in behind me. Her long legs hug me as she slides in closer—the engine roars, rumbling between our thighs. Promise wraps her arms around my torso, presses her lips close to my ear, her warm breath on my skin causing my cock to swell. "Rev it up." I grin remembering the other night. I twist the throttle a few times before taking off down the road.

A short time later, we pull up in front of Twisted Throttle. Backing my bike alongside the others, I kill the engine and dismount. Promise removes her helmet, and I hang it on my handlebar. She looks around. "Come on." I hold out my hand, helping her climb off.

"What are we doing here? The bar isn't open yet."

"We need a place to talk about the case." I open the front door, stepping to the side for her to enter, and the smell of my brother's jambalaya assaults my senses.

"Something smells delicious," Promise remarks. The moment she walks in, she freezes, noticing the bar full of people. "Come on. Let me introduce you to everyone." I take her by the hand, and she follows without hesitation.

Everyone is scattered around the bar, sitting at the tables, eating. "Hey, dad." Piper makes her way toward me, then wraps me in a hug.

"Hey, Bean. How are you feelin'?" With my free hand, I pull her to my chest, kissing her forehead.

Piper tilts her head back to look at me. She carries no physical marks on the outside from her assault, but I worry about what could be going on inside her head, and most importantly, her heart. Those are the bruises and scars I can't see, and it pains me.

"I'm good, dad." She smiles at me, and I try my best to believe her. It only takes her a moment to introduce herself to Promise. "Hi, I'm Piper." My daughter keeps one arm around my waist as she extends her hand.

Promise smiles. "Hey, and I'm Promise."

"That's such a cool name," Piper tells her.

Needing to get introductions out of the way, I begin with my brother. "You may notice a few faces from yesterday, but not my brother, Abel. Most call him Riggs. He's the club's President." Promise looks between Riggs and me with a surprised look.

"Twins. What was that like growing up?"

My brother laughs. "He was a pain in my ass." I can't even defend myself. I was a pain in the ass. My ass was always doing something that got us into trouble. "Nice to meet you, Promise." Riggs turns and waves his wife over. Luna, who is holding their daughter, crosses the room. "This is my woman, Luna, and our daughter Aria," he signs as he speaks.

"Nice to meet you," Promise returns, and Luna signs her hello, keeping her voice to herself.

"Over there," I gesture to my right, "At the bar is Wick, our VP, beside him, his woman Vayda. Everyone here calls her Tequila."

Wick gives Promise a chin lift, raising the beer in his hand, and Tequila waves.

"Tequila, huh? I bet there's a good story behind that name," Promise remarks, earning a light laugh from Tequila.

"The guy sitting over there, holding the guitar is Fender, and our Viking lookin' friend over there is Kiwi."

"How ya doin'?" Kiwi greets her.

Finally, I point to the three sitting at a table close by. "Big guy there is Everest, and these two lovely ladies are Payton and Josie." All three say hello.

"It's nice to meet all of you." Promise holds my hand a little tighter.

"We just sat down to eat lunch." Piper points over her shoulder, "Why don't you join us? Uncle Abel makes the best jambalaya in Louisiana," she boasts.

Grabbing Promise by the hand, I follow my daughter to the table. We take our seats, and Payton walks over, sitting a bowl of food in front of us, along with a slice of cornbread. I watch Promise crumble her cornbread over her jambalaya, mixing it all. Wanting to get more pressing issues out of the way, I mention one of the reasons I needed to see her today. "Is there a possibility the charges against me can be reduced?"

Her eyes scan the room before she turns her body and looks at me. "We don't have to talk about that now. We can wait until it's the two of us."

"We can discuss it now. Everyone here is family."

"Alright." Promise places her spoon in her bowl, then wipes her mouth with a paper towel. "As I said before, if we get the right judge, it's possible. My hope is for you to get no more than a few hefty fines. Probation isn't being ruled out either, but it is far better than sitting behind bars for a few months."

"What about the fucker who touched my daughter?" My words come out harsher than intended. When I look at Piper, she's staring into her bowl, pushing her food around.

"From what I know, he bonded out a few hours after you. The police have your daughter's statement. All of that will be presented in court on the day of his hearing." Promise shifts her attention to my daughter. "Piper." Promise slides her hand across the tabletop, placing her palm on my daughter's arm. Piper lifts her head. No tears visible, but emotion present behind her hazel eyes. "I know you've been through a lot, and there's a possibility you may need to testify against your attacker. But, if I can get a chamber meeting between you and the appointed judge for your dad's case, would you be willing to tell him, in your own words, what took place the other day?" Promise asks, her voice soft, but firm. "It could help."

Piper cuts her eyes at me. It's her call. I won't make her do anything she isn't comfortable with. She looks back to Promise, holding her head higher. "Yes. I'll do anything to keep my dad out of jail."

The bar room falls silent a beat, while my brothers and I share similar looks. All of us are probably thinking the same. If we have it our way, we'll exact our brand of justice, making sure the sorry son of a bitch never has the opportunity to put his filthy hands on another woman again.

For the rest of the day, we sit around, enjoying good food over easy conversation. Promise doesn't say a whole lot. Mostly she listens, fully absorbing interaction between me and the others, never once hinting at being uncomfortable. One thing she did mention was her and her friend, London are lookin' to start their own firm, and that little nugget of information gave me an idea, which I plan to act on later, when the time is right. I mostly watch the way Promise and my daughter interact. The fact Piper is at ease around her, being her usual chatty self, only cements the thoughts and developing feelings I have toward the vibrant woman sitting next to me.

When she is ready to leave, we get on my bike. The ride is the same as before, comfortable, and welcoming. All too soon, we are pulling up in front of her apartment complex, and I'm walking her to her door. Snaking my arm around her waist, I pull her into my body, her palms resting against my chest as she lifts her blue eyes to mine. "Thanks for the ride," Promise tells me.

"I appreciate what you did today."

Promise scrunches her face. "What do you mean?"

"You talked freely with my family and made my daughter feel like she could trust you." I lean in closer, feeling her breath on my lips.

"Piper is as protective of you as you are of her." A look of longing crosses Promise's face. "She adores you, and I can tell family means the world to all of you."

"My family is my life," I say with conviction.

"I like that about you," Promise admits, surprising the fuck out of me just before her lips touch mine. Her kiss is soft and sweet. Not at all what I'm used to. My cock hardens, and I pull her closer, wanting her to feel the effect she has on me. She lingers there for a moment before breaking our connection.

I press my forehead against hers. "I want nothing more than to sweep you off your feet, press your back against that door, and make you come on my cock," I admit freely, hiding nothing. Her breathing increases, and even though I know she wants it too, I let my arms fall to my sides, releasing my hold on her. "Soon," I promise her. Though I warned her that I wanted her, I want to show Promise I'm after more than what's between her legs. I want all of her. This woman is worth waiting for.

Promise steps away, turning her back to me as she unlocks the door. "Um," she says, her face flush, "I'll call you once I find out your court date." After stepping inside, she faces me, her smile giving me the confidence that I made the right move.

"Alright," I answer back, and she stands, unmoving, her eyes locked on mine. Cocking my head, I grin. "I'm not leavin' until I hear you lock the door, Sugar." Her smile grows as she closes the door, and her beautiful face disappears. Rooted in place, I wait to hear the locks engage before jogging down the stairs. The ride home felt a little empty without her on the back of my bike.

10

PROMISE

The next morning, I'm quietly sitting on the sofa, with a throw draped across my legs and a mug of coffee in my hand, as I search real estate listings online. I'm desperately trying to concentrate on the task at hand, but Cain keeps invading my thoughts. Focus.

"Hey, you." London greets me as she pads into the kitchen. "Why are you up so early? It's not like you need to get to that dreaded job anymore. You should relax, sleep in a little, take a long hot bath, and prune like a raisin." She pops a pod into the coffee machine and waits for it to brew.

I sigh and rub my temples. "I couldn't sleep. I've got a lot on my mind." I continue to stare at my laptop screen.

Strolling into the living room, London places a plate stacked with several doughnuts on the coffee table, then sinks to the sofa beside me. She tucks her legs beneath her and takes a sip of her coffee. "Your insomnia wouldn't have anything to with a particular biker, would it?" Looking up from the screen, I find my best friend smirking at me from behind her mug. "Maybe a little," I decide not to lie.

"Girl. I don't blame you for losing sleep over that man. He is fine. And don't get me started on the way he looks at you. That man wants you bad." Setting her mug on the coffee table in front of us, she steals part of the throw I'm covered with.

"I'm not sure he's what I need in my life, Lon."

London twists her body to face me. "He's exactly what you need. Not everyone is like Brad." She says his name like it leaves a bad taste in her mouth. "I have to admit, at first, I was a little hesitant, knowing who he is. But, honey, the chemistry between you two is off the charts. Hell, I need a man like him."

Damn. What do I say to that? Nothing, because London is right. I can't deny the way I feel around Cain. He's also nothing like Brad. Maybe that's what makes me a little hesitant to move forward into a relationship with him. Hell, I haven't even caught my breath since getting out of the last one. What if Cain isn't capable of long term?

"I hear those gears turning in your head, Promise. Stop overthinking this—whatever it is between you and Nova." Leaning forward, London grabs a donut from the plate on the table. "Just go with it." Tearing a piece off, she pops the bite of pastry into her mouth.

"I'm not getting any younger, Lon. I want to get married and have babies one day."

London shrugs. "Maybe Nova is the one to give you all those things. Then again, maybe he isn't." My friend falls silent for a moment as she eats another bite. "Sweetie, let it happen naturally. You never find love—it finds you."

Plucking a Danish from the platter, I take a bite. For a few moments, I try to let London's words sink in. I've been chasing all forms of love and acceptance my whole life.

"So, what's on the agenda today?" London asks. "I'm free. What do you say we do a little retail therapy?"

I smile. "Sounds good to me," I agree as I open my emails.

Spotting a response from my acquaintance down at the

courthouse, I open it. She was kind enough to email the court dates I needed. It looks like Cain's hearing is not for another couple of weeks due to the docket backlog. Grabbing my phone off the arm of the sofa, I send a text to Cain, letting him know. I wait for his reply, but my phone rings instead. "Cain."

"Hey, Sugar."

My insides melt, hearing his voice. My eyes cut to London, finding her eyeing me with a shit-eating grin.

" I sent you the date of your hearing, but there is a possibility it could be pushed back to a later date."

"Yeah, babe. I got it, but I wanted to hear your voice." His tone sounds husky like he just woke up, and my mind immediately thinks of lying in bed beside him.

"If I need any more information before then, I'll be sure to let you know," I tell him.

"I'd like to see you today," he says.

"Today?"

"Yeah, babe—today."

At my side, London hangs on mine and Cain's conversation, and I think back to what she said earlier about letting go and just have fun. My silence goes unnoticed as I continue to overthink the invite.

"Have a drink with me—tonight, before my shift starts at the bar."

"Are you asking me out on a date?" My stomach flutters with excitement.

Cain chuckles, and I can hear the smile in his tone when he answers. "Yeah, Babe. I guess I am."

Trusting myself, I jump into the deep end. "I'd like that." My reply has London throwing her hands in the air.

"I'll pick you up around seven," Cain confirms before I hear the sound of water running.

Thinking that I'll be spending the day with London, I tell him,

"I can just meet you there." I hear him sigh heavily on the other end of the line. For a minute, I think he's going to go all caveman on me again.

"Alright, Sugar." I smile. I have a feeling that giving in was not easy for him. "I'll see you later, babe."

"Bye, Cain." The call ends, and my hand falls slowly to the couch, amazed at myself for stepping outside my comfort zone.

"Feels good, doesn't it?" London looks at me over the rim of her mug.

"What's that?" I pick at the remaining portion of my pastry.

"Having fun," London proclaims. My best friend sets her coffee down, then stands. "Come on. We've got some shopping to do."

I have one hour before meeting Cain for a drink or two down at the bar his club owns, and I'm nowhere close to being ready. Do I dress for comfort or wear something sexy? Ugh. Why am I so nervous? Hell, I've slept with the man already. Closing my eyes, I think about our night together. "Stop it," I scold myself. I do not need to show up ready to hump his leg for Christ's sake.

Walking to the foot of the bed, I stare down at the outfit options laid out and opt for a pair of curve-hugging jeans, and a cropped band tee, paired with black mid-calf boots with a three inch heel. Finally dressed, I take one last look in the mirror.

"Damn, girl. If you weren't practically my sister, and I didn't like dick so much, I'd fuck you." London says from the doorway of my room. Grabbing my bag from the bed, I dig out my car keys, then slide it onto my shoulder.

"Does it send the wrong message?"

"You're kidding, right? Honey, you could wear a potato sack and still look just as good," London boasts, giving me an extra boost of confidence.

"What would I do without you, Lon?" I hug her, then head for the front door.

"Don't do anything I wouldn't do," she calls to me after I step into the hallway, and I smile.

Thirty minutes later, I'm pulling up to the bar, and spot Cain, leaning against the wall outside, smoking a cigarette. Lifting his head, he spots me walking in his direction. His eyes lock on mine, and my body heats and my skin prickles from the intensity of his stare. His arm snakes around my middle when I come within reach, and he pulls me close. "Hey, babe."

God, he smells good. "Hey."

"You look good," he compliments as his fingertips graze my exposed skin. He drops his hand, taking mine in his. "Come on." He leads me inside.

The bar isn't busy yet. Only a dozen people are sitting around enjoying the music playing from the speakers mounted in the corners of the room. Cain seats us in the same spot at the end of the bar we sat the night we first met. "Old Fashion?" he asks, and I smile because he remembered. Suddenly any lingering nerves I had before disappear. We sit and talk for an hour or two, keeping the conversation light and not too personal. Small talk about each other. Cain made it a point to make me feel at ease. He dialed his intensity back to make me more comfortable. He was giving me what I wanted. Cain proved to me I was more to him than another notch in his bedpost.

Before I know it, time passes by, and Cain has to start his shift for the night, which means I need to go.

"Sure I can't convince you to stay?" Cain's hand slides up and down my arm. As much as my body is telling me to stay, I shake my head no. "I'll walk you to your car." Cain's fingers link with mine as he leads me out the door to my car.

Letting go of his hand, I cast my eyes down as I dig in my bag for my keys.

"Promise," Cain says, my name as I continue to dig.

"Yeah?" Where the hell are my keys?

Placing his finger beneath my chin, Cain brings my eyes to his. He brushes the hair from my face. My heart starts thumping against my chest, and my breath hitches. I find myself hoping he will kiss me, and my eyes close without thought. Then, I feel his lips against my forehead. "I had a good time."

My eyes open. "Me too."

It's dark by the time I leave Twisted Throttle, and I can't stop myself from smiling as I sing along to the radio. My cell rings. Turning the music down, I reach over to the passenger seat and dig it out of my purse. I smile when I see it's Jackson calling.

"Hello."

"Hey." His voice sounds hesitant.

"What's up?"

"I uh...I wanted to check on you. See how you were holding up after what happened."

This is why I love my stepbrother. He never fails to look out for me. "I'm good, Jackson. Really good in-fact."

I hear him exhale over the phone. "That's good. I've been worried about you. You didn't return my call yesterday."

"I'm sorry about that. Yesterday was..." I let my sentence hang as I blow out a breath. Yesterday I was still reeling from what went down with Thomas and Avery.

"I know, Promise. You don't have to tell me. I will say I am fucking proud of you, though. I love my dad and my sister, but they deserved the verbal ass-kicking you gave them. I'm just sorry I missed it." I can hear the smirk behind his tone when he says that, and I smile.

"It was pretty epic. It felt so damn good too. Not just saying what I said but choosing to finally walk away. I meant what I said. I'm done with them." I'm silent for a beat and my smile drops from my face. "I hope what happened doesn't affect you and me. You're the closest thing I have to a brother and I'd hate to lose that. But I will understand if things have to change between us. Thomas and Avery are your family."

"Stop!" Jackson cuts me off. "You're my family, too, Promise. I'll always be there for you. Always."

"Thanks, Jackson."

"Uh...one more thing before I let you go. Mr. LeBlanc came into the office the other morning. I told him where he could find you. I hope you don't mind."

"Of course not. And he found me. I'll be handling his case."

"You're a great attorney, Promise. I'm not surprised he was adamant you be his lawyer. His visit to the office was quite entertaining."

"Oh, I bet it was. I can't imagine Thomas taking the fact one of his clients chose me over him, well."

"You are one of the best attorney's in New Orleans, Promise. I mean that."

"That means a lot coming from you, Jackson."

"I only speak the truth."

Stopping at a red light, I cover my mouth and yawn.

"Look, you sound beat. I'm going to let you go."

"Okay. Is it okay if I call you and we meet up for lunch soon?"

"You better."

"Great. I'll talk with you later, Jackson." "Sounds good," he tells me.

"Bye."

Hanging up with Jackson, I drop the phone in the cupholder just as the light turns green. Peering over in the rear-view mirror, I notice a truck trailing behind me, and for some strange reason, I get an uneasy feeling in my stomach. I drive another mile while keeping my attention on the truck but let out a sigh of relief when the person makes a left turn and is no longer behind me. I shake my head. "Get a grip, Promise." It's been a strange week, and now my head is playing tricks on me.

Pulling up to the apartment, I don't see London's car. She texted me earlier saying she would be a little late getting home. Grabbing my things from the passenger seat, I climb out of my vehicle then press the key fob, locking it. Climbing the stairs, I let out another yawn just as I reach the door. With my keys still in hand, I unlock the door. Just as I push it open, something heavy crashes into me from behind, or someone, which sends me flying to the floor, landing hard on my knees, and I cry out. Next, I'm grabbed by my hair and flipped over on my back. Everything happens so fast I am not prepared for the fist that strikes my left cheek, making my teeth clatter. A hand clamps down over my mouth muffling my screams.

"Shut the fuck up, bitch." Hot, rancid breath fills my nostrils, making me gag.

Somewhat recovering from the punch, my senses come back to me, and I blink my eyes open. Crouched over me on the floor is a man with dark hair and even darker eyes. His face is twisted into a sneer as he keeps his grip on my hair.

"Listen to me, cunt. I have a message for your boyfriend. You tell him and his club they better watch their backs. You tell him if they don't quit snooping around, my men and I are going to finish what I started with that bitch daughter of his. My club will have fun passing her around and turning her into our whore. He's going to pay for what he did to me." My hair is yanked on once again, causing my head to snap back. "Do you understand me, bitch?"

My body starts shaking with fear, and I struggle to find my words. My lack of an answer earns me another blow to my face making my cheek feel like it's going to explode. "I said do you fuckin' understand?"

"Yes," I rasp. "Yes, I understand."

The man raises off of me. "And don't even think about calling the police, or I'll be back to finish you off."

When he turns and exits the apartment, I see he is wearing a leather vest. One similar to what Cain and his club wear. Only the one this man is sporting has Hell's Punishers MC on it.

I don't know how many minutes pass as I slowly try to pick myself up off the floor when I hear London's shocked voice ring out and the lights to the apartment flicker on. "Oh my God! Promise! What happened?" My best friend drops to the floor beside me and starts helping me up. My knees are weak, and my legs feel like lead as she guides me over to the sofa. "Are you okay? I'm calling the police." London hurries across the living room to where she dropped her purse on the floor by the door.

I call out. "No! No, police!" I say in a rush, remembering the man's threat.

"What! Are you crazy, Promise? You were assaulted."

"No police," I say again, adamantly. "Find my phone and call Cain."

"Cain?" her face falls. "Promise..."

I cut her off. "Please, Lon. I need you to call Cain." I slump against the back of the sofa, bringing my hand up to my cheek when I feel wetness trickling down the side of my face. When I pull my hand back, I note my fingers are covered in blood. The sight makes me queasy. "Shit. Okay, I'll call him."

I watch as London shuffles over to where my purse is and retrieves my cell. I listen as she places the phone to her ear and starts talking to who I assume in Cain.

"No, it's London."

"We need you to come to our apartment. I just came home and found Promise on the floor. She's been attacked." London delivers the news with a shaky voice.

Seconds later, I hear Cain's deep voice ring out as London's eyes go big, and she looks at me with a worried expression. She hangs up the phone and swallows. "He's on his way."

I breathe a sigh of relief, knowing Cain is coming. Just the thought of having him near makes me feel safe.

"I'm going to get something for your face. It's swelling pretty badly." London goes to the freezer and pulls out a bag of frozen peas. Sitting down next to me, she places the bag against my cheek, and I wince. "Sorry," she whispers.

Ten minutes later, London and I look at each other when we hear the rumble of a bike. A few seconds later, the door to the apartment bursts open, nearly breaking from its hinges. Nova's large frame fills the doorframe, with a look that can only be described as murder marring his face. His eyes appraise every inch of my body. He takes in my disheveled clothes and ratty hair. Then when I drop the ice pack from my face, he growls. "The motherfucker is dead."

In two strides, Cain is in front of me taking my battered face in his hands. I close my eyes and rest my face against his warm palms.

"Brother." Everest steps into the apartment and takes in the scene. His face hardens when he gets a look at me. He then turns his attention back to Cain.

"You see anything?" Cain asks Everest.

"Nothin,' man."

Cain grits his teeth. His eyes never leave mine. "Tell me?"

I know what he is asking, so I tell him everything. I tell him about the uneasy feeling I got when I thought I was being followed. I tell him about the man sneaking up on me when I arrived, and how he shoved me into the apartment, pinned me down on the floor and punched me in the face. I told him what the man said about Piper and his club. I didn't leave a single detail out. By the time I'm done, the fury coming off Cain is palpable but somehow, he manages to tamp it down and gain control of the situation.

Palming the uninjured side of my face, Cain brushes his lips against mine. "You're safe now, babe. I'm going to take care of this shit." Cain stands, facing Everest. "Get on the phone with Kiwi. Check on him and Piper. Give him the low down on what happened here, so he knows to be vigilant. Then call Fender and have him bring the cage. He can bring my bike back to the clubhouse. Also, have Doc meet us there. I want her to check Promise over."

"You got it, brother," Everest nods.

Next, Cain addresses London. "I want you to pack some shit. You two will not be stayin' here tonight."

"Where are we going?" I interject.

"London will go back to the clubhouse with Everest. She'll be set up in a room. You'll be coming home with me," he states.

"Cain, I..."

He holds up his hand, cutting me off. "Some motherfucker comes up in my woman's place, putting his filthy fuckin' hands on her, making threats against my daughter and my club. You will be comin' home with me where I can keep my eyes on you. End of fuckin' discussion."

Too tired to argue and sensing Cain is hanging on by a very thin thread, I relent. "Okay."

Thirty minutes later, I'm woken up by Cain sliding his arms under me and pulling me from his truck. I must have fallen asleep. "Where are we?"

"Clubhouse. Doc is here to check on you, and then I'm taking you home."

I start to wiggle in his arms. "I can walk, Cain."

"Nope. Not lettin' you go, Sugar."

Lifting my head from Cain's shoulder, I take in my surroundings. The Kings clubhouse sits on a large lot, next to an old paper mill, no longer in use. The building itself looks like an old two-level warehouse, and just behind the building runs the Mississippi River.

When Cain steps through the doors of the clubhouse, we are met by London and Everest, who arrived just before us. Cain strides across the room to a large leather sofa and sets me down. London walks over and sits beside me, studying my face. "You okay?" she asks me.

I nod. "I think so. What about you? Will you be okay staying here? Would you rather call Ruby or Sadie and stay with one of them?"

"Naw. It's late. Let's not worry them with all that's happened tonight."

The sound of the clubhouse door opening and heels clicking on the floor draws my attention to a beautiful woman walking in. She has long blonde hair and is wearing a black knee-length pencil skirt and a beige satin blouse, paired with black four-inch heels. Her eyes land on Cain first with a look of warmth and familiarity as she smiles. An unwelcome reaction settles over me —jealousy.

"Nova," the woman greets him.

"Doc," Cain nods, not moving from his place beside me. "I need you to check on my woman."

The moment Cain says the words 'my woman,' the lady snaps her gaze away from him over to me. The woman studies me for a moment. She is quiet as her eyes move between me and Cain. There is no missing the possessive arm Cain has wrapped around my waist. I'd be lying if I said I didn't like it. Finally, the woman in front of us smiles and her face lights up. "I'm happy for you, Nova." Something passes between Cain and the woman before she turns her attention back to me. "Hi. I'm Doctor Teagan. Are you okay with me looking at those marks on your face?"

"Sure. And I'm Promise."

"It's good to meet you, Promise." Over the next fifteen minutes, Doctor Teagan examines my face and asks a series of questions. "Well, the good news is the cut to your cheek doesn't need stitches. The bad news is you will most likely wake tomorrow with a black eye and be sporting a bruised face for a few days. I recommend some over the counter pain reliever for the discomfort. If any other problems arise, I want you to call me. Okay?"

"I will. Thanks, Doctor."

"You're welcome, Promise." Teagan gathers her things, then turns to Cain. "Take care of her."

"I will."

Thirty minutes later, after making sure London was settled in the clubhouse, we arrive at Cain's house. The moment we pull up, his daughter Piper comes flying out of the front door with Kiwi behind her. The two of them stand on the porch and watch as Cain helps me from the truck. When we step up on the porch, I take in how upset Piper looks. "Daddy?"

"She's okay, Bean. Come on, let's get inside."

I give Piper a reassuring smile. My heart melts at how sweet this girl is to be concerned about me.

"Let's get you upstairs, babe," Cain murmurs. "Kiwi, thanks for hangin' with Piper. You can head out."

Kiwi nods. "No worries, brother. Call if you need anything."

Once Kiwi leaves, Cain places his palm on my lower back and guides me toward the stairs.

I stop. "Um...maybe I should sleep on the sofa."

"Not happenin'."

"Cain," I argue. "I think I should sleep downstairs." I lift a brow and nod toward Piper.

Piper and Cain are both looking at me with amused grins. "Bean, you don't have a problem with my woman sleepin' upstairs, do ya?"

Piper rolls her eyes and giggles. "You two are cute." Lifting on her tiptoes, she kisses her dad's cheek. "I'm going to go to the kitchen and make Promise some warm tea while you get her settled. I'll bring it up in a few minutes."

"Appreciate that. You're the best, baby girl." Piper disappears around the corner into the kitchen, and Cain brings his attention back to me. "Come on, Sugar."

"So bossy," I huff as I make my way up the stairs and to his bedroom. When we step through the door, Cain kicks it shut with his booted foot. Next, he strides over to the dresser, pulling out a t-shirt. He then turns and makes his way back to me. "Arms up, babe."

Once I'm standing in nothing but my bra and panties, Cain reaches behind me and unclasps my bra then tosses it to the growing pile on the floor. Reaching over to the bed beside us, he grabs the t-shirt he retrieved from the dresser and slides it over my head and waits for me to thread my arms through. The shirt smells of laundry detergent and hangs down to the tops of my knees.

"I like you in my shirt, babe," Cain says, his voice husky. Reaching up between us, I fist the front of his shirt while tilting my head back and getting lost in the depth of his heated gaze.

"Cain."

Leaning down, his lips brush lightly over my bruised and swollen cheek. He then trails kisses down my jaw and neck— eventually, his lips capture mine. I waste no time opening my mouth, allowing his tongue to tangle with mine. Seconds later, our connection is interrupted by a knock at the bedroom door.

"Get in the bed, babe, while I let Piper in."

Snapping out of my lust-filled daze, I round the corner of the bed, pull back the blanket and climb in just as Cain lets Piper in. She smiles as she carries a steaming cup of tea toward me. "I wasn't sure how you liked it, so I made it how I normally do, with honey and lemon."

"That's perfect. Thank you, Piper."

"You're welcome."

Walking back over to her father, Piper hugs Cain. "I'm going to bed. You need anything else, Daddy?"

"No, Bean. We're good. Go on and get some sleep."

"Okay. Goodnight." Piper gives me a little wave over her shoulder.

"Goodnight, sweetie."

Once Piper is gone, I smile over at Cain. "You have an amazing daughter. You're fortunate."

His face goes soft. "Yeah. The best thing to ever happen to me." I take a few sips of my tea before setting the cup on the nightstand and settling back against the pillow.

"You going to be okay while I jump in the shower?"

I let out a deep sigh. "I'm good, Cain. I promise. Just tired." When he disappears into the bathroom, I turn on my side and settle deeper into the blanket. Before I know it, my eyes grow heavy, and I'm out.

The next morning, I wake to an empty bed. When I reach over and feel Cain's side, it's cold. Sitting up, I stretch my arms above my head and work out the soreness in my back. Wondering what time it is, I scan the bedroom for my purse which holds my phone but don't see it. It must be downstairs.

Climbing out of bed, I make my way into the bathroom where I get the first glimpse at my face and I gasp. "Holy shit." The swelling has gone down, but I have one hell of a shiner and my cheek is black and blue. No amount of concealer is going to cover this up. Shaking my head, I sigh. What I need is a shower. Turning, my eyes get big when I finally take time to admire Cain's bathroom. Holy shit! I take in the size of the shower stall, and the digital keypad on the wall that must operate it. You could fit six people in there and still have room. His bathroom is a dream.

Deciding I need to take time to enjoy a proper bath in that exquisite tub, I opt for a quick shower instead. After turning the water on and letting it heat, I rummage through Cain's drawer coming across a hair tie and fix my hair in a messy bun at the top of my head. I strip out of Cain's shirt and my panties, then step inside the tiled stall and close my eyes as the hot water beats down on my body.

I spot a bottle of body wash, flick the top open and realize I have found the source of one of Cain's many scents. Pouring a generous amount onto a sponge, I lather my body from head to toe, liking the fact I now smell like him. When I'm done, I cut the water off, step out of the stall and wrap a towel around my body. Opening the bathroom door, I pad over to the dresser, pull it open, finding a pair of Cain's boxers and another t-shirt to wear until I can ask him where he put the bag London packed for me. Now that I'm showered and feeling somewhat human again, I decide to head downstairs in search of some coffee. As I'm descending the stairs, I hear murmured voices. When I walk into the kitchen, I'm met by Piper, who is standing at the stove cooking what looks like pancakes, and Kiwi, who is sitting at the table watching her while he drinks coffee.

"Morning," I announce.

Piper looks over at me and smiles. "Morning, Promise. Are you hungry? I can make you something else if you don't want pancakes."

"I'm good, sweetie. I could use some coffee, though."

"Sure. I have a fresh pot made. The cream and sugar are on the table."

"Where is Cain?" I ask as I shuffle over to the counter and pour a cup of coffee.

Kiwi is the first to answer. "He had some club shit to take care of. He should be back any minute, though."

I nod, taking my cup over to the table and sitting down just as Kiwi stands and takes his empty plate to the sink. "I'll be on the porch havin' a smoke."

I don't miss the way he leans in toward Piper and says something in her ear. And whatever he says has her blushing. Hmm. Interesting.

When Piper takes a seat at the table across from me, I lift a brow but say nothing, which causes her to turn redder. After several awkward moments, Piper is the first to break the silence.

"My dad likes you."

Her admission makes me smile. "I like him too."

"No, I mean he REALLY likes you. Dad has never brought a woman home before. He's never even had a girlfriend." I stare at Piper, stunned. "It's true. Dad is a man whore." Piper says her last statement the same moment I take a sip of coffee, and I choke. "Oh, crap! Are you okay, Promise?" Piper hands me a paper towel to dry my face and the little bit of coffee I spilled on the table.

"It's okay, Piper. You just caught me off guard with that one."

Piper winces. "Yeah. I tend not to have a filter. It's the truth though. My dad thinks I don't know things, but I do. He's a good guy, though. The greatest in-fact. He's...I don't know. Guarded. He's never let a woman get too close." Piper's shoulders slump. "I think it has something to do with my mom. I don't remember her because she left when I was a baby, but I think she's the reason he is the way he is. Until you. I see it, Promise. You're different. Dad would never have brought you here if you weren't."

"Hmm. Maybe. The truth is, Piper, I'm not sure what we are yet."

"That's okay. From what I can tell, dad is sure enough for the both of you," she giggles.

"You know what, Piper?" I grin. "I see a whole lot of your dad in you, girl."

"Since I think my dad is the best person in the whole world, I'll take that as a compliment."

"You definitely should take that as a compliment, sweetie."

Piper is silent for a minute as she studies me from across the table. "I like you, Promise."

My smile gets even bigger. "I like you too, Piper."

11

NOVA

I hated leaving my daughter and Promise this morning but needed to meet with the rest of my brothers to discuss the shit that took place last night. Knowing Kiwi is with them puts my mind at ease.

Pulling up to the clubhouse, I punch in the code, and the gate rolls open. Parking my bike beside Wick's, I head inside, finding him, Fender, Everest, and my brother sitting at the bar, enjoying cold beers. "Hey, brother."

"How's it goin'?" I step to the bar.

"How's your woman fairin' this mornin'?" my brother asks, knowing most of what went down last night. He was the first one I made a call to the moment Promise described the cut the guy had on.

"The piece of shit roughed her up a bit, but she's handlin' the situation pretty well." Anger builds in my gut, thinking about the bruise on her face. I'm pissed at myself that she is caught up in a feud she has no part of. "I had Kiwi stay behind. I'll fill him in on what we discuss later."

My brother nods. Standing, he tosses his empty bottle in the trash. "Alright. Let's head to church and formulate a plan." He strides across the room, and the rest of us men follow.

The four of us sit around the table. Fender slides a pack of cigarettes across the table toward me, along with a lighter. Taking one from the box, I light it, pulling a toke. "What do we know about the Hell's Punishers?" Riggs directs his attention to Fender.

"The club is from north Louisiana. They've been around for years. The President goes by the name Crow. The one Nova gave a beating to; they call him Creep," Fender informs us, and I scoff. Creep. The goddamn name suits his sorry good for nothing ass. Fender continues. "Not only is he the President's brother, but he's the club's VP."

"How many members are we lookin' at?" I ask.

"At least a dozen," Fender states.

Shit. They have more significant numbers than we do. "They sent a clear message last night. They want some restitution, and that they won't be leaving the city any time soon." I snub out my cigarette. "I should have finished the job," I admit.

"Well, lucky for you, the bastard is still alive."

"For now," I grit my teeth.

"Shit went down in a public place, during a public event," my brother adds. "If Wick didn't get there when he did, you would have been lookin' at a murder charge."

He's right. I fuckin' hate when he's right. I wouldn't have let up until he was lying on the floor with no life left in him. "He touched my baby girl."

"And he deserves to be six feet under for it." Riggs' features harden. "This shit with the Hell's Punishers and the vendetta they have against you—against the club—is just as personal to the rest of us as it is to you, brother." My eyes scan the table, looking at the faces of my brothers. "You forget, Wick and I helped raise Piper. I think I speak for both of us when I say what happened to her feels as if it happened to our own child." My eyes shift between him and

Wick. "They fucked with our family. Plain and simple. If Hell's Punishers want to start a war, they'll get one."

The room falls silent for a beat. I feel the tension in the room heighten. It wasn't so long ago that we dealt with a threat to the club. "What is our option here? Do we go to them, put this shit to bed, or do we hang back and wait for their next move? Cause I've got to tell you, my gut is tellin' me they want to play games with us. Try and fuck with our heads. They assumed Promise was a useful target just by seeing her with me. What's to say they aren't watching us as we speak. I don't want to sit around on my ass waiting for one of those fuckers to strike again." At this point, my nerves are frayed, and I'm fucking furious. My entire body is shaking with rage.

"Fender, do we know their whereabouts?" Riggs asks.

"Negative."

"Then we wait." My brother's eyes cut to me. "We can't fight what we can't see."

I push myself from the table, my chair falling to its side, skidding across the floor. Holding my words, I pace the floor, with my fists balled at my sides.

"We play this smart. The Hell's Punishers are loose cannons. They displayed that not only at the event, but last night as well. Going off half-cocked like that can make a man stupid and make mistakes. You have to trust me on this one, brother," Riggs says, getting me to see reason, but vengeance has me bloodthirsty and blind at the moment. "Everest, you and Fender ride the streets today. Dig up a little intel on our visitors. The city has eyes and ears everywhere." Riggs stands, and I stop pacing. "Cain, go home and keep Kiwi with you. Have him tap into street camera feeds or if they possibly had surveillance cameras anywhere in the vicinity of the apartment complex Promise was staying." Riggs slaps his hand on my shoulder. "We'll get the motherfuckers. You hear me?" I nod. He then addresses all of us.

"Until we know where these assholes are hiding, we travel in pairs. Got it?"

Church ends, and we head back to the bar, where Josie places cold beers in front of us. "Does the club still own the building across the street from the tactical store?" I ask before lifting my bottle, downing half of my drink.

"Yeah, brother." Wick is the one to answer.

"Any plans for it?"

"What do you have in mind?" Wick turns to face me.

"Promise and her friend, London are shootin' around the idea of opening their own firm together. The practice London works at now is state-run and a real shit hole, in a less than desirable part of town. What would the club's thoughts be on leasing the building to them both?"

"Start their own firm?" Riggs runs his hand down his beard, giving my idea some thought. "Is this you admitting you're going after this woman? You claimin' her?" he pauses a beat. "To be honest, I never would have thought you'd go for a woman like her. Hell, I never thought you'd settle down. Now here you are only knowin' this woman a week and you're tied up in knots. My brother, the Casanova, has fallen hard. And you've set a record doin' it." My brother smirks, and the others wait for my reply. He's not wrong either. They don't call me Nova for nothing.

"What the fuck is that supposed to mean?" My body tenses.

"Calm down. All I'm sayin' is your reputation for the choice of women you've bedded is less than stellar. This one has her act together. She has class." Riggs eyes me. "You got it bad for her, huh?"

"She's mine." I try hard to hide my grin, but fail. Promise stole my fucking soul the moment her eyes locked with mine. My brothers hoot, and hollers fill the air, and Riggs clinks his beer bottle against mine.

"You deserve it, Cain." The others chime in agreeing.

Wick stands and pulls a bundle of keys from his pocket. Working a silver key off one of the rings, he tosses it to me. "Overlook the boxes sitting around. We've been using it as storage space for the bar and tactical store."

Once outside, I straddle my bike and fire it up. I stare at the key in the palm of my hand before slipping it inside my pocket. Having Promise in my home last night and waking to her still there this morning felt fucking incredible. I think back to the other day at the bar when she met my family. She meshed well with them as if she belonged.

Promise blindsided me. I never saw it coming. She knocked me on my ass. If I'm honest with myself, finding the one is something I've wanted for some time. All I do is think about Promise. I want her on the back of my bike, and her body pressed firmly against mine. I want her in my bed—in mine and my daughter's life.

A short time later, I'm rolling up the driveway, and spot Kiwi sitting outside, smoking a cigarette. Parking my bike in the garage, I join him on the front porch. "The girls, okay?" I ask, leaning against the porch railing.

"Oh yeah, mate." He offers me a smoke, and I take it. "What's the word?" he asks.

"We wait."

"No shit, bro?"

"Yeah. Riggs is right. We need to know where these fuckers are hiding before we can flush them out of our city like the turds they are."

"What are my orders?" Kiwi asks.

"See what images you can get from cameras in the area near London's apartment, and camp out here for a while. Help me look after Piper and Promise."

"I got your back, brother."

"Appreciate it," I tell him.

Putting out his cigarette, Kiwi stands. "I got to use the

bathroom. Give me a few hours to dig up some feed. I'll let you know what I come up with later tonight."

An hour later, I'm in my truck with Piper and Promise. With the threat of further retaliation lingering, I'm hyper-aware of our surroundings as we travel down the road. But with Kiwi following behind us, my mood has shifted for the better. "Okay. I sent the address to London. She should be there soon." Promise looks up from her phone. "Are you going to tell me what we are doing?"

"I'll explain when we get there," I say, expecting her to protest, but she doesn't. I glance back at my daughter sitting in the back seat. Piper knows the address and smiles. She doesn't know my plans but knows me well enough to know I'm up to something.

The rest of the ride, I listen to Piper and Promise sing along to songs on the radio. I settle into the comfort of the two of them getting along well and think to myself; *This is what the rest of my life could be like.* Forever with one woman doesn't feel so foreign anymore. Though I've only known Promise for a fraction of time, it feels like much longer. Like a missing puzzle piece, she fits so perfectly in the picture, making it complete. For a second, the Hell's Punishers push through my happy thoughts. My grip on the steering wheel tightens, and my knuckles turn white.

"Are you okay?" Promise asks, her voice soft with worry, and I glance her way.

"Yeah, Sugar."

She breathes in and out with a heavy sigh. "Does it have anything to do with what happened last night?" The tone of her voice wavers.

"Try not to worry about it, babe. The club will handle it." I'm vague while trying to reassure her worries.

"Telling me not worry is like telling me I can't eat chocolate ever again. That's just never going to happen." Promise pauses, looking out the window. "Is that the reason you left so early this morning?"

"Sorry, Sugar. I won't discuss club business." I'm quiet for a moment, then add, "You'll also be staying at my house while we handle shit with this other club."

"Okay," Promise is quick to say, taking me by surprise.

"Yeah?"

She shrugs her shoulders. "Yeah. I trust you, honey."

Honey? Shit, why do I like the sound of that? "You're fuckin' perfect," I say, my tone low as we finally pull up to our destination, Kiwi parks his bike beside my truck.

"Don't place me on a pedestal like that." Promise stares at her lap, wringing her hands together. "I'm nowhere close to being perfect, Cain."

"Says who?" Piper unbuckles, leaning between the front seats. "None of us are flawless, but we are all perfect in our own ways." I stare out the windshield listening to my daughter. She just went through hell herself, and she's lifting Promise with her kindness. My heart swells. "So, who's to say you're not perfect just the way you are?" Piper throws her arms around my neck. "Take my dad, for instance. He is the best damn waffles maker in the world. He can build a motorcycle from the ground up, and is an artistic genius, but the man doesn't know how to put the toilet seat down." My daughter kisses my cheek. "But I think he's pretty damn perfect."

Promise throws her head back with laughter, and my shoulders shake with amusement. "You two are too much." Promise continues to giggle.

A small car pulls up beside my truck, and I recognize London behind the wheel. Climbing out of the truck, I open my daughter's door, before moving around to Promise's side. She swings the door open. "I can open my own door, Cain."

"Not when I'm around." I hold out my hand for her to take as she steps down.

"Damn. The man opens doors for you, and he's fine," Promise's friend London says, rounding the front of the truck. "So, what are we here for?" She looks around before her eyes settle on me.

"The two of you serious about opening your own firm?" I ask as I insert the key into the deadbolt, unlocking the front door to the building. London looks to Promise, her brow raised. I push open the door, allowing Piper, Promise, and London to step inside, then look to Kiwi who's still sitting on his bike. "Keep watch," I order and he nods.

Letting the door close behind me, I walk around, lifting the shades covering the four large windows. Sunlight filters in, showing more of the space. The girls walk around, taking it all in. "How did you find this place?" Promise asks as she runs her hand across the shiplap walls, then over the exposed brown brick of the fireplace.

"The club owns it. It used to be a boarding house back in the day. As you can tell, this space has been completely gutted, taken down to the original woodwork. There was once four separate rooms and one bath, but that was all ripped out by the guy we bought it from a few years ago. Anyway, with a little work, I think you two could make it into something."

London's eyes widen. "You're shitting me." Her head whips in the opposite direction to look at Promise. "Is this guy for real?" "Cain. It's too much." Promise locks her eyes with mine.

Crossing the room, I pull her body against mine. "You need a job, correct?"

Promise swallows, her eyes falling to my lips. "Yes, but..."

I shift my attention to London, still speechless. "London, are you happy with your current employment?"

"Fuck no," London says, then turns to Piper, who is standing beside her. "Shit, excuse my language." This causes Piper to laugh.

"Trust me; these ears have heard worse."

"Thank fuck," London sighs. "I don't exactly have a filter," she admits.

"You should fit in just fine," Piper offers London a red licorice stick, which earns her a smile. "Well," Piper looks my way. "Proceed to swoon."

My kid. I shake my head.

God bless the man who catches her. They'll be in for the ride of their life.

I clear my throat, my eyes settling on Promise's blue ones. "What do you say?"

"I need to talk with London. Maybe give it some thought." Promise bites her bottom lip.

"What is there to discuss? I say hell, yes. It's what we've always wanted, Promise. I'm all in if you are." London steps forward.

Promise finally nods, her eyes lifting to mine again. "You're sure about this? I mean, what if we don't stay together? What if this," Promise waves her hand between us, "doesn't work?"

"Like I told you before, babe. This—you and me. It's happening. I believe in you, and so does the club." Tears pool in her eyes, one slipping down her cheek.

"You believe in me?" Her voice comes out as a whisper.

I cup her face in the palms of my hands, my mouth watering with the need to press my lips to hers. "I believe in you, Sugar. The place is yours if you want it." I keep my eyes fixed on her face.

"Okay." Promise gives me an easy smile, and I grin like the lovesick fool I am, then capture her mouth with mine, leaving both of us breathless when I pull away.

12

PROMISE

"Can you take me to get my car?" I ask Cain as I lean my hip against the railing of the porch and take a sip of my coffee.

"What for?" he hedges, looking up from where he's crouched down on the ground next to his bike with a wrench in his hand.

"I need to go over to Brad's apartment and pack up my things. I texted him yesterday and told him I'd be by around 10:00 am today. I don't have much. Mostly clothes and a few personal items. I won't be gone long."

Cain stands, wiping his grease-covered hands on a rag. "I'll take you," he clips.

"You don't have to take me. London already said she'd help. It's seriously no big deal."

Cain tucks the rag into his back pocket and stalks toward me. "Not a big deal?" One booted foot hits the step and then the other until he is standing in front of me, the smell of motor oil, laundry detergent, musk and the faint scent of his minty breath fills my senses. "My woman wants to go to her ex-fiancé's apartment, a place where she shared the same bed with another man, yet it's

121

not a big deal?" he says in a dangerously low tone I have yet to hear before.

"I...yes?" My response comes out as more of a question than an answer.

"Wrong, babe. You won't be going anywhere near that cocksucker. Not without me."

I set my mug down on the railing and prop my hands on my hips. "For your information, Brad won't be there. I told him I didn't want him around while I was getting my things."

"And you believe that fuck is going to listen?"

"I can handle Brad."

"Not without me," Cain counters, not backing down.

I roll my eyes. "Fine."

Grabbing the back of my head, Cain leans down and covers his mouth with mine, stealing my breath with a hard, toe-curling kiss. When he releases me, he grins. "Glad you see things my way, Sugar."

"So, how did you end up with that dickhead anyway?"

I turn in the passenger seat of Cain's truck and think about his question for a moment. He has one hand hanging out the window, and the other propped on the steering wheel with a cigarette between his fingers. "Brad started working at my stepdad's firm a few years ago. We started seeing each other soon after. Then he proposed, and I said yes."

"How long ago did he propose?"

"Two years." I shrug.

"How long have you been broke up?"

I begin to fidget in my seat at his last question. "A little over two weeks."

Cain chuckles. "That explains it."

"Explains what?" I narrow my eyes.

He takes a drag from his cigarette and cuts his eyes at me. "The night you and your posse came into the bar. You were celebratin' cuttin' that asshole loose. Lucky for me, I happened to be in the right place at the right time, and it was me who got a taste of that sweet pussy. Fuck of a way to celebrate, Sugar."

"Cain!" I swat his arm. "Must you be so crude? It wasn't even like that." I feel my cheeks heat. "You're so cocky."

"Not cocky, babe. Just statin' facts. Tell me, Sugar. Your pussy ever get wet for that asshole like it does for me?" My tummy flutters at the memory of how well Cain worked my body and I squirm in my seat. "That pussy hungry for my cock now? Bet if I put my hand down your pants, I'd find you soaked." My breathing picks up, and I bite my bottom lip. "Fuck," Cain growls. "I should pull this truck over and have you ride my cock right here on the side of the road, but I won't." Cain reaches across the console, grips the back of my neck, and brings my eyes to his. "Tonight, you're mine," he growls and my sex clenches. Something to look forward to.

Fifteen minutes later, I use my key to unlock the door to Brad's apartment. When I step inside, Cain is directly behind me. "Let's get your shit so we can get the fuck out of here."

"Okay. All my stuff is in the bedroom." I head down the hallway, and Cain follows. In the back of the closet, I pull out two large suitcases. "All my things should fit in here."

"Any of the furniture yours?"

"No."

"Good," he mutters. "I'd burn the shit anyway."

Once I have my clothes packed, I walk across the hall to the second bedroom Brad uses as an office. The closet in there is where I kept a box of memorabilia from my childhood. Mostly photos and small momentos; things that belonged to my mother. When I walk back into the living room, Cain is out there patiently waiting on me. "I'm takin' the suitcases down to the truck. That everything?" he nods to the box I'm carrying.

"Yep." We go to leave the apartment when I remember one last thing. "Oh, wait. My spare laptop is on the nightstand in the bedroom. Let me grab it, and I'll meet you downstairs."

"Alright, babe."

Cain leaves, and I jog back down the hall to the bedroom. I snag my laptop from the table beside the bed and the charger cord. As I'm leaving, I stop, reach into the front pocket of my jeans and pull out the diamond engagement ring Brad gave me and set it on top of the dresser. Then movement out the corner of my eye catches my attention. It's Brad. He looks at me then at the ring and takes a step forward. "Promise."

"Brad. You're not supposed to be here. I told you I didn't want to see you."

"I know you did, but I wanted to see you. We need to talk."

I shake my head and brush past him. When I walk back into the kitchen, Cain is there with his back propped against the kitchen island as he casually smokes a cigarette. "Hey, babe."

"What the hell is he doing here?" Brad comes up behind me, his eyes on Cain with a look of disgust. I take in Brad's attire. Slicked back hair, pressed suit. He's the complete opposite of Cain who is wearing faded jeans, ripped at the knees and a black t-shirt under his cut.

Cain answers for me. "I'm here because she's my woman."

Brad ignores Cain's statement. "If you'll excuse us, I would like to talk with Promise alone."

"Not fuckin' happenin'." Cain flicks his ashes on the kitchen floor.

"You don't speak for Promise."

Cain grunts. "You want to talk to this prick, babe?"

I look at Brad when I answer. "Nope."

"There ya go. My woman doesn't have shit to say to you."

Brad continues as if he didn't hear a word Cain said. "Promise, sweetheart, we can work this out. Don't throw away the last three years."

Hitting a nerve, I turn away from Cain and face my ex. "Don't throw away the last three years?" I take a step closer to Brad. "That was all you—you fucking asshole!" I scream.

"You're saying all the blame lies on me? That you didn't play a role in anything?"

"Are you serious right now? I'm not saying I'm perfect. I know I've been distant, and things were off between us, but that doesn't excuse a partner for cheating. No matter how difficult things are, I would never cheat."

"Promise..." Brad tries again.

"You know how I feel about them." Brad flinches. He knows I'm talking about my stepfather and Avery when I say 'them'. He hears the hurt in my voice when I speak again. "You know about the things I went through after my mom died, and you know how it was for me growing up with Thomas and Avery. You could have chosen anyone, but you chose her."

Brad's shoulders slump. "I'm sorry, Promise. I'm sorry I hurt you."

I look over my shoulder to Cain, who is watching. I give him a small smile. "I'm ready now, honey."

Just as I turn to leave, Brad speaks again. "I do love you, Promise. Even though I know you didn't feel the same, I still wanted us to work."

I turn back to face Brad. "You were wrong for cheating, but I was wrong for allowing our relationship to continue as long as it did. God knows I wanted it to work, but I didn't love you." I swallow past the lump in my throat and take a deep breath. "I'm sorry too, Brad."

Cain pushes off from the counter, holding his hand out to me, and I take it.

"Promise," Brad calls out, stopping me. "I hope you find what you've been missing."

I close my eyes and squeeze Cain's hand. I already have.

On the ride back to Cain's house, I can feel his gaze burning a hole in the side of my head. I get the feeling he wants to ask about things that were said back at Brad's apartment but doesn't want to upset me. So, I decided to bring the subject up. "The day before you and I hooked up, I caught Brad fucking my stepsister in his office."

"I gathered that," Cain replies.

"I've never had a good relationship with Avery. She was just as horrible when we were younger, and still is an adult. Avery is your typical spoiled daddy's girl. When we were kids, I could never figure out why she hated me so much. I think it had something to do with her dad marrying my mom. Thomas' wife passed away when Avery was around five, and Jackson was a few years older. I know her hate for me never wavered."

"You sayin' the bitch fucked your fiancé just to get to you?"

"Yep. She did the same with my college boyfriend too."

"Are you fuckin' serious?"

"Oh, yeah. I came home to my dorm after a study group session to find my boyfriend screwing Avery."

"Shit, babe. That's fucked up. What about your stepdad? He have anything to say about his daughter and her bullshit?"

"Are you kidding? In his eyes, Avery can do no wrong. Besides, to Thomas, I was just the stepdaughter he was stuck with when my mom died. It didn't matter that I never got into trouble or that I even went on to follow in his footsteps. I was an inconvenience."

"That's fucked, babe. I'm sorry you had to go through that."

"Yeah, well, I don't have to anymore. I'm finally free. It took me a long time, but I realized they aren't worth the pain anymore."

"You're strong, babe. Good for you." Cain reaches across the console and squeezes the back of my neck.

"Will you tell me about your mom, and what happened to her?"

"My mom passed away from complications due to a skiing

accident when I was sixteen." I close my eyes and smile as I remember her face. "I look just like her. The same hair, the same height and build. She was my best friend. Before she met and married Thomas, it had always been the two of us. It was her and me against the world. I remember being nervous when she told me she was going to get married. It felt like she had been taken away from me. I kept thinking she wouldn't have time for me anymore. But she did. Even though she had a new husband and two new stepchildren, she always made time to do the things we used to do. Like every Friday after school, we'd go for ice cream, and Sundays were for playing at the park. She still read to me every night before bed. I couldn't have asked for a better mom." I wipe the tears rolling down my cheek when I finish telling my story.

"What about your dad?" Cain asks.

"My father was in the Army. Two months after mom found out she was pregnant with me, he was deployed. She was eight months pregnant when he was killed. At dad's funeral, mom said she stood next to his casket and promised him she would do her best to make him proud and to love me enough for the both of them. That's why she named me Promise."

When we arrive back at Cain's house, he parks the truck, hops out, and strides around to my side, opening the door before I have the chance. He takes my face between the palms of his hands. "You are somethin' special, Promise Bailey." Then he kisses me. The moment is broken when we hear a car pull into the driveway behind Cain's truck. I look to my right, seeing Piper climbing out of her car.

"Hi, daddy—hi, Promise."

"Hey, sweetie," I wave.

Piper walks up to her dad. "Are we still going to Gampy's tonight?

"Yep. Go on in and get ready. We leave as soon as I get my truck unloaded." Piper takes off in the house, and Cain turns to me. "I'll bring your stuff in."

I wave my hand. "I can handle my things. You and Piper go."

"Babe, you're comin' with us."

"What? You have family plans, Cain. I can stay here."

"Hell, no, you're not. You're comin' with us. I want you to meet my Pop. He's having a BBQ, and the whole club will be there."

"Are...are you sure?"

Cain places his finger under my chin and softly touches his lips to mine. "Yeah, babe. I'm sure. Now, go inside with Piper and get ready while I unload the truck." He swats my butt, and I smile.

Cain mentions a BBQ, and knowing we will be spending a lot of time outside, I know the exact dress I want to wear. After I have finished with a quick shower, I walk back into the bedroom. Seeing my suitcases, I go straight for the one that has a few of my summer dresses. Finding the one I want, a white sleeveless wrap dress, I drop the towel from around my body and pull on a pair of white lace panties. Next, I slide the dress on over my shoulders, then tie the sash at my waist. I pair the dress with some simple gold sandals. Not wanting to make a big fuss with my hair, I tie it up into a high ponytail. Once I'm done, I swipe my purse off the bed and make my way out of the bedroom. As I'm passing Piper's room, she and Cain's hushed voices draw my attention and the most beautiful sight greets me. Piper is sitting on a stool in front of a mirror while her dad stands behind her executing a perfect fishtail braid with his daughter's long brown hair. He does it with such ease, like he's done it a thousand times before.

I watch as a rugged, six-foot four-inch biker braids his daughter's hair. It's at this moment I realize Cain has something in common with my mother. He's both father and mother to Piper.

By the smile on Piper's face and the adoring way she looks at her dad, I'd say he did a fantastic job at both.

"Hey!" Piper catches sight of me in the mirror.

"Hey, sweetie."

"I have never been able to do a fishtail, and dad is the master." Piper hooks a thumb over her shoulder toward Cain.

"She insisted on wearing it like this to school every day when she was eight. I had no choice but to figure the shit out. I had to carry my ass down to the hair salon in town and let Mrs. Betty teach me." Cain finishes by securing a tie at the end of Piper's hair.

His daughter stands then kisses him on the cheek.

"That's what makes you the best."

With Cain's grandfather living close, we opt to walk to his place. And by the looks of things when we get there, we are the last to arrive. As we stroll hand in hand into the backyard, there is a round of fist bumps and pats on the back between Cain and his brothers.

"Alright, out of my way. Get, get," a male's voice calls out from behind everyone. Cain's brother Riggs and his wife Luna, who is holding their baby girl, along with Fender, Kiwi, Wick, and his woman Tequila, all back away while laughing as an older gentleman who I know must be Cain's grandfather, steps forward. He looks to Cain, then to me and back to Cain before a huge smile takes over his face. "Why I never thought I'd live to see the day. Don't just stand there, son. Introduce me to your girl."

"Pop, this is Promise. Promise, this is my grandfather Abraham LeBlanc."

I hold out my hand. "It's nice to meet you, Mr. LeBlanc."

"Oh, child. Call me Abe or Pop." Instead of taking my hand, he pulls me in for a big bear hug. For an older man, he sure is strong.

"Pop, can I have my girl back now?"

"Not yet. Why don't you go help your brother with the grills while Promise and I get to know each other."

I can't help but giggle when Cain walks away grumbling. Left alone with Abe, he turns to me. "Join an old man on the porch for a glass of sweet tea?"

"I'd love to."

Abe holds out his arm, and I place my hand in the crook of his elbow letting him lead me across the yard and up the steps of the porch where a couple of rocking chairs sit. Like a true gentleman, he waits for me to take my seat before he lifts a pitcher of tea sitting on the table beside me, pours me a glass then hands it to me.

"Thank you." I take a sip as Abe sits in the chair next to me.

"I like to give Cain a hard time, but I always knew this day would come." I look at Abe as he continues. "Cain has never brought a woman home to meet his family. That tells me you're something special. It's written all over his face."

I shake my head. "I don't know, Abe. What I feel for Cain scares me a little. I mean, we hardly know each other."

"I knew my wife, God rest her soul, was the woman I would spend the rest of my life with the moment I laid eyes on her. I told her as much on our first date. She thought I was nuts. It didn't matter much though. No way was I lettin' her go and I didn't." Abe looks out at the water's edge, where the sun is beginning to set. "I see it in Cain's eyes. In the way, he looks at you. I'd recognize that look anywhere because it's the same one I had all those years ago. It's also the same one Abel had with Luna." Abe looks away from the sky and sets his attention back on me. "It doesn't matter how long you have known someone. Time is just time. What matters is what your heart tells you. Cain is listening to his. The real question here is are you going to listen to yours?"

A couple of hours later, Cain is lounging in a chair near the water's edge with me on his lap. The sun disappeared behind the river a while ago and is now dark. The only thing lighting the sky is the moon's reflection and lightning bugs dancing along the bayou.

"You and Pops have a good chat?" Cain nuzzles my neck.

"We did."

"What did you two talk about?"

I shift on Cain's lap and rest my head on his shoulder. "We talked about you."

"Figures," he sighs, and I giggle. I'm quiet for a moment then add, "You're fortunate to have the family you do."

'"They're your family now, too, Promise."

"Cain," I breathe.

Cain grips my chin, and I have no choice but to look at him. "You are mine," he jerks his head toward the men and women sitting with us. "You belong to us and we belong to you. Me, Piper, Pops, and the club, we're your family now. I know you're scared shitless at how fast things are moving, babe. But I don't know any other way. You're it for me, Promise and I don't plan on wastin' any time fightin' this pull we have. I sure as fuck hope you don't either." I swallow past the lump in my throat as I try to find my words—the sincerity of Cain's seen in his eyes. "Now tell me this, Sugar. You takin' this ride with me?"

Reaching up, I run my palm over his cheek and through his beard I love so much and take a deep breath. "Yeah, honey. I'm with you."

13

NOVA

The moment Promise says she's with me, I grip the back of her neck and cover her mouth with mine. I find myself drowning, as the kiss becomes desperate and full of emotions we have yet to profess. I kiss her like she's the very air I need to breathe. She squirms on my lap, rubbing her ass against my growing erection, causing me to growl, before reluctantly breaking our connection. Promise is breathless as she locks eyes with me. "Cain, you have no idea how fast my heart beats when I'm near you. I need you so badly, it frightens me." Her confession has me standing, and she stands with me, my hold on her never wavering. Her body is humming with want and my desire for her feeding off of it. My palm skims down her arm. Then, I take her hand in mine. Before I can get the words in my head out of my mouth, I catch my brother trying to grab my attention from across the yard near the back porch. He's huddled with my other brothers. Shit. I guess my early departure will have to wait.

I sigh, willing my hard-on to subside. "We'll finish this later, Sugar. I need to talk with my brothers for a moment." Promise lets out a heavy sigh of her own, and I feel her frustration too. "Why don't you grab a drink from the cooler and join the women by the fire?"

Promise reaches her hand up, caressing the nape of my neck, her fingernails lightly scraping against my skin, causing electricity from her touch to shoot down my spine and straight to my dick. "You sure we can't leave now?" The tone of her voice makes me want to say to hell with it and get her into my bed NOW.

"Shit, babe. Keep touchin' me like that, and I'm going to lose my shit. I don't need to walk around sportin' a hard-on the entire night," I admit, and Promise's eyes sparkle as her smile brightens her face. She's enjoying the effect she is having on me, and I'm loving every minute of it myself. I give her a look, then reiterate what I said before. "Soon, babe."

With one final sigh, followed by a soft kiss on my cheek, I watch Promise as she makes her way toward the bonfire, settling into a seat between Piper and Luna, her eyes cutting to me once before she eases into conversation with the rest of the women.

Striding across the yard, I step beside the men. "What's up?" Reaching around Fender, I lift the lid to a cooler sitting a few feet from the rocking chair Pop is currently seated, sipping on a glass of sweet tea, looking off toward the waterfront. With a cold beer in my hand, I twist the top off, then lift the bottle to my lips, waiting for Riggs to say whatever is on his mind.

"Kiwi found something interesting. Looks like Hell's Punishers left town, all except for about five, who happen to be checked into an extended stay hotel on the other side of town," Riggs tells us.

"Any word why?" I ask.

"That, I haven't figured out yet," Kiwi jumps in. "But word is spreading that we are lookin' for them. The manager of the hotel himself happens to be the source who gave me this information. He says they've been keeping to themselves."

I huff. "And that sorry son of a bitch known as Creep?"

"No sign of him." Kiwi pauses long enough to down the rest of his drink, then tosses it into an outdoor trash can nearby. "No feed available from the other night near your woman's place, either."

Figures. Thinking a beat, I process the new information. "I'm tired of waitin'. This piece of shit made it clear he wanted blood."

"True," Wick mentions.

"Yeah, but I'm not sold on the idea their entire club wants your ass skinned." Riggs leans against the porch banister. "I've looked into the Hell's Punishers. They don't seem to be the type of club to pussyfoot around."

"So, what is our next move? Continue to sit on our asses?" My mood shifts drastically.

"They're waitin' for a reason. We need to find out why," Wick adds.

"We invite them for a sit-down. See what in the hell their end game is. If they were lookin' to stir up more shit, they would have by now."

"Give them a chance to explain why the hell their member attempted to rape my daughter?" I growl, keeping my voice low. My brother eyes me for a second.

"I know it's not the answer you want to hear, brother, but I've got to go with my gut on this one."

I don't like his final words on the subject. I want the satisfaction of ridding this world of the bastard who put his hands on my daughter, then my woman. But, over the years, I've come to trust Riggs' intuition on things. He can be a little more level headed than me. It's also what makes him a damn good leader and our Prez. "When?" I ask him what the rest of us are waiting to find out.

"As soon as possible. I'll get word to them first thing tomorrow. Tonight, although we are all a little uptight with the threat looming, we do our best to enjoy the family."

I look out across the yard, as do the rest of the men. We take in the smiles on the women's faces and heads thrown back in laughter with whatever they are discussing. I smile at the sight of Piper holding her cousin on her lap as she roasts a marshmallow.

"Anyone else's ears burnin'?" Wick snorts, and I laugh, knowing there is a good possibility they are talking about us men.

"I'll catch you guys later. I'm about to round up my girls and take them home." Riggs lifts the beer in his hand. "Wick, you got my six?"

"Yeah, brother. Tequila and I will be right behind you," Wick informs him. He gives the rest of us a nod before striding across the yard to his woman as well.

"I'm going to follow them to town and make my way back to the clubhouse," Fender states then looks past my shoulder. "Hey, Pop. Mind if I wrap some food up for Everest and the girls back at the clubhouse?" he calls to the place where Pop is still rocking at the other end of the porch.

"You sure can. And make sure you take them ladies some of that chocolate cake Mrs. Monroe from church made for me," Pop replies and Fender shoots him a smile along with a nod before walking inside the house. "Cain," Pop calls to me. "Come sit with me for a moment, would you, son?"

Kiwi is the only one left beside me. He looks across the yard, then back to me. "I'm going to hang around the fire until you get ready to leave, mate." Then he walks off.

Stepping on to the porch, I stride toward my grandad, then lower my ass in the rocking chair beside him. I stare out at the still water and take in the bright reflection from the moon on the surface. The small breeze beginning to blow is cooling to my exposed skin. Pop's begins to rock again, taking in a deep breath of muggy air.

"There's a storm brewin'." He keeps his gaze forward, and I'm not sure if he's remarking on the faint smell of a pending rainstorm, or if he overheard our conversation moments ago and is voicing his concerns. Either way, my reply will answer both accurately.

"Yep."

"She's pretty special. Smart too," Pop says, and I know he's talking about Promise.

"That she is." I pause a moment, then continue. "Piper thinks so too." Out of the corner of my eye, I notice the edge of Pop's lips lifting slightly.

"You got deep feelings for her."

"I do." I take a deep breath of night air. "Crazy, right? Seeing that I've only known her for a short time." I focus on the lightning bugs dancing above the water. "I can't explain it, Pop. The moment I laid eyes on her it felt like lightning striking, knocking me flat on my ass." I hear Pop chuckle and shake my head. "For once in my life, I see myself settlin' down."

"I suspected as much." Pop's reaches beside him, lifting a cigar from the small round table between us. I eye him as he lights the end, smoke billowing in front of him as he stokes the flame. "Your grandma knocked me on my keister all those years ago. Funny how women, the right woman, can do that to a man." Pop finally looks at me. "I'm damn proud of you, Cain." His words grab at my heartstrings and I swallow the emotions they evoke. "I may not say it as often as I should, but it's true. You've done what most men wouldn't. You've made something of yourself and raised a daughter on your own."

"I didn't raise Piper by myself. You and the rest of my family helped. I could never have done it without all the support," I admit.

"Don't go sellin' yourself short. We lifted you when you needed it, but it was you, Cain. Look at her." With the cigar between his fingers, Pop points in the direction of the bonfire where Piper sits with Promise on one side and Kiwi on the other. "You helped her bloom into the beautiful young woman she's becoming. That smile on her face comes from the love you have for her." Pop sets his eyes on me once more. "And now, you've found someone you can see yourself watchin' sunsets with for the rest of your life." I fight the smile lifting my lips as I picture sharing the rest of my days with Promise. "Trust what you're feelin' for Promise. Let it be your compass. You deserve to love and be loved, and so does she." Pop's clears his throat. "Your grandma would be so proud of you. You and your brother."

I look at Pop, noticing his eyes are a bit misty. Instead of trying to find words, I say nothing. Seconds tick by as silence falls between us. How do I respond to all of that? I've always known my grandparents are proud of me. Since grandma passed away, Pop has never wavered over the years to be there for Piper or me. "I love you, Pop." They are the only words with enough importance to say at the moment, but they hold a lot of weight.

"I love you too, son." He rocks in his chair.

I sit with Pop for a few more minutes until I notice the sky flicker with lights in the distant sky. "Looks like rain."

"Better be gettin' the family home before the bottom falls." Pop snubs out his cigar, leaving it sitting in the tray, then stands, and I stand with him. "I didn't say anything before while you boys were chattin', but I couldn't help but overhear..." I go to interrupt him, but he stops me before I get the words from my mouth. "I know. It's club business. Nevertheless, know I'm here and that I'm always watching."

"Thanks, Pop." I pull him in for a quick hug.

"Hell. Just doing my job." Reaching above his head, he takes down the shotgun mounted out of sight that he always keeps nearby while he's sitting on his porch. "Kiwi staying with you still?" he asks as he swings open the screen door.

"Just until we know things are safe." I won't say more. No need to. He knows what happened to Piper and Promise. And even though I haven't shared anymore with him about the club in town,

I'm sure he already knows. There isn't much Pop doesn't know. He has his ways of finding shit out all on his own. "I'll be by tomorrow," I tell Pop as I step off the porch.

"I'll be here," he replies.

Promise spots me as I make my way toward them. "Hey." She smiles at me. "The others went home a while ago."

"Yeah. They have a long drive home." Reaching for Promise, I pull her close. "Rain is movin' in. Time to head home." I turn to Piper. "Bean, run over and hug Gampy's neck before we go," I say, then shift my attention to Kiwi. "You mind grabbing that water hose over there," I point to the side of the house, "and douse the fire, in case the rain misses us?"

"You got it, mate." Kiwi walks away.

A few minutes later, Promise, Piper, Kiwi and I are strolling down the road, heading home. Halfway to the house, the sky rumbles with thunder behind our backs, and the heavens let loose a steady rain. With nothing to keep us from getting wet, the four of us make a run for it. By the time we hit the steps of the porch, and I've unlocked the door, our clothes are soaked, and we are all laughing. "It's late, Piper." I step to my daughter, kissing her wet head. "Get upstairs and put some dry clothes on."

She continues to laugh as she pulls on her wet shirt. "That was the best." Her eyes light up. "Goodnight, ya'll." And she climbs the stairs.

"That'll sober you up." Kiwi grins. "I'll catch you two later," he says, and jerks his chin as he heads to the spare room he's using, leaving Promise and me standing in the foyer.

Water drips from the ends of her hair, and her dress is clinging to her body like a second skin. Grabbing her ass, I lift her, and Promise wraps her legs over my hips. I climb the stairs with her wet body against mine. Stepping into the bedroom, I close the door with my foot then stride over to the bed where I lay Promise down. She peels her soaked dress from her body, as I rid myself of my drench clothes.

Laid out in front of me like the goddess she is, her body slick from the rain, and her dark hair spread out on my pillow, I hover above my woman, unmoving. I take a moment ingraining this perfect vision of Promise into my brain. My woman reaches between us, taking my cock in her skillful little hand, effectively bringing me out of my daze.

"Cain, I need you."

I run my finger along her pussy, feeling how ready she is for me. "You need my cock, babe?"

"Yes. I can't wait any longer," she pants.

Brushing her hand away from my dick, I drop down and claim her mouth. I kiss my woman the way I always kiss her—hard. And because she was made for me, Promise takes what I give her. The noises she makes in the back of her throat urges me to give her more. Licking the seam of her mouth, Promise opens for me, and I waste no time taking what I want. Her taste fuels my need to claim every inch of her body. I can't get enough of my woman.

Releasing my lips, Promise kisses my jaw then trails her mouth down my neck. "I want you inside me."

Sitting back on my haunches, I run my hands up between her thighs, over the dip of her stomach until I cup both breasts. I give them a firm squeeze before rolling her nipples between my fingers. "Oh, God," she groans, her breathing turning erratic.

Promise becomes impatient as her hips shift and rise off the bed. "Honey," she whimpers as my hands skim back over her ribs.

"Wrap your legs around me, babe." I reach underneath her and lift, bringing her body flush against mine, her pebbled nipples digging into my chest. Taking her hair in my fist, I tip her head back. With her neck exposed, I lick and nip at her glistening skin. With her body overcome with need, Promise starts grinding her wet pussy against my cock—the feel of her heat is my undoing.

Grabbing hold of her waist, I raise her. "Guide me in."

With her breaths coming out in pants, Promise reaches behind her, takes my heavy cock in her hand, and places it at her opening. The moment her pussy kisses the tip of my cock, I lower her down until I'm buried completely. Her head falls back, and she sighs. "Eyes on me," I snap. "Keep your eyes on me, so you know who's fuckin' you. I want you to know it's your man fuckin' this pussy. I want you to watch me take you." Promise does as she's told and keeps her beautiful eyes on mine. With my hands cupping her ass, I guide her to move. "Ride me."

My woman is good with instructions. She wastes no time bracing her hands on my shoulders as she grinds down on my cock, bouncing up and down, swiveling her hips. "Fuck, this pussy is good."

"Oh, God. You're so deep like this. I'm going to come."

"Not yet. You come when I do." Bending forward, I lay her back on the bed while keeping her ass in my lap and my dick in her greedy pussy. "Look down, Promise. Look down and watch me take you."

Once her eyes dip down to where we are joined, I start driving my cock in and out of her. Her fingers grip the sheets, and I know she's trying to hold off her orgasm, but I'm not quite ready to be done with her, so I buck harder, causing her breast to bounce.

"Fuckin', beautiful. My woman's pussy is fuckin' beautiful."

"Cain, I need to come."

Leaning forward, I order, "Wrap your arms around me." Promise wraps her arms around me the same time I flip us over, me on my back, and her straddling me. "Take what you need, babe, and take me with you."

With my hands on her hips, I push up into her pussy the same time Promise starts riding me hard, taking what she wants. The moment her pussy flutters, clamping down around my cock, it triggers my release. Promise throws her head back and screams with my name on her lips as I fill her with my cum.

14

PROMISE

Blinking my eyes open, I immediately feel the loss of Cain's heat, and I know he is no longer in bed with me. The clock on the bedside table reads 4:58 am. Wondering why he would be up this early, I climb out of bed and snag his shirt from the floor and cover my naked body. Once I have finished my business in the bathroom, I head downstairs to see if he is there, but I come up empty. I walk into the living room to also find it empty. I start to worry about where he could be when I catch a flicker of light flashing through the kitchen window to my left. Padding further into the kitchen, I reach over the sink and pull back the curtain to get a better look. Cain's back yard is enormous, and at the back of the property sits a massive industrial size metal building with the roll-up door that is open. I see flashes of light that look almost like fire and a shadowy figure moving around. What is he doing out there?

Curiosity getting the better of me, I open the back-sliding glass door, step out onto the patio, and make my way across the lawn, my toes sinking into the fresh, lush grass. I'm not prepared for what I find when I step through the entryway of the shed. Cain is standing with his back to me in front of a heating chamber. He is shirtless, wearing a pair of faded jeans that hang low on his hips. The bright fire from the chamber is lighting up his skin making him sweat. Cain is holding a long metal pipe and is twisting it while holding it over the flame. I watch as he works the tube, his muscles flexing with each twist. Stunned speechless my eyes shift from him to the large angel sculpture sitting on the table behind him. I then scan the shelves lining the wall of the shed and see several pieces of glass art. "Oh my God," I gasp covering my mouth alerting Cain to my presence. He turns and smiles that smile. "Hey, Sugar."

I watch as Cain carries the long metal pipe in his hand to a metal table where he begins twisting it, rolling the molten glass on end, shaping it. I'm so mesmerized by what he is doing that I don't speak. I keep watching him. Cain then sits on a stool, picks up what looks like a big wooden spoon, cups the glass with it and twists the metal pipe again, shaping the glass into something rounder. With ease, he holds the pipe in one hand and puts a thick padded glove on his other hand. Once he is finished putting the glove on, he picks another tool and cuts the upper part of the glass. The piece falls away, landing in his gloved hand. Cain stands, strides over to a metal box, opens it and places the glass inside then closes the door. By this point, I finally find my voice. "This is amazing," I breathe. "You do all of this?' I point to the pieces lining the shelves and to the partially finished angel in front of me.

"Yeah," Cain shrugs like it's no big deal. Only I see it as a huge deal.

"How long have you been glassblowing?" I start to walk around his workspace and look at some of the pieces sitting around.

"Since I was a kid. My grandmother did it as a hobby. I used to love watching her work. One day I asked her if she'd teach me. I was probably fifteen at the time. Been doing it ever since. Before I had Piper, I worked out on the rigs and didn't do it as much, but once I had her, I quit roughneckin'. I had a daughter to raise but didn't have any direction. All I knew was I needed a job that allowed me to be home with Piper, so I decided to make a go of sellin' my pieces. The rest is history. I used to sell my art in a few shops around New Orleans but now I mainly do custom orders."

"Like this?" I point to the angel.

"Yeah. A brother of mine who is the VP of The Kings out in Montana is havin' it made for his woman, Bella."

I run my fingers along the wings of the angel. The angel itself is transparent in color except for the wings which are blue and green. "So beautiful," I breathe.

Next, I inspect a few pieces he has on a shelf. One is a bowl. It's shaped like an oyster shell and is rainbow-colored. I pick it up and begin admiring its eccentric colors up close. When I flip it over, I nearly drop the bowl. The name LeBlanc next to a Flor De Lis symbol. "Oh my God! You're that LeBlanc?"

Cain shakes his head and chuckles. "I take it you've heard of my stuff."

"Heard of you? Cain, you're like the biggest name in the glassblowing industry! Some of your smaller pieces sell for thousands of dollars!" I nearly shout. And on that thought, I carefully set the bowl down. "Wait here. I'll be right back." I dash out of the shed without waiting for a response from Cain and run into the house and up the stairs to the bedroom. Dropping down to the floor of the closet, I dig through the box of stuff I keep my mom's mementos in. Finding what I'm looking for, I hold it close to my chest and hurry back out to the shed where Cain is still standing in the same spot I left him. Stopping in front of him, nearly out of breath and panting, I hold up an orange, red and blue glass butterfly. "Three months before my mom's accident, she took me to the flea market. That was our thing. We loved them. The last one we went to I saw this butterfly and was immediately drawn to it and my mom didn't hesitate to buy it for me." I flip the butterfly over to show Cain the stamp on the bottom.

"Fuck, babe. I remember this. I must have been twenty-five or so when I made it. I remember because Piper was just a baby, but she was fascinated with butterflies. I also never create two similar pieces. Piper has one but hers is pink. I sold a few in some local shops in town."

"Lucky for me, I got this before you made a name for yourself. I've looked up your work, Cain. I bet whoever sold this to me sixteen years ago is kicking themselves now," I chuckle.

Closing my eyes and holding the butterfly close to my chest. "I can't believe I've had a piece of you with me this whole time," I tell him as tears begin to pool in my eyes.

He cups my face. "Fuck, babe."

"Your art is beautiful, Cain. It means something to people. Every time I look at this butterfly, I think of my mom and that perfect day we spent together."

Cain kisses my lips. "I'm glad you have that, babe."

"Me too, honey."

Later that day, London and I are at our new office getting things set up. Our furniture was delivered an hour ago, and since Cain is off doing club business, Fender and Kiwi are here helping us since Piper went to hang at the clubhouse with Josie and Payton. Currently, we're breaking for lunch. London and I are sitting on our new sofa eating the Shrimp Po' Boy sandwich and fries Fender brought us while he and Kiwi are outside on their phones and smoking.

"So, you and Nova are getting pretty serious," London speaks through a mouth full of food.

"I know it's fast," I shrug, "But it feels right, you know."

"I'm happy you're happy, Promise." London looks at me like she wants to say more.

"Why do I feel a but coming?"

"I worry about you. I mean how much do you actually know about Nova and the club?"

"I know Cain is a great father and a devoted friend to his brothers. I know he's caring and protective. And the more I get to know him, the more I like him. As for the club, I don't know much. We both know of the rumors, but I have not directly asked him."

"Do the rumors about The Kings scare you?" London asks.

I ponder her question a second. "No. Not just Cain, but his brothers, Kiwi, Fender, and all the guys have never given me a reason to be scared of them. Besides, rumors are not something we should base our opinion on."

"Yeah, you're right."

Deciding to change the subject, I ask, "What are you doing tonight? Cain is working at the bar, and I'm going to hang out there with him. Do you want to come have a drink?"

"Sorry, I wish I could. I'm going to my parents' for dinner. It's been a few weeks and mom is beside herself with questions about our new venture."

I laugh. "Well, tell them I said hi."

"I will. Is it safe to assume you won't be staying at my place tonight?"

Two days ago, the club hooked London's apartment up with a new steel door and a top-notch security system, so she is now back home and no longer staying at the clubhouse. I, however, am still at Cain's. He hasn't brought up my leaving and neither have I. I think it's something I need to talk with him about tonight. I don't want to overstay my welcome.

"I'm not sure yet. I'll text you later tonight and let you know."

We both eat our meal in silence a few minutes before London

lets out a sigh. "I sure will miss staying at the clubhouse. Everest is one mountain I wouldn't mind climbing."

I toss my napkin at my best friend. "You're too much." We both laugh.

"What! I speak the truth. These men are fine as in F.I.N.E. And don't get me started on your man who is a twin. A TWIN! God made two of them, Promise." London waves her hand in front of her face fanning herself.

The rumble of Harley pipes reverberating off the walls of the office, which grabs mine, and London's attention. We glance at the front office window where I see Cain pull up on his bike and park. I smile when he walks through the door. "Hi."

"Hey, Sugar." Cain prowls toward me, leans down, grips the back of my neck, and kisses me. And not just a peck. Cain has no qualms with public displays of affection. He proves it by sticking his tongue in my mouth any chance he gets. And me being the greedy hussy I am, I let him. I love the way he tastes.

A throat clearing brings me out of my lusty haze, and I break away from Cain. London is looking at the two of us with a goofy grin. Cain gives her a chin lift. "London."

London mimics Cain's gesture. "Nova."

She then grabs her purse off the table beside her and slings it over her shoulder. "Well, I'm out. I'll call you tomorrow, Promise."

"Okay, girl. Give your mom and dad my love." London gives us a wave over her shoulder as she leaves.

"You have any more shit to do here, babe?" Cain asks.

"No. I'm done for the day. Thanks to Kiwi and Fender, we were able to knock everything out early."

"Good. You're on the back of my bike then. Get your shit, and we'll head to the bar."

"Oh. I was going to go back to your house and change first."

Nova appraises me. "You look fine, babe."

I peer down at my cut off jean shorts and old Def Leppard t-shirt, and shrug. "Okay."

When Cain and I step outside, I lock the door to the office and drop the keys into my purse. Taking my bag from me, Cain places it in the saddlebag on his bike. As I'm putting my helmet on, I notice Cain's body stiffen. When I peer up at his face, his attention is on something over my shoulder. When I look behind me, I see Leon Velasco step out of the back seat of a black SUV. What the hell?

"Stay here. Don't move," Cain orders just as Kiwi and Fender come up behind us. Fender flanks Cain while Kiwi places himself in front of me, blocking my view of Cain and Leon. I can't hear the words that are spoken, and I can't see Cain's face, but his body language says he doesn't like the fact my former client is here. I'm a bit shaken by it too. It's been days since the last flower delivery. I was thinking he had moved on from trying to gain my attention.

A minute later Leon gets back into his vehicle, and Cain appears again in front of me, his face hard. "Let's go," he clips.

"Cain. What did he want?"

Cain ignores my question as he straddles his bike.

"Cain?"

"On the bike now, Promise."

The tone of his voice gives me pause, and I decide not to press. I do as I'm told and climb on behind him. I want to tell him about Leon Velasco, but maybe now is not the right time. I make a mental note to tell him later, once he's cooled down

By the time we arrive at the bar, Cain is still visibly pissed. He continues to say nothing as I follow him inside. The bar is mostly empty aside from a group of older men sitting at a round top at the far corner.

"Cain," I try again, and he still ignores me as he makes his way into the back. I follow him into what looks like a stock room. When we enter, I call his name once more. "Cain?" His silence makes me nervous, and I begin to worry his reaction to Leon will not be pleasant with each passing second. "Look, is this about Leon Velasco? Because I have no plans to represent him again. I'll tell him I no longer work with Thomas's firm. I have no intention of taking those sorts of cases in the future. Also, he's been..."

My words are cut off by Cain's mouth crashing down on mine. He backs us up until he has my body pressed against the wall and his hand wrapped around my neck. His grip is firm but not tight and surprisingly, it doesn't scare me.

"You won't be sayin' shit to Velasco," he grits his nostrils flaring. "What Velasco wants has nothing to do with your professional services."

I go to open my mouth to say something, but nothing comes out because what the hell am I supposed to say? During the time I represented him, Leon Velasco made several passes at me and has been sending flowers every week for months. I knew he was interested but no way in hell would I go there with a man like him. I guess Cain knows of Leon's agenda too. Now I'm more curious about their conversation.

"Oh," I say.

"Yeah, and needless to say, Velasco didn't take too kindly to the fact that you are my woman. But if he's smart, he will heed my warning about stayin' away from you," he informs me.

Suddenly the conversation I had with London about what kind of man Cain is and what sort of things the club does come rushing back. "Uh, what kind of warning, Cain?"

"The kind that lets motherfuckers like Leon Velasco know I will bring a world of hurt down on his ass if he so much as looks in my woman's direction."

"Wh...what kind of hurt?"

"Don't ask me a question like that, Promise, unless you are prepared for the answer."

"Does that threat involve something illegal?" I ask.

Cain doesn't hesitate to lay it all out. "The club doesn't run shit as we did in the past. But the club does what it has to do to protect the ones we care about. Sometimes our way of doing those things may be frowned upon by the law. The Kings are tight with the law here in New Orleans because we help keep the streets clean, so that means the law sometimes overlooks some of the things we do."

I blink up at him. "Okay."

"Okay?" he asks, his hand still around my throat only now his thumb is gently rubbing my pulse.

"Yeah, Cain. Okay."

Cain searches my eyes. "Does what I said scare you, Sugar? Do you understand what livin' in my world will be like?" "Nothing about you scares me, Cain," I tell him truthfully.

"Fuck you're perfect," he says just before claiming my mouth.

It doesn't take long for our kiss to become heated. The next thing I know my hand slips down between us, and I'm undoing his belt. Sliding the zipper to his jeans down, I wrap my hand around his cock.

"Fuck," he grunts, spinning me around to face the wall. The next thing I know, my shorts and panties are ripped down my legs. A second later, Cain thrusts his cock inside me, and I scream.

"Ahh!"

Each thrust is powerful, I have no choice but to brace my palms against the wall, taking what he gives me. "Oh, God. Don't stop."

"Never," he growls. "This pussy, these tits," Cain palms my breasts over my t-shirt, "these lips," he kisses me. "All belong to me." Hearing Cain says those words does something to me and my pussy clamps down around his cock.

"Fuck, yeah. You like knowing you belong to me, don't you?"

"Yes!" I scream through my orgasm as Cain continues to pump in and out of me.

"Fuck, your pussy is stranglin' my dick," he grunts through one final thrust before he buries himself in me completely, filling me with his release.

Cain stays inside me while resting his head against my shoulder as we both catch our breath. Finally, he speaks "I love the thought of you spendin' the rest of the night with my cum inside your sweet pussy."

I wasn't expecting him to say that, but I'd be lying if I said I didn't like it too.

It's near midnight, and I'm sitting at the bar with Tequila while Cain tends to the customers. I try to focus on what Tequila is saying but my attention is on the woman sitting three stools down. The blonde is wearing a top cut so low her boobs are practically spilling out onto the bar as she leans over talking to Cain. Cain is doing his best to ignore the skank while he tends to the other patrons but that seems to only make the woman try harder.

"Bitches," I hear Tequila mutter as she takes a shot of whiskey. "Here." She pours another shot and slides it in front of me. "Down this, then go handle that shit." She nods over her shoulder at the woman who I have been watching for the last ten minutes.

"This is Cain's place of business. I can't just go over there and start shit with a customer."

"Customer my ass, girl. Take a look around. You see that table over there?" Tequila points to a table where four other women are sitting, all with their attention on Cain.

"Those bitches are just waiting their turn. As soon as the blonde strikes out, the next skank will make their move. That's how it's always been here."

My stomach knots. "I know Cain used to be a manwhore. I didn't expect to have it thrown in my face."

"Yeah. And that sucks. But my question is, what the hell are you going to do about it?"

I think about Tequila's question a second. When I look over her shoulder again to see the blonde reach across the bar and run her hand down Cain's arm, I lose it. Standing from my stool, I pick up the shot of whiskey and down it. "I'm going to show these bitches my man is claimed."

"Fuck yeah, you are." Tequila stands with me. "And I'm going to watch."

With my blood boiling, I sidle up on the stool next to the blonde. I don't miss the amused look Cain gives me, one that says he knows what I'm about to do.

"You can go now," I tell the woman.

The bitch takes her eyes off Cain and looks at me. "Excuse me?"

Tequila, who has taken the stool on the other side of the blonde, decides to have my back. "My girl didn't stutter."

The woman looks at Tequila then dismisses her by flicking her hair over her shoulder then sneers at me. "What's it to you where I sit?"

"This is what it is to me." I twist in the stool and look at Cain whose amused gaze has suddenly turned heated. I lick my lips and lean over the bar. "Honey."

"Yeah, Sugar." Cain spreads his arm out while bracing his palms on top of the bar.

I reach over and fist his shirt. "Come here." Cain meets me halfway as I thread my fingers in his hair then proceed to show every single bitch in Twisted Throttle who he belongs to by sticking my tongue in his mouth.

"Hell, yeah! Now that's how you claim your man, girl!" Tequila shouts the same time the entire bar breaks out into cheers. By the time I pull away from Cain, the blonde is no longer sitting beside me.

15

NOVA

After waking up to Promise kissing my neck this morning, and delivering a repeat performance of the night before, I hate that I had to leave the bed at all.

"You sure I can't tempt you to stay?" Promise is sitting in the bed, with her back against the padded headboard. She lets the sheet covering her body fall, pooling around her waist, exposing her breasts to me as I continue to dress.

My mouth waters and my cock jumps with the need to taste her again. Fuck. I stay hungry for Promise twenty-four-seven. I can't seem to get enough of her. Pulling my cut over my shoulders, I stroll across the room. "As much as I'd like another taste of your sweet pussy, Sugar," I grab my phone and wallet and shove them into my pocket, "it will have to wait." Promise sighs, sticking her lower lip out. The pout she's giving makes me harder. Her eyes drop to the bulge in my pants. Leaning forward, she crawls on her hands and knees to the edge of the bed. I watch her body as she slinks toward me with a feline-like movement.

My feet move on their own accord, stopping at the end of the bed. Sitting back on her heels, Promise reaches out, popping the button on my jeans, then slowly slides the zipper down. Her blue eyes never leave mine. She's sexy as fuck, as she frees my cock. There is no fucking way I'm telling her to stop now, and by the twinkle in her eyes, she knows it.

Her eyes fall as she strokes my shaft. All I can do is watch her. The moment her tongue darts out, and she licks the head of my cock, I almost lose my shit. When her hair falls, hiding her face, I gather the long strands and wrap them once around my hand, so I can watch her. Without hesitating, Promise takes my cock in her mouth, and I hiss. "Fuck, babe. Your mouth feels good." She takes as much of me as she can into her mouth until I feel the back of her throat. "Reach between your legs and touch yourself for me. I want to watch you come while you suck me off." My grip tightens on her hair as I watch her do as I say.

Finding her center, Promise rubs her clit and moans. The vibration from her throat as she continues to get off on pleasuring herself, with her mouth full of my cock, causes me to growl. Synchronizing her mouth with the strumming of her clit, my woman increases her speed, giving me the most intense blowjob of my fucking life. "Goddamn, Sugar. That's it." I end up taking my eyes off her for a moment—only for a second because the way she moves and how she is working me right now feels too damn good.

Suddenly, without warning, my thigh muscles convulse, and I break out in a sweat. I explode in her mouth with so much force I'm sure she can't take it. Without missing a beat, Promise moans with pleasure as she rides out the rest of her orgasm while giving a few more strokes to my cock with her mouth, swallowing every last damn drop.

Never has a woman got me off so fast.

Promise releases my cock, her eyes locking with mine as she licks her swollen lips. My hand falls from her hair, and I wipe the beads of sweat slowly sliding down the sides of my face, with the back of my forearm then adjust my cock back in my jeans.

Still sitting on her heels, I lift her, pressing her naked body into mine. "Fuckin', hell, woman." I press my lips to hers in a heated kiss, then pull away, gazing into her eyes.

"You're going to be late." Her mischievous grin is contagious, and my lips lift in a smile of my own. Promise fastens my jeans, lifting the zipper back into place. "Will you get in trouble?" She leans in, pressing her lips along my neck just beneath my ear, knowing it drives me crazy.

"Probably," I tell her the truth.

"I'm sorry—sort of. I couldn't help myself," she admits, then softly kisses my lips.

My palms skim across her soft skin until they reach her sweet ass. Gripping her cheeks, I give them a firm squeeze. "Totally worth the hell I may catch, Sugar. Absofuckinglutley worth it." My tongue tangles with hers one more time before pulling away. I walk back to my dresser, opening the top drawer where I keep my weapon, held securely in the holster, then clip it at my side. "Kiwi will be ridin' out with me, but Pop will be hangin' around while we're gone. To keep an eye on things."

"You guys still worried about that biker and his club?" Promise slides her legs over the side of the bed, grabbing her silk robe nearby. Standing, she slips it on over her bare body.

"The club is takin' every precaution." Once my boots are on my feet, I close the space between us, and she steps into my open arms. "Piper wants to run to town later. I want you to ride with her and Pop. Don't want you sittin' out here alone."

"Okay," Promise agrees.

I kiss her forehead. "I'll see you later, Sugar."

Fifteen minutes later, Pop arrives, and Kiwi and I are on our bikes heading toward town. It's an unusually cold day for this time of the year, but the sun is bright, and the sky is blue. We're on our way to the clubhouse to discuss in further detail what we talked about last night. Being a Sunday traffic is less hectic, so we end up making good time as we head for the other side of town.

Rolling to a stop, just outside the gate as we wait for it to slide open, I take in the fact everyone has already arrived, making Kiwi and I the last ones to show. Backing our bikes up alongside the others, we kick the stands down and cut the engines. Kiwi removes his helmet, hanging it on the handlebar of his Harley. "We're late for the party, mate."

"Yeah." I can't help but grin knowing the reason, and Kiwi doesn't miss it either.

He laughs as I dismount my bike, and we stroll toward the clubhouse. "You don't have to say anything, brother." Kiwi pulls open the door. "That shit-eatin' grin you're sportin' speaks for itself." He walks inside and I follow.

We spot Payton, and Josie in the main room, cleaning, and Payton looks up from her task behind the bar. "Hey." She brushes fallen hair from her face. "The others are in the room waiting for you," she says, then goes back to cleaning.

The door's close when we approach it, so I hit my knuckles against it before swinging the door open and walking in. "About fuckin' time," Riggs barks, leaning back in his seat, with his hands clasped behind his head. "Care to explain why you've kept us waitin' on your asses for," he drops one hand, peering at his watch, "forty-five minutes?"

Kiwi pulls his chair from the table, taking a seat, and so do I. "Nope." I give my brother a look.

"Shit," he shakes his head, holding back a chuckle, and the rest of my brothers, fight back their amusement. Riggs sighs. "I get it." He leans forward, placing his forearms on the table. "But, next time, try draggin' your love drunk ass to church, when it's supposed to be here."

"Absolutely," I reply, knowing full damn well it will happen again.

"Alright. Let's get down to the bare bones of things," Riggs states. "I sent word to the Hell's Punishers, and it traveled fast." He looks around the table. "They have agreed to a meeting."

"No, shit?" I'm genuinely surprised.

"Yeah—today," Riggs declares, and the rest of us exchange looks across the table.

"Where?" I ask.

"They're waiting on me to decide." Riggs leans back in his chair once more. "We need a safe place. Not the clubhouse, but still on our grounds."

"The whole damn city is our turf," Wick proclaims, crossing his arms over his chest.

"True. But we don't need our business in the streets either," Riggs tells him.

"What about the bar?" I cock my head. "We're closed all day, and it will be private enough to keep shit low key," I suggest.

Riggs nods, running his hand down his beard, as he thinks. "The rest of you cool with that?" he asks our brothers.

After a beat, everyone agrees to Twisted Throttle being ground zero for the two clubs to have words. "Alright. I'll make a call. Everyone hang here. We all ride out together."

It doesn't take long for word to get back to us that Hell's Punishers will meet us at Twisted Throttle at noon, which is an hour from now. Filing out of the clubhouse, Riggs, Wick, Fender, Kiwi, Everest, and I mount our bikes. The vibration from all six Harleys as we rev our engines energizes us, getting us jacked up for what could come.

Sliding my shades over my eyes I see my brother roll out first, then the rest of us pull into formation as we hit the city streets, causing a few heads to turn as we pass by some of the shops that are always open. A few short minutes later, we're parking our bikes in front of the bar. I spot Luna sitting out on the balcony above us with Aria as we maneuver inside the building and wave. Luna waves back, pointing for my niece to look down in my direction. When she spots me, she clasps her hands together. "She's getting so big," I say to my brother, who watches the exchange.

"Like a weed." He smiles at his family. Luna blows him a kiss before standing from her seat, and she and Aria disappear into their home above the bar. "Come on. Let's have a drink before company arrives." He claps me on the back.

Inside, Fender goes behind the bar, grabbing several beers from the ice cooler and a bottle of whiskey from the top shelf, handing them to Everest who takes them to one of the center tables where we gather. Seconds later, Fender sits several glasses down, sliding one to each of us. The bottles pass around the table, everyone pouring themselves a shot. I fill my shot glass to the rim, lift it to my lips, and throw my head back. The heat from the alcohol as it wets my mouth and slides down my throat acts like gasoline to a flame. We have no idea which way this meeting will go, but we are all prepared in case shit hits the fan. I, for one, want answers. One way or another, I want their man to pay for his actions.

Silence falls as the minutes tick by. Not one of us speaking, as we sip on our beers. The bar becomes so quiet I can hear the slight ticking from the neon sign hanging on the wall as it flickers. We shift in our seats the moment we hear the distinct rumble of bikes approaching, the noise becoming louder with every breath I take. Riggs stays seated as the rest of us stand. Like finely tuned soldiers, we check our weapons, before the roar of engines is right outside the bar.

Once more, silence falls. Everest is at the door in a few strides, ready to greet our guest. He opens the door and the light from outside floods inside the darkened bar room. A minute later, a large frame eclipses the entrance. Instantly I recognize the man from the evening Piper was attacked as the biker Riggs brawled. He strolls toward us, his eyes scanning the room before landing on my brother. Four more of his members follow close behind as they enter the bar. Everest closes the door and stays at his post.

"Riggs?" The burly biker directs his words to our Prez.

Riggs nods. "Crow?" and the guy nods his reply. "Have a seat." Crow pulls the chair from the table, sitting across from my brother. Riggs grabs an extra glass sitting on the table and reaches for the whiskey. "Drink?"

"I won't say no," Crow says, his eyes shifting to me, then back to Riggs. "Twins, huh?" he questions as he accepts the drink.

"My brother, Nova," he tells him, pouring a shot. Crows eyes shoot my way, lingering for a beat. His gaze begins to get under my skin, pissing me off. Wick must sense my mood change, and places his hand on my shoulder, giving it a firm squeeze.

"Before this meetin' goes any further, I'd like to clear a few things up." Crow places his glass in front of him after downing it. "What happened to the young girl the other week should never have taken place."

"You're damn right about that, motherfucker," I lunge forward, but Wick stops me. "Your brother," I growl, "would have raped my daughter if I hadn't gotten to her when I did." The tension in my neck increases as my anger doubles.

"What Creep did was apprehensible, and when he's found, he will pay."

"You're damn right he will. I'll see to it that he rots in hell," I threaten.

My brother, levelheaded as he is, doesn't waver after my outburst. "Glad to know we're on the same page when it comes to your man." Riggs levels Crow with a hardened stare. "I also didn't miss the fact you said when he is found."

"We haven't seen hide nor hair of him since he bonded out of jail. I also heard about the shit he pulled soon after." Crow's eyes cut to mine. "The scare he put into your woman, and the threat made toward you and your club has nothin' to do with Hell's

Punishers." He then settles his attention back on my brother. "My club has no quarrels with The Kings of Retribution, and I'd like to keep it that way."

"And the reason you're still in my city?" Riggs demands to know.

"To find my brother before he makes another mistake, which may cost more than his life. To stop him from starting a war," Crow admits, leaving us all lost for words.

"Damn." Riggs leans back, crossing his arms over his chest. "That has to be a hard pill to swallow, givin' up your own brother like that."

Crow is willing to give up his brother to keep the peace? I can't even begin to imagine what type of relationship the two of them have. I don't care how fucking pissed I get at my brother. I could never turn my back on him. Whatever. I brush the thoughts from my head. Crows family shit is not my problem. Getting my hands on his brother and making him pay is.

"Look. Don't get me wrong. He's my blood, but me and him," Crow shakes his head, "we're far from family." He sighs, running his hand through his hair. "Creep has been a fuck up for a long time—most of his life to be precise, but him puttin' his hands on a woman, attempting to take something from her like that, my club won't tolerate and I won't stand behind."

"You realize which way things could go if my men get a hold of him?" Riggs eyes Crow.

If? I scoff. It's not a matter of if, but when.

"I do," Crow nods.

"Then, my club has no beef with you." My brother extends his hand, and Crow accepts. "Let's hope it stays that way." Releasing hands, Riggs stands, but Crow stays seated. His eyes drop to the table.

"There's another reason we haven't left town." His words cause all of us to tense, and his men take it as a threat. Moving forward, their hands reach for their weapons, and we go for our own. I have mine out and the end of the barrel directly in Crow's face before either of his brothers manage to pull guns on us.

"Tell your men to stand down before I put a bullet in your head," I warn him.

"Stand down," he barks, and his men holster their guns. Unfazed, Crow continues, as he looks to my brother. "I have someone waitin' outside that I'd like you to meet." Then his eyes settle on my face. "L.A," he calls one of his men. "Bring her in." Crow's eyes never leave mine.

What the fuck kind of games are they playing?

"You got it." His brother, L.A, turns toward the door, but Everest won't let him pass. "Think you could tell the mountain here to move?" He looks over his shoulder.

"I'm not playin' games here, Riggs. My old lady is no threat to you or your club." Crow is quick to reassure us, but I don't give two shits. I keep my gun on the fucker, just in case.

"Let him pass," Riggs orders Everest, and he steps aside. Looking down at Crow, my brother tells him, "Let's hope, for your sake, you're right. I'd hate to see my brother make a mess all over my barroom floor."

His man L.A opens the door, leans out, motioning to grab someone's attention. A tall, thin brunette steps inside, with her face, cast down to the floor as she approaches. The wringing of her hands as she keeps them clasped in front of her tells me she is nervous.

The moment she lifts her head, I'm staring at a ghost from my past.

"Holy fuckin' shit," my brother exhales on a heavy breath.

Never in my lifetime did I think she would ever show her face again. "Hello, Cain." Her voice sounds the same. Why did I think it wouldn't?

Seventeen years bubble inside of me and the hate I thought

was long gone surfaces. "Madison." My eyes leave hers, looking to Crow. "I don't know what you're playin' at bringing her here," my finger itches to pull the trigger. "But you're a hair away from me losin' my shit."

"Wait," Madison steps forward, throwing her hands up. "Please. Me being here right now has nothing to do with Crow. I mean, it does because of his brother, but" she pauses, and I notice her hands shaking. "Cain. I've always planned to stay out of the way, but after what Creep did to our daughter..." "Daughter?" Kiwi voices behind me.

"Yeah," Wick speaks. "Meet Piper's mom." The anger I hear in Wick's voice resonates with me.

"Mind removing your gun from my face?" Crow asks, but I don't comply.

"Brother," I feel Riggs at my side, placing his hand on my forearm. "Stand down." Only then do I lower my weapon, putting it back in the holster.

"You are not welcome here." My eyes narrow to slits as I say the words to Madison.

"Cain. Please."

"I need a drink," I proclaim. Grabbing the whiskey bottle from the table, I fill a glass and take the shot.

"Look, I know you hate me—" Madison starts but I cut her off.

"Damn right, I do. You abandoned my daughter. You left her without lookin' back. And now, you roll into town, on the back of a Harley as someone's old lady thinkin' you can waltz right into her life as if you never left?" I shake my head and run my hands through my hair.

"You have every right to be furious with me. What I did was wrong." Madison pauses then continues. "But at the time, it was the right thing to do for me." She pats her chest. "Not a day goes by that my heart doesn't hurt, or that my arms don't ache to hold my daughter." Tears stream down her face, but I can't bring myself to keep my attention on her. "Drugs and a string of bad choices were ruining my life." When she says that, my eyes snap to hers. My face saying what words won't. "Yes, Cain. I used for a short time before I found out I was pregnant. As soon as I did, I ran. Ran from the drugs, and from the man who eagerly provided them to me." She wraps her arms around herself, and Crow stands, pulling her to his side. "I fought like hell for the rest of my pregnancy. I left town, mostly running from the man I'd been staying with. I found sanctuary at a halfway house in Mississippi. They took me in and kept me safe—more importantly, kept me clean. I bailed the day I was released from the hospital." Crow helps her to sit in the chair he was occupying before. "I knew I wasn't strong enough to keep our daughter. I had too much baggage, and she needed to be kept safe." Her eyes lift to mine again. "I knew you would give her what I couldn't at the time. You also had the support of your family, which is something I didn't."

All the words she says are cycling through my head, but none of them matter. "What do you want, Madison?" I rub my temples.

"A chance. A chance to meet my daughter—to be her mother," Madison pleads, breaking down, her body wracked with sobs.

The bar becomes silent. Madison sobbing is the only noise heard as I process the fucking shit show brought to my feet. I'm pissed—mad as hell knowing she used for a short time while she was pregnant with Piper. Relieved, she sobered up for her but furious, nonetheless. And the goddamn old lady to the president of Hell's Punishers? All this time she's been living a few hours away, and not once could she find the guts to bring this shit to my door before now. "Your timing is for shit." My eyes harden even more if that's even possible when I look at her. "You wait until somethin' horrific happens to my daughter before you decide you want to have anything to do with her?"

Crow hands her a handkerchief he pulled from his back pocket, and she blows her nose. "I've been keeping tabs on Piper for a long time," she admits. "You've done such a good job raising her, Cain. I had no intention of causing problems."

"Yeah, well..." I leave the rest of my thoughts unsaid.

Crow clears his throat. "I think we've all had enough for one day." He pulls Madison to her feet. "We'll be staying in town for a few more days. You know where to find us if you need me." Crow directs his words to my brother.

"Can I see her?" Madison asks between breaths as she collects herself.

"If it was up to me, you know the answer." Her face falls. "But it's not. That choice is Piper's and hers alone," I clarify. I may not be ready to forgive Madison just yet for walking out on Piper, but I damn sure won't project my feelings for the matter on her. If she was to tell me today she wanted to see her mother, I would support her decision.

Madison nods her understanding.

We follow Crow and his men out the door and watch them mount their bikes. As Crow and Riggs shake hands, I hang back and bum a cigarette from Fender. "You okay?" he asks.

"Not sure, to tell you the truth," I admit.

Just as the words leave my mouth, I spot Pop's truck parked down the road at the Blue Star Cafe. Shit. I forgot to tell Pop to stay clear of this area because of the meeting being here at the bar. Not a second after my thoughts, and kicking myself in the ass, Piper can be seen jogging our direction as her, Pop, and Promise exit the restaurant.

"Daddy, wait." She holds up a brown paper bag, and immediately my eyes dart to Madison. My body stiffens when her eyes hon in on Piper. Relief washes over me as she stands unmoving beside her man's bike. I also feel my brother's eyes burning a hole right through me for my mistake.

Piper makes it to me and catches her breath from the run. "I wanted to make sure you ate lunch." She shoves the bag clutched in her hand at me. "Here—your favorite. Fried boudin balls with some of Annie's famous comeback sauce." She smiles not realizing what she walked into. Not that she is in any danger. We've established that as much. I'm confident the Hell's Punishers want no harm to come to her.

She finally looks around, noticing several faces she doesn't recognize, then takes in her uncle's irritation. "Crap. I shouldn't be here, huh?"

"No, Bean, you shouldn't. That's my fault." I kiss the top of her head.

"Daddy," she whispers, "who is the lady staring so hard at me right now?" My head turns, and I eye Madison, who takes a small step forward, her expression full of hope.

There's a struggle inside me to tell my daughter the truth, and for a moment, I don't think I can, but I stomp those feelings down because I won't have her find out from anyone else but me. "Bean," I place my finger under her chin and have her look at me. "That woman over there is your mother." Piper's eyes widen, and she looks over her shoulder, staring intensely at Madison, then looks back at me. Her eyes fill with unshed tears that she is struggling so damn hard to hold back and my heart crumbles.

"Why is she here?" Her bottom lip wobbles.

Piper doesn't need to know much, just the basics about her question. "To see you," I force out.

Piper straightens her back, and a couple of tears trickle down her sweet face. "I don't need her. I only need you, and the rest of my family. She means nothing to me." I didn't expect her words to be so harsh, if at all. Most of all, I didn't expect her words to make me feel a twinge of pain for Madison. Piper buries her face in my chest, and I hold her to me, stroking her hair. Down the street, I notice Pop and Promise looking on, but hanging back.

I shift my attention to Madison, shaking my head, letting her know without words, Piper wants no part of her right now.

Madison clutches her chest but doesn't put up a fight as Crow swings his leg over his bike, holds out his hand, and helps her settle in behind him. Crow looks my way, and gives me a short nod, before firing his engine, and pulling out into the road. Once the Hell's Punishers are gone, my brothers walk back into the bar, except for Riggs and Wick, who hang back.

"You okay, Sweetheart?" Riggs asks, and Piper turns to look at her uncle.

She sniffles. "Yeah."

"You sure?" Wick also asks, just as concerned.

"I'm sure."

"Good. Give me a hug." Wick opens his arms, and Piper goes to him wrapping her arms around him.

"Bring that hug over here." My brother opens his arms, and Piper hugs him too.

Pop pulls his truck up to the bar and yells out the window. "Don't go into explaining nothing. I saw her with my own two eyes."

I walk my daughter to the truck, and Promise opens the door, getting out so Piper can slide in. "I'll be home soon, Bean." I kiss her forehead, and she climbs in next to her Gampy.

"Everything okay?" Promise asks with worry.

"Yeah, Sugar."

"She's crying, Cain." Promise cocks her head. "Why?" The protectiveness in her voice is firm but gentle, and it cements my feelings for her even more.

"She just stared into the face of someone she hasn't seen in seventeen years, babe," I explain.

"Who?" Promise scrunches her face.

"Her mother."

16

PROMISE

It's been two days since Cain came home and told me about what went down with Piper and her mom. He didn't divulge the details of what is happening with this other club, but he did give me the rundown on Madison. Cain and his daughter have been thrown for a loop, discovering that her mom is now the old lady of the President of Hell's Punishers. And not only that, she has been in the same state for several years now. She was even keeping tabs on Piper.

Now Piper has been held up in her bedroom for the last two days. Cain has talked to her, but we both can see her shutting down. It kills him to see his daughter struggling and not have a clue about how to help her. He has confided in me his experience with his own mother, and he too knows about mine, but Piper's is different. Cain and I can understand her pain, but we can't relate. I know someone who can, though.

"Would you allow me to take Piper out today?" I ask Cain, who is sitting on the edge of the bed, lacing up his boots while I stand in front of the dresser putting on my earrings.

"Sure, babe, if you can get her to go. What do you have planned?"

"I don't want to overstep, but I called London last night for some advice on Piper."

At that, Cain peers up at me. "What do you mean?"

Sighing, I sit down on the bed beside him. "London was adopted by her stepmom when she was five. Her birth mother left her and her dad when she was just six months old. Her dad remarried when she was two, and later her stepmom, Faye, adopted her."

"Shit. That's rough, babe."

"It wasn't for a long time. Not until London was fifteen. One day out of the blue, her birth mom showed up. She had her issues and her reasons for the choices she had made with London but had wanted to get to know her daughter finally. I won't go into detail because it's not my story to tell, but I feel London can help Piper. She wants to help. The same confusion and hurt Piper is feeling is something London can relate to because she too has been in Piper's shoes. And if you're okay with it, London and I would like to spend the day with Piper. I think some retail therapy and a trip to Sadie's salon is just the medicine she needs. I want her comfortable enough to open up to us and not make it feel like we are staging an intervention."

Cain grips the inside of my thigh and squeezes. "You're fuckin' amazin'. Thanks for caring' about my girl like that."

"Well, I think your daughter is pretty wonderful, and I can't stand to see her hurting the way she is. So, if there is anything I can do to help ease her pain, I want to do it. As long as I'm not overstepping."

"You're not oversteppin', babe. I plan on you being in mine and Piper's lives for a long time. That means I want you to feel comfortable about the permanent role you will have in this house."

The thought of Cain seeing me as an actual part of his family, makes my heart soar. "Do you see me like that?"

"Fuck, babe. Have you not been payin' attention? Have I not said you belong to me?"

"Yes. But..."

Cain shakes his head. "No buts. You're mine, Promise. This thing between us is not fuckin' casual, and it doesn't have an expiration date. You're it for me. So, get that through your head now and know when I say somethin', I mean it."

He studies me for a minute to make sure his words are sinking in. "We clear?"

I nod. "Yeah, honey. We're clear."

"Good, now give me your mouth so I can go. I have shit to do."

"So bossy," I mutter and give him my mouth

After Cain leaves, I walk down the hall to Piper's bedroom and knock on the door.

"Come in," she calls out.

Opening the door, I find her sitting on a chair in front of the window, with a notebook and pen in her hands.

"Hey. London is on her way over. We're going to hit up the mall and then go to my friend Sadie's salon and have a mani-pedi.

Want to come?"

Piper gives me a small shoulder shrug. "Sure."

Her response isn't very enthusiastic, but I'll take what I can get. "Great! Meet me downstairs in ten minutes."

Piper, London, and I spend our first three hours in the mall going from store to store and talking about mundane things. I ask Piper about school and graduation. She asks London and me how we met and about our time together in college. Piper is still undecided about what college she wants to attend. After leaving the mall, we decided to grab some burgers and fries before heading to Sadie's.

"I don't know if I could go out of state," she says, popping a fry in her mouth.

"Why is that?" London asks.

Piper takes a sip of her soda. "I've never been away from dad for more than a night and never as far away as another state. I know I give him a hard time about letting me go, but the truth is, I don't want to let him go either. My dad and the guys...I think I'd miss my family too much." Piper stops talking and gets a faraway look in her eyes, and I can tell her mood has shifted. Reaching across the table, I place my hand on her arm. "London and I are here if you want to talk about it, sweetie."

Piper remains quiet while looking at her lap. London and I share a look, and I give her a nod.

"My birth mom left my dad and me when I was six months old," London says, and Piper snaps her head up. "Like you, I have an amazing dad. Also lucky for me, he married an equally amazing woman who adopted me when I was six."

Piper doesn't say anything but keeps her gaze locked on London, so London takes that as her go-ahead to continue. "When I was fifteen, my birth mom showed up. Just like that," London snaps her fingers. "She shows up on our doorstep with her own story about why she left and that she was ready to have a relationship with me."

"Really?" Piper asks. "What did you do?"

"At first, nothing. I was angry and I was hurt. I didn't understand how she could walk away from her child. Then, after all those years, she suddenly decided she wanted to see me."

"So, what happened?"

"It took some time, but after a few months, I agreed to meet with her. After I got over the initial shock of the situation, I decided I wanted answers. Answers I knew only my birth mom would have."

"Did finding the answers help you?"

"They did. And I can tell you now, I have a solid relationship with my birth mom. I'm not as close with her as I am to the woman who raised me, but I'm no longer in a place of resentment. It took me years, but I finally realized we all have a different journey in life. I can honestly say that mine was exactly the way it was meant to be. I'm incredibly lucky to have been raised by two of the most loving parents. Had my birth mom not made the decision she did, my life could have turned out differently."

Piper is quiet as she absorbs each word London says. "So, you're saying I should talk with my mom? That it might help me to understand why she left?"

London shakes her head. "I can't make that decision for you. It's something you have to figure out on your own. You have to do what is right for you. Telling you my story is to let you know you are not alone. I understand, and I'm here for you. So is Promise and your dad. Don't be afraid to talk to them. Don't bottle up your feelings and close them out."

"London is right, sweetie," I jump in. "Your dad will understand any decision you make. He will back you up one hundred percent, and so will I. Nobody wants to force you to do anything you're not comfortable with. Your dad is just worried about you because you have crawled inside yourself instead of leaning on him to comfort you."

Piper swipes the tears rolling down her cheek. Sliding out of my seat, I settle into the one next to her. I pull her into my arms. "I've just been confused. I don't know what to do," she says.

"Oh, sweetheart," I tuck her hair behind her ear. "It's okay to be confused. You are allowed to feel whatever you're feeling. Just know that talking about what's going on inside your head helps.

Let the people who care about you be there for you. Okay?"

Piper sniffles and nods. "Okay. And you're right. I already feel better. I promise to talk to dad when we get home."

After our lunchtime talk, Piper was feeling emotionally

drained, so we put a raincheck on our mani-pedi and went home. The second we walked through the front door we found Cain standing at the stove making dinner, Piper went straight up to her father and wrapped her arms around him. I offered to finish making dinner while the two retreated upstairs to talk. An hour later, Cain walks into the kitchen where I'm currently sitting at the table, takes my hand, urging me to stand and without a word pulls me into his chest. He holds me for the longest time, not saying a word. After several seconds he speaks. "Thank you for today; for givin' my little girl what she needed."

I melt further into his embrace. "You're welcome, honey. Did she talk to you?"

Cain pulls away. "Not yet. She's sleepin' now."

I sigh. "She's had a long day."

Sensing Cain had a bit of a day himself, I lean up on my toes and kiss his neck. "How about I put the spaghetti sauce on to simmer, and we have a beer out on the porch?"

Cain cups my face and kisses the tip of my nose. "I'd say that sounds fuckin' perfect, Sugar."

A week has passed since the drama with Piper's mom and whatever has been going down with the Hell's Punishers. Cain still hasn't told me all the details surrounding the man who attacked me; only the club is continuing to look for him. He's also assured me I'm safe. I believe him. Being with Cain makes me feel protected. For instance, no matter where I go, one of the guys is with me. Today it is Fender. I'm at the grocery store picking up a few things when my cell rings. I smile when I see it's Jackson calling. I answer. "Hey!"

"Promise." The tone in his voice is off, alerting me to something being wrong.

"Jackson, is everything okay?"

"Look, I'm not sure I should be calling you. You probably don't want to know, but I felt you should."

"Know what? Tell me?"

Jackson sighs. "It's Thomas. He had a heart attack. I found him slumped over at his desk this afternoon."

A lump forms in my throat. Thomas and I are not on speaking terms, but he is still my stepdad. "Is he...is he okay?"

"He's stable for now, but the doctors say his condition is serious. We're at University Medical."

"I'm on my way. I'll see you soon, Jackson."

"You don't have to come, Promise." Jackson's voice sounds pained.

"I know I don't, but I'm coming anyway. I'll be there in fifteen minutes." I hang up with Jackson, abandon my shopping cart, and rush out of the store. Fender is at the entrance waiting on me when I come out.

"What's wrong?" he asks, taking in my current state.

"I got a call from my brother. My stepdad had a heart attack. I'm heading to the hospital now."

"I'll follow you."

Fender straddles his bike the same time I climb into my car. Less than fifteen minutes later, I pull up to the hospital, and Fender follows me inside and up to the fifth floor. Jackson is standing at the nurse's station when I step off the elevator.

"Jackson!" I call out to him.

He takes in Fender, who is behind me with a confused look but doesn't ask questions. "Hi, Promise." Jackson pulls me in for a hug. He then holds his hand out to Fender. "Hi, I'm Jackson, Promise's stepbrother."

Fender takes Jackson's offered hand, and they shake. "Fender," he grunts. He then nods toward a small waiting area. "I'll wait over there."

Leaving Fender, I walk with Jackson, following him into a hospital room.

"What the hell is she doing here?" Avery's voice rings out the moment I step in.

"I called her," Jackson informs his sister.

"What for? She's not wanted."

"Promise is still a part of this family, Avery."

Avery scoffs. "The bitch is no family of mine."

I'm about to say something, but a voice over my shoulder beats me to it. "You'd be smart to watch the way you talk to my woman."

I turn to see Cain standing behind me just inside the door to the room. Fender must have called him when I got the news about Thomas.

"Your woman?" Avery looks to Cain and then back to me. "You sure don't waste any time moving on from Brad. And you call me a slut."

Closing my eyes, I pray for the strength to not be petty. Lucky for me, my man doesn't wish for the same thing because Cain has no problem defending my honor. "Well, in my book, an unattached woman, no matter how long she has been that way, goes out and finds another man, does not make her a slut. A woman who spreads her legs for engaged or otherwise attached men is the definition of a slut." Cain's gaze stays on Avery as he enunciates each word, leaving Avery with her mouth gaped open. It takes every ounce of self-control not to laugh. Considering my stepdad is lying in a hospital bed five feet away, laughing would not be appropriate. Although the current show between Avery and Cain is far from proper.

Just as Avery goes to open her mouth again, Jackson cuts her off. "Zip it, Avery. Now is not the time for your shit."

Only Avery doesn't listen. She never does. "This is so typical. You're always taking up for Promise. Everything is always about her."

Is she serious?

"Avery, I have no clue what you are talking about, but Jackson is right. Now is not the place or time."

"Shut up, Promise. You don't get to come in here acting like the perfect daughter when you haven't been around in weeks."

"For Christ sakes, Avery. What is your problem? Your father just had a heart attack and is laid up in this bed," I point to my left, "and all you want to do is run your damn mouth."

"You're my problem." Avery points an accusing finger at me.

"I've never done anything to you, Avery!" I yell, having had enough of her bullshit.

"It's because of you my dad is in here!" Avery yells, and I'm taken aback by her accusation.

"Me? How is Thomas having a heart attack, my fault?"

"Dad and I fought last night. He was saying it was my fault that you and Brad quit. He said I needed to get my act together, or he was going to kick me out of the house."

"Wait a minute," I hold my hand up. "Brad quit?" This was news to me.

"Yes. He said he was moving back to Florida. Now, dad is blaming me for everything."

"That's because you are to blame, Avery!" Jackson cuts in. "When you go around playing your little high school games and fucking with people's lives, there are consequences."

"See! This is what I'm talking about. It's all about Promise. You and dad both have always liked her more than me."

"Are you nuts! Thomas barely tolerates my existence."

"Really?" Avery sneers. "Then why has he spent my whole life comparing me to you? Avery, why don't you make good grades like Promise? Avery, how come you can't stay out of trouble like your sister? Avery, why won't you go to college and make something of yourself like Promise?"

I stand here with my mouth gaped open because not once

have I heard Thomas talk like that. He has not once given me praise.

At Avery's confession, things start clicking into place. Her extreme distaste for me. I have spent years baffled as to why my stepsister hated me so much. Now I know. And though it is no excuse for the horrible things she has done to me, I, to some degree, empathize with her.

Feeling Cain's heat at my back and his hands on my shoulders, I close my eyes and take a deep breath.

"Excuse me." A nurse walks into the room. "I'm going to have to ask that you all leave. We are getting complaints about the noise coming from this room. I'm going to have to ask you all to take your family dispute elsewhere."

"No problem. I was just leaving," I say, looking at the nurse then at Jackson. Stepping out of Cain's hold, I hug Jackson. "If you need anything, I want you to call me day or night. You can keep me updated on Thomas's condition, but I won't be back up here."

Jackson squeezes me back and then gives me a look that says he understands. Finally, I turn my attention to Avery. "I'm sorry you were hurt by Thomas's constant comparison to me for all these years. A fact I knew nothing about, considering the man never showed me anything but resentment. I wish things could have been different for us. I would have given anything to have a real sister. But the truth is, what happened to your dad is not on me. It's time you grow up, Avery, and take responsibility for your actions and the consequences caused by them."

My parting words help to close a painful chapter in my life. Feeling a weight lifted from my shoulders, I walk out of the hospital, ready to start a new one.

17

NOVA

It's been a few days since the shit show took place at Twisted Throttle, and I'm still unsettled with the fact Piper's mom wants back in her life after all these years. Madison and her old man, along with the other few members who were with them the other day, are still in town. Part of that has to do with how they're searching for their ex-member as much as we are. I'm beginning to think he's left town because there has been no sighting of his sorry ass on the streets.

Sipping my coffee, I sit out here on my back deck, looking out over the water, and the dense fog hovering above it. I love mornings like this, where the bayou is hidden amongst the mist. The world around me becomes quiet and still—the kind of peace a man needs to think. My thoughts drift back to when I arrived back home after leaving the bar the other night, and Piper was locked away in her room. She didn't want to talk much about seeing her mom. So, I did the only thing I could do—held her while she softly cried. My daughter is not a crier, but that night she did. Years of hurt she's never shown before poured from her as she wept, while I stroked her hair.

I wish I could rid her of the turmoil she must be feeling. If my embrace could fix the hurt, or extinguish the anger inside her, I would hold her forever if that meant I could shield her and protect her from life's disappointments. Hearing the door open, then close behind me, pulls me from my thoughts. Looking back over my shoulder, I see Piper. "Hey, Bean."

She rounds the corner of the outdoor sectional, sitting beside me with a mug of warm tea in her hands. "Good morning, Daddy." Piper sighs, slowly looking out at the water. We sit quietly for a few minutes. Just the two of us enjoying the silence only a bayou morning can bring. "Daddy?" she finally speaks softly.

"Yeah?" I down what remains of my coffee, then set the mug on the table in front of me. Leaning back, I drape my arm across the back of the wicker sofa.

"Does it make me a horrible person if I say that I'm not ready —to meet her?"

"No, baby girl." It breaks my heart that she would even think such a thing. There isn't a mean bone in Piper's body. Not vindictive or purposeful anyway. "You'll know when the time is right."

Her eyes fall to the mug in her hands. "What if that never happens? What if it never feels like the right time?"

"Come here." I motion for her to scoot closer. When she does, I wrap my arm around her, kissing the top of her head. "I can't answer that for you, Bean. You're the only one with that answer. The only advice I can give is that your heart will know. Give it time. When it speaks, listen."

Silence falls between us again.

"I see her when I look in the mirror now," Piper states. "Her heart-shaped face, long brown hair. Everything about me reflects her image—all but my eyes." My daughter turns her head to look at me with eyes like my own. "Those I got from you." The smile gracing her beautiful face is small, but it speaks louder than her words. It lets me know even though she's struggling right now, she's okay.

I smile back. "You're beautiful, Piper. Just as your mother is, but so much more. The kind-hearted person you are makes your light and beauty shine brighter than hers ever did. You got the better part of both of us. Don't compare yourself to her, or me," I tell her. "You are one of a kind, baby girl. It's not about who you look like. It's who you are on the inside."

"Part of me hates the fact I see her likeness in myself. Another part of me feels this tug—a pull deep inside my..." Piper stops herself from saying more and leaves her sentencing hanging.

I pull in a deep breath. "It's okay to want to know your mom, Bean. Is that what you're struggling with?"

It takes her a moment to reply to my question, which is fine. I'll wait. She can have all the time she requires. I'm just happy that she is finally opening up to me. I was grateful she confided in Promise yesterday, but I must admit, I'm delighted she's coming to me now. "Kind of—yeah. Even though for most of my life I haven't given it too much thought. Not having a mom I mean. I didn't realize just how much it actually bothered me until it—until she was right there in front of me," Piper confesses, and I feel the weight of her words.

"I'm not goin' to sugarcoat how I feel about your mom. I was angry for her actions all those years ago, and I'm fightin' mad now that she wants to be apart of someone's life she gave up on, regardless of her reasons." My voice hardens with anger over the situation. Breathing in, I calm my inner turmoil. "But those are my issues, not yours. I'm always here for you, Bean. I'll support any decision you make regarding your mom." I fight against the rage swirling in my gut because Piper doesn't deserve to see that from me. Especially now.

Sitting together, we watch the fog lift from the surface of the water, revealing a large heron, perched upon a broken tree stump protruding above the waterline. Both of us keep whatever thoughts we have to ourselves.

Piper breaks the silence. "I'm blessed, Daddy. And so grateful that you never gave up on me. I don't know what choices I'll make when it comes to my mom, but right now," she pauses, "my life is full. I'm happy, and I know without question that I am loved." Piper lays her head against my shoulder, and I hug her tighter. "I love you, Daddy."

Damn. Piper got me all choked up. Taking a moment to absorb what she said, I pull in a few cleansing breaths and respond. "I'm the one who is blessed, baby girl." I kiss the top of her head once more. "I love you past the moon and beyond the farthest star."

Piper smiles at what I used to say when tucking her into bed at night when she was little.

The back-door creaks open and Promise pokes her head out.

"Hey."

"Hey,"

"Mind if I join you two?" she asks.

"Bring your pretty ass over here," I pat the spot on the other side of me, and she walks out in a white summer dress that floats around her bare feet as she pads across the deck, then settles in beside me, tucking her body close to mine.

The three of us sit together, content with being in the moment, and I couldn't ask for anything more than what I have right now.

Later that afternoon, with time to myself, I attempt to work on the piece I need to finish for Logan. A phone call from Kiwi halts my progress before it even starts. "What's up?"

"We have a situation."

My body becomes rigid. "I'm listening." Placing my tools down, I walk outside.

"Seems Velasco has been following your woman around town."

"How'd you find this out?" My blood begins to boil.

"You know we installed security at her place of work the day they moved in and set up shop. Well, who we now know to be a couple of his goons were caught snooping around, trying to get a peek inside during the middle of the night," Kiwi explains.

The other night while lying in bed, Promise talked about how that motherfucker sent her flowers constantly, and the many advances Velasco made toward her during the time she represented him. I nearly lost my shit when she went into detail about the time he approached her in the parking lot of the courthouse after his trial. Promise admitted she had been meaning to tell me but with everything that's been going lately, she forgot.

"Shit." This guy is becoming a thorn in my fucking side.

"That's not all. I was checking the security feed across the street at the gun range and came across footage of Velasco himself making a few drive byes. The image is a bit grainy, but I recognize his expensive car." I think the only thing this guy loves more than himself is his dirty money. Fuckin douche. This guy has a hard-on for my woman. That shit doesn't fly with me.

"You happen to have an address? I think it's time I reintroduce myself."

"I figured you'd asked. I'll send it to you," Kiwi replies. Before he hangs up, he asks, "Need backup?"

"Meet me there," I tell him, knowing we may run into trouble. Velasco doesn't seem like the type to dirty his hands, but he'll damn sure send his men to try and do the job.

"You got it." The phone goes silent.

Closing up the shop, I walk back to the house, while I wait for Kiwi to send the address. Grabbing my keys off the kitchen counter, I head for the garage. Throwing my leg over my bike, I start the engine. My phone vibrates in my hand, and I look down at the screen. I huff. Figures. The ugly bastard lives in a penthouse in the Warehouse District.

He likes to flash his money around. Probably the only way his ass gets any pussy.

It takes me forty minutes to reach my destination. As I round the street corner, I spot Kiwi sitting on his bike, casually having a smoke. I pull my bike along the curbside behind him. Getting off his bike, he steps beside me as I take off my helmet. "Look at this place, mate." Kiwi leans his head back, looking up toward the building. "I was a little curious about what it costs to live in a place like this. This fuckin' penthouse is going to cost a bloke seven figures."

"I can think of much better ways to spend that kind of money," I pocket my keys as we stride to the front door. Then ride it to the top floor of the building.

The second the doors slide open, two armed men are standing in the hallway. Taking in our appearance, they become defensive, and reach for their weapons, causing us to do the same. "I wouldn't do that if I were you," I warn them.

"Let them in." Velasco's voice drifts into the hallway. His men stand down, and Kiwi and I stroll past them stepping inside. "You two didn't think you'd catch me with my pants down, now did you?" Velasco says, lounging in an oversized leather chair with a cigar dangling from the corner of his mouth.

"I wouldn't need no element of a surprise if I wanted you dead, Velasco." Scanning the room, I find he's the only one in here, and his only protection standing outside in the hall. The fucker isn't very bright. He's just left himself wide open. I could put a bullet in his head before his two men outside could bat an eye.

Velasco tokes his cigar. "It amuses me that you think so highly of yourself."

"Seems you haven't heeded the warning I gave you the first time to stay clear of my woman." Spotting his expensive array of whiskey nearby, I walk across the room, helping myself. I pour myself a shot's worth in a glass tumbler and toss it back. "Consider this visit your final warning because there won't be another." I level him with a murderous stare.

"Is that a threat?" Velasco abruptly stands, and I'm in his face before he has time to draw another breath.

"Motherfucker." I grab him by his cheap-ass tie and tighten it around his thick neck. Kiwi pulls his weapon, and presses the end of the barrel against Velasco's head. "It's a fuckin' promise. If I find out you or one of your men have been within a hundred yards of my woman, I'll cut your dick off, shove it down your fuckin' throat and watch you choke to death on it." Loosening my hold, I cut Velasco loose. Kiwi keeping his gun aimed at him, backs away as well, and we make our way to the door.

"You'd better watch your back, biker. You just fucked up. You're a dead man. I'll see to it myself." Velasco's words fall on deaf ears.

Let him try coming for me.

"I'll have a bullet with your name on it, Velasco, whenever you're feelin' man enough to try."

18

PROMISE

"What is it like being with a man who is a twin?" Sadie asks as she stands behind Piper, who is sitting in a chair, getting her hair trimmed. Sadie also makes sure to face Luna, who is sitting with her feet soaking in some water as she waits for a pedicure. "Do you two ever get them mixed up?"

Both Luna and I scrunch up our noses at the question. "No," I say the same time Luna's soft voice says, "Never." Luna and I giggle at each other.

"But they look exactly alike," Sadie huffs.

I shake my head. "Not to me. To me, they are so different. Especially their demeanor." Luna nods in agreement.

"I'm afraid I'd have to agree with Promise on this one," Tequila pipes up. She wasn't excited about a mani-pedi girls' day that us women had chosen to do earlier while sitting around the clubhouse, but when her niece Sydney perked up at the idea, she couldn't say no. Another perk to having Tequila spending the day hanging out with us—no babysitter. "Riggs and Nova are like night and day in my eyes. Then again, I've known them since I was a kid so..." Tequila shrugs.

"All done, sweetheart." Sadie unfastens the nylon cape from around Piper's neck.

"Thanks, Sadie." Piper looks in the mirror as she runs her fingers through her long strands.

"You're welcome, Piper. I have some snacks and soda in the refrigerator in the back if you and Sydney want some before I start on your nails," Sadie offers.

"Sure." Piper looks to Sydney. "Come on." The two girls make their way toward the back of the salon to where the break room is.

Once the girls are out of earshot, London is the next to put her two cents in. "If we are going to talk about the twins, then how about you two," she points to Luna and me, "compare notes on how they are in..."

"London!" I screech, cutting her off before she could finish her sentence. I know what was about to come out of that dirty mouth of hers. I know by the mischievous smile she casts my way.

"What? You can't blame a girl for being curious."

"Stop asking me that. I told you last time I wasn't going to tell you," I laugh.

"That's because you're no fun, Promise."

London turns her attention away from me to Luna. The way her cheeks have reddened, I'd say she understood what London was asking.

"Ignore my best friend. She's highly inappropriate." I look directly at Luna, letting her read my lips and smile.

"Again, I have to agree with your girl. Nova and Riggs are like my brothers. I don't want those kinds of mental visions haunting my dreams." Tequila mock shivers causing everyone to laugh. Thank God the subject was shut down because Piper and Sydney emerge from the back a second later.

"Those are some awesome cookies you have back there, Miss Sadie," Sydney says with a soda in one hand and a cookie in the other.

"Thanks, sweetheart," Sadie smiles. "How about I wrap some up for you to take with you. I have plenty left at home so you can have what I brought with me today."

"That would be great. Thanks," Sydney beams.

A few minutes later, the subject changes when Tequila asks, "How's the new office coming along. Fender says the last of the furniture arrived the other day."

"It's coming along great. London and I officially open next week. We've already had a couple of former clients reach out to us too."

"I have an excellent feeling you and London will do great," Sadie adds.

"Thanks, girl. I have a good feeling about our new venture too. It's a fresh start."

Tequila's phone rings, cutting into our conversation. She pulls it from her pocket just as the ringing stops. "That was my dad. I need to call him back." She stands. "I'm going to grab some coffee from across the street while I make my call. Anyone want me to bring them back anything?"

We all decline Tequila's offer.

"Can Sydney hang with you all? I'll only be a few minutes."

"Of course," I tell her.

Once Tequila slips out of the salon, the room falls into a comfortable silence. Sadie goes about painting Luna's toenails while Piper and Sydney sit on a small sofa with their noses buried in their cell phones. Everyone is relaxed and off in their own little worlds when a man in a baseball cap walks into the salon. The bell above the door alerts Sadie to his arrival.

"Can I help you, sir?" Sadie greets.

A second later, it's Piper's gasp that sets me on alert just as the man in the hat reaches behind his back and produces a gun. Sadie screams while London and Luna rush over to the sofa where

Sydney and Piper are sitting. The gunman points the weapon in Sadie's direction. "Shut the hell up, bitch!"

I stand and place myself in front of Sadie, blocking her from the aim of the gun. "You need to leave." My voice shakes as I put my hands out in front of me.

"Oh, I'm not goin' anywhere, bitch," the guy sneers.

It's then I recognize the stranger's voice. It's the voice of the man who attacked me in London's apartment. The guy is wearing jeans and a wrinkled t-shirt. His long greasy hair is sticking out from under his hat, and he has a crazed look on his face. "I see you remember me now, don't ya you, fuckin' whore." The man takes a step closer toward me. "I'm not leavin' without a little payback. It's because of you and that bitch over there," the man jerks his chin toward Piper, "my fuckin' club and my own brother has turned their backs on me." The guy darts his eyes back and forth between Piper and me before they finally settle on Piper. Piper lets out a whimper as Luna and London huddle closer to her and Sydney, shielding them. "She's comin' with me," the man points his gun at Piper. "I'm going to finish what I started with the bitch and teach that piece of shit club you belong to you can't fuck with me."

Piper begins to cry even harder at the guy's words. And when he takes a step in Piper's direction, I grab his arm. "You're not going to put your filthy hands on her."

The man whips around, shrugs off the hold I have on his arm, and backhands me across my face, making me stumble and fall to the floor. Flashes of light dance in my vision. Sadie screams again, falling to the floor beside me.

"Who do you think is going to stop me, cunt?" Spittle flies from his mouth as he crouches down on the floor, getting in my face.

Jumping into action, Sadie tries to push the guy away from me. Her effort to protect me earns her a blow to the left side of her face with the butt of the man's gun. Sadie cries out in pain from being pistol-whipped. She falls back on her butt, holding her eye as blood seeps between her fingers.

That's when I see red.

Lunging for the man, I start to hit and claw at his face. "You asshole!" My assault on the guy goes on for several seconds. I manage to get a few licks in before he backhands me again, this time splitting my lip. I pray that London or someone is using the distraction to call Cain.

From the corner of my eye, I see London and Luna rise from the sofa, and I know they are about to try making a run for it with the girls. Unlucky for us, the asshole over me clocks them about two points five seconds after I do. He stops our struggle by placing the barrel of his gun to my head. I freeze.

"Get your asses back over there and sit or I'll put a bullet in her brain," the guy warns London and Luna, his breath heaving. And by the wild look in his eyes, I know he'll not think twice about pulling the trigger. Seeing the same look on his face Luna and London do as they are told.

"Here's what's going to happen." The man stands and pulls me up with him by the hair on my head. "I'm taking both these cunts with me. Any of you bitches makes a move I don't like, you'll be eatin' a bullet."

As the guy rants, I catch sight of Tequila through the window of the salon. Her phone is against her ear. She shakes her head at me and puts her finger to her lips just as she ducks out of sight. I close my eyes and take a deep breath. I know she has alerted Cain and the club to the situation.

19

NOVA

I still have adrenaline coursing through my veins from my face to face with Velasco when I roll my bike up to the clubhouse gate. That guy is a piece of fucking work, and fucking delusional if he sincerely believes my woman will give him the time of day. Inching my bike near the keypad, I begin to punch in the security code, just as Riggs comes busting through the front door in a full-on sprint.

The fuck?

With his phone pressed to his ear, Riggs swings his leg over his ride just as the gate rolls open. It only takes a second for me to pull my bike alongside his, my body becoming rigid as I take in his expression. I don't get the chance to hear his side of the conversation before he's shoving his phone in his pocket. My brother levels me with a rage-filled stare.

"Talk to me, brother."

"Creep has our women at gunpoint," he growls as he starts his engine.

My stomach falls. "Where?" I yell over the sound of both our motors running.

"Sadie's salon," Riggs says, and my gut churns. Promise and Piper. The two of them went with Luna, Tequila, and Sydney for another girl outing today. Fuck. I white knuckle my handlebars.

Riggs takes off, and my back tire flings loose gravel everywhere as I speed off toward the compound exit behind him. As the two of us race down the road, weaving through traffic, my mind has time to play out every unthinkable scenario. "Goddammit!" I roar through clench teeth.

After what feels like an eternity, we start closing in on the location of the salon, and my gut clenches tighter than it already was knowing my family is in danger. Following my brother's lead, I slow down, stopping a few buildings down from our destination. From where we are, I clearly notice the shades in the salon windows closed, keeping what's going on inside from passersby. We cut our engines, and dismount. On instinct, I go to rush past my brother, needing to get to my girls. His hand shoots out, grabbing the back of my cut with a firm tug, jerking me to a dead stop. "What the fuck?" I lash out, my anger getting the better of me.

"Cool your shit, brother," Riggs demands, his voice low with warning. "My woman is in there too, but we need to access the situation—get our bearings before barging in there with our guns blazin'."

Fucking hell.

Why does he always need to be right?

"You talk to the others?"

"Not enough time for that." Riggs takes in our surroundings. "We may be goin' solo on this one." The streets are bustling with pedestrians. Slowly approaching the building, we stop as we reach the side of the salon. "That was Tequila I was talkin' to when you arrived at the clubhouse. For whatever reason, she stepped out of the salon, leaving the other women to do their thing. The motherfucker just so happened to make his move during this time."

A whistle catches our attention. Looking at the backside of the building, we spot Tequila. Keeping to the narrow space between the salon and the building beside it, Riggs and I make our way toward her. The moment we get to her, and step behind the building, I spot a blue rusted out van parked near the dumpster.

"You reach the others?" Riggs asks Tequila.

"They're on the way. It will take them a bit longer coming from the gun range," she informs him.

"That his?" Riggs motions to the van.

"Has to be." She keeps her voice low.

"When was the last time you had eyes on the women?" I want to know.

"It's been at least ten minutes since he directed Promise to lower the blinds. Up until then, I was able to see what was going on."

"Anyone hurt?" Riggs is quick to question.

"Promise's friend, the one who owns the salon, was bleeding. From where I don't know. I watched Promise struggle with the guy until he got the upper hand, but Piper is okay."

An ear-piercing scream coming from inside has my feet moving. Riggs and Tequila are on my heels as I sprint toward the back door, pulling my weapon from the holster at my side along the way. I don't wait for my brother to give the word to go. I try the handle.

"It's locked," Tequila informs.

"Goddamnit!" I yell, taking a step back, and attempt to kick the door in with my heavy boot.

"It's the only reason I haven't gone in myself," she adds, but at the moment, her words don't deter me from what needs to be done to get inside.

Another scream, followed by a loud crash, causes an animalistic roar to escape me, and my kicks become frantic. From the corner of my eye, I watch Riggs retrieve his gun. Before anyone has a chance to stop me, I take a step back and point my weapon at the deadbolt. I don't give a fuck at this point if gunfire is heard. All I care about is getting to my girls. Tequila and my brother back away from the door. I fire off several shots, leaving splintered holes in the wood surrounding the lock. Then together, using both our strength, Riggs and I kick the door in. Fragments of wood pieces are sent flying as we finally gain entrance.

"You fuckin' cunt!" Creep's voice carries from the front of the building.

Knowing the likelihood my gunshots were heard by the bastard inside, the three of us move around stacked boxes, rushing to the front of the salon, stopping dead in my tracks when I see the gangly son of a bitch hovering above Promise, holding his head as he points the barrel of his gun at my woman, who has Piper shielded behind her back.

"You'll pay for that, bitch," he sneers, kicking away a large glass bowl at his feet.

That's my girl.

But then, Promise catches sight of me trying to inch my way forward without being detected. Her eye movement causes the already tweaked out motherfucker to turn his head. "Oh, hell, look who showed up to the party." His lips turn up in an evil smirk. "Must be my lucky day." He laughs maniacally. "I get to kill you and fuck your pretty little girl here." He looks back at Promise, pressing the barrel of his gun against her forehead. Then his head swings back in my direction, locking eyes with me. "But first, I think I'll let you watch your whore die."

The fucker shouldn't have taken his eyes off my woman. Using the narrow window of opportunity, I watch Promise as she brings her arm up, hitting his hand away. I hear the sound of his gun firing as I surge forward, closing the several yards between him and myself, and tackling him to the ground. Losing his grip on the gun in his hand, it skids across the tiled floor. Before he has the opportunity to put up a fight, I have him pinned against the wall, the barrel of my gun is pressed firmly against his chest, and my hand wrapped around his throat.

He laughs.

The motherfucker laughs as my hand tightens, restricting his breathing. "Must be my lucky day," I use his words.

"You don't have the balls," his strangled voice croaks and the cords in my neck tighten. "Kill me, asshole." He forces the breaths past his compressed windpipe.

"Nova, the others are here. We need to go before someone calls the law." From the corner of my eye, I notice Fender and Kiwi making their way over.

"Daddy." Piper's scared voice causes me to look to my side, where she's being held by Promise, her eyes filled with fear. I chance a look around finding Riggs with Luna, and Wick and Tequila consoling Sydney, London and Sadie.

Shit.

I won't kill a man in front of my daughter. "It's going to be okay, baby girl," I assure her, then look at Tequila. She's kneeled beside Promise's friends, who is bleeding from a cut on her head. "Tequila," I call to her, and she looks over her shoulder. "Get them out of here. Take them back to the clubhouse and get a hold of Doc."

"Cain." Promise stands as Tequila helps Sadie off the floor. I don't look at her. Not now. She and my daughter don't deserve to see murder in my eyes. "Promise. Go with Tequila."

"Don't..." her voice shakes, and I know what she wants to say, but she doesn't. There are things a man is willing to do. Some things he is ready to sacrifice to keep the ones he loves safe. The tone of her voice hints at those things I'm capable of. Instead, I hear her sigh, as she moves away, with my daughter tucked at her side.

Once the women are no longer in sight, my brother joins me.

"Luna?" I ask.

"She's okay. Shaken, but not harmed."

"And him?" I ask about the motherfucker in my grasp, who begins to struggle, and I squeeze, putting more force on his windpipe, watching his eyes bulge from the pressure.

"Your call," Riggs tells me.

My eyes narrow and twisted thoughts manifest in my mind. I want him to suffer before I end his sorry existence. "Take him with us."

Kiwi and Fender flank both sides of me. Reaching into a duffle bag he's carrying at his side, Kiwi produces a roll of duct tape, ripping a strip off, then slapping it across the bastard's mouth. From there, I finally drop my weapon and release my hold on his scrawny neck. I take a couple of steps back, watching as they bind his hands behind his back. Not once does he resist. The entire time the asshole stares me down. He knows his time is coming.

With nothing to transport the motherfucker back to our compound, we opted to fish in the asshole's pockets for his keys. Shoving him in the back of the van he intended to use for my daughter, I slam the back doors shut. Needing to be with my daughter and my woman, I turn to my brother, who already knows.

"Go. I'll wrap shit up here."

With no words, I jog back to my bike, parked down the street.

In no time, I'm at the clubhouse and bursting through the front door to find the women seated on one of the sofas. I rush to them, falling to my knees, then pull them close. I hold my girls for several seconds before pulling back to get a good look at them. Tears stain Piper's face, and it guts me. "I'm so sorry, Bean. Shit. I'm so fuckin' sorry." Guilt eats at me because she was in harm's way once more.

"I'm okay, Daddy. I'm not hurt. Scared a little, but I'm okay." Her palm touches my cheek.

And I'm supposed to be the strong one.

I brush the hair from her face, kissing her cheek, then lift my eyes to Promise quietly sitting beside her. That's when I get a closer look at her, and the deep purple welt on her cheek. My insides coil with rage. Her hand lifts, touching her face. "It doesn't hurt much, but my wrist hurts like hell." My eyes fall to her lap. Reaching out, I carefully inspect her wrist, and Promise winces, sucking in a sharp breath.

"Shit, babe. Doc will be here soon. She'll take a look at it." Grippin' her chin lightly, I guide her lips to mine, kissing her. The distant roar of motorcycles lets us all know the rest of the men have arrived. I hate leaving Piper and Promise. "I got to go."

"I know," Promise says, her expression one of understanding. As I stand, Promise takes my hand, and I look down at her. "Don't worry about us. I've got this," my woman assures me.

With the women being cared for by Payton and Josie, I walk away. Once outside, I watch as Teagan drives her souped-up Jeep through the gate. She pulls her car to a stop, and rolls her window down, hiding her eyes behind sunglasses. "Nova." She turns the vehicle off and climbs out. Going to her back door, she opens it, retrieving her bag from the backseat.

"Take care of my girls, Doc."

"You got it," she responds.

My brothers are waiting for me to make it across the property. I had in mind to have a little fun with the bastard before offing him, but all I can think about is getting back to my girls. Pulling my gun, I walk past my brothers, flinging the heavy metal door of the shed open. My target sits on a wooden chair, in the center of the room, with his arms bound behind his back and his ankles tied to the bottom chair legs. I rip the tape from his lips, taking half of his mustache with it.

He roars from the sharp pain it must have caused, and blood

rises to the surface of his skin where flesh is missing. "Why don't you kill me, motherfucker—go on—do it you..."

He doesn't get to finish the final words he'll ever speak again. Raising my weapon, I aim, pulling the trigger. A single bullet ends his worthless life, and I feel nothing but satisfaction.

20

PROMISE

The ride from the salon to the clubhouse was a blur, and now Cain and the rest of the guys have disappeared, to where I have no clue. I suspect it has something to do with the asshole who tried to kidnap Piper and me. Honestly, I don't want to think about it. I could care less what happens to him. I know Cain won't tell me the details, but I'm confident the club will make him pay.

When we arrived here at the clubhouse mere moments ago, I could see the struggle in his eyes. He didn't want to leave his daughter, and he didn't want to leave me. I felt the only thing I could do was to assure him we'd be okay. Him taking care of business with his brothers was a priority. I know Cain needs to make sure the situation is handled so that guy would no longer be a threat. I saw the storm brewing inside him, in his soul. He needed to release his rage on something, and that something was the man who had threatened his daughter and his woman. So, once I assured him I have Piper, he disappeared out the front door of the clubhouse. And right now, I have no time to think about what is happening outside these walls. My only concern right now is for Piper and Sadie. On that thought, my attention is diverted to my friend, who is sitting beside me on the sofa. The cut over Sadie's eye is swelling by the minute. And by the looks of it, it will need stitches.

"I'm so sorry, Sadie," I choke out. "I'm so sorry."

Sadie removes the ice pack that Payton gave her from her face. "It's not your fault, Promise."

Josie interrupts when she comes into the room. "Can I get anyone anything?"

I shake my head and give her a weak smile. "I think we're good. Thanks, though."

Feeling Piper fidget beside me, I turn my attention to her. "You holding up okay, sweetie?" I wrap my arm around her shoulders. Piper nods the same time she swipes a tear from her face. "I know you were scared, but I promise I'll never let anything happen to you. Your dad wouldn't either."

"I know. I knew you wouldn't let that man take me. And I knew dad, and Uncle Abel would show up. It's just..."

"Just what?"

Piper takes a deep breath. "When that guy had the gun to your head, I...I thought my dad and I were going to lose you," Piper sobs, and I pull her in closer to me. I hold her tight and stroke her hair.

"Oh, sweet girl. It's all going to be okay. It's over now. You know that, right?"

Piper doesn't speak, but I feel her nod.

Over the next several minutes, I continue to comfort Piper as the room falls silent. Soon, the door to the clubhouse opens, and Doctor Teagan walks in. Her eyes cut to Piper first, as if to check her state before they landed on me and then on Sadie. Once she takes in Sadie's state, her gaze doesn't falter. I can tell she has gone into doctor mode. With her four-inch heels clicking against the floor of the clubhouse, she goes straight to my friend. Doctor Teagan sits on the coffee table in front of the sofa where Sadie is perched. Setting a brown leather bag down next to her, Doctor Teagan pulls out a pair of latex gloves and puts them on. She gently assesses the cut above Sadie's eye, causing her to flinch.

"I'm sorry," she murmurs. "I'm going to need to close this cut. I'll use some Dermabond Adhesive instead of stitches. The scar should be minimal. Before I do that, I want to check you for a concussion." Reaching into the bag, Doctor Teagan retrieves a penlight. While she examines Sadie, she starts asking her questions.

"At any time did you lose consciousness?"

Sadie answers, "No."

"Do you remember what happened?"

"Yes."

"Do you have a headache?"

"No. The only thing that hurts is the area around my eye."

"Any nausea?"

"No."

Doctor Teagan puts the penlight away and pulls out some gauze and some solution. She begins cleaning the cut. "What about your vision? Any flashes of light or blurriness?"

"No. Nothing like that."

"Good. I don't believe you have a concussion. I would like for someone to stay with you for the next twenty-four hours, though. If you start experiencing any of those symptoms I listed, I want you to go straight to the hospital."

"Okay," Sadie agrees.

Over the next few minutes, I watch as Doctor Teagan tends to my friend. I take the time to study the woman. The woman I know Cain once had a thing with. There is still a twinge of jealousy that wants to creep in, but I also know it's not warranted. We all have a past. It's just hard having Cain's so close to home.

Finished with Sadie, Doctor Teagan says, "All done. I want you to take some pain reliever and try to get some rest."

Josie stands. "I can show you to where you'll be sleeping tonight if you want."

"I'll go with her," London calls out.

I rub Sadie's back. "You should go with London. I'll come to check on you in a bit."

Sadie nods, then she and London follow Josie. I watch them retreat across the room until they disappear down the hallway.

My attention is back on Doctor Teagan as she turns toward Piper. "How are you doing, Piper?"

"I'm okay. Just tired."

"That's understandable. Are you hurt?"

"No. I'm not hurt."

I cut in, "Why don't you go on and lay down too? You need some rest, sweetie."

I look across from me and catch Payton's eye. We give each other a look, and she nods.

"Why don't I make you and Sydney some hot cocoa, and we can put a movie on in my room until you fall asleep?"

Both Piper and Sydney agree as they head off to the kitchen with Payton. Josie and Payton have proven to be lifesavers tonight. Once the room is empty, Doctor Teagan looks at me. Her tone is soft when she speaks. "I'm going to clean the cut on your lip."

She gives me a crooked smile as she daps an antiseptic wipe across my cut. "I could feel your gaze drilling a hole into the side of my head the whole time I was tending to your friend."

"Was I that obvious?"

Doctor Teagan's lip twitches. "A little." I sigh. "I get it. You're curious about Nova and me. Right?" she asks.

"Maybe a little, " I mumble.

Doctor Teagan stops what she's doing. "What Nova and I had in the past was casual. He wasn't my boyfriend, and I had no preconceived notions where he was concerned. I'm married to my job. I don't have time, nor do I want a serious relationship. Nova is a great guy and a good friend. Now that he has you, I have no intention to interfere. From now on, my only involvement with Nova will be what I'm doing now. If the club calls on me, I will be here. But that's where things end. You have my word."

Don't ask me why, but I believe her.

"Thanks for saying that, Doctor Teagan."

She smiles. "You don't have to call me Doctor Teagan. Teagan will do just fine."

I nod, and the subject of her and Cain drops.

Once my cut lip has been cleaned and Teagan asks me some of the same questions, she asks Sadie, she turns her attention to my arm.

"Is your arm bothering you? You've been cradling it close to you since I got here."

She's right. My wrist is throbbing. It started hurting earlier, but I wanted her to take care of Sadie first. "Yeah. My wrist hurts and feels like it's on fire. It wasn't too bad before, but I think that was the adrenalin numbing the pain. It's probably just a sprain."

"Could be, but I'd like to take a look anyway." I hold my arm out in front of me. When Teagan takes my wrist in her hands, I notice the swelling. "Girl, that's not a sprain. Your wrist is broken."

"Really?"

"Oh, yeah. I can't fix that here. You'll have to come down to the hospital for an x-ray and a cast."

"What's going on?" A deep voice echoes through the clubhouse as Cain comes into the room.

Teagan speaks first. "Promise has a broken wrist. I'll need to treat that at the hospital."

"Fuck, babe." Cain appears in front of me and gently examines my wrist. "Shit, babe. I'm sorry you've been sittin' here all this time in pain."

I try to calm him. "Seriously, Cain. I just now started hurting. I thought it was just a sprain or something."

He shakes his head. "No excuse, Sugar. I should have checked you over better. This shit is on me."

"No, honey, it's not." I try to take the blame off Cain, but I know he's not hearing me.

Then Riggs comes into the room. "You two good? I just talked to Josie. Sadie and London are sleepin', and the girls are with Payton."

Cain stands and turns to his brother. "You good here for now?"

I'm takin' Promise to the ER." "What happened?" Riggs asks.

"Promise may have broken her wrist. Doc needs to see her at the hospital."

"Shit. Yeah, brother, I have us covered here. Take care of your woman."

Before I can go to stand, a pair of arms slide under my legs and against my back. "Cain, I can walk." I try to wiggle from his hold.

"You'll stay right where you are."

I go to protest again. "Cain."

He cuts me off and stops mid-stride in the middle of the clubhouse. "You bein' hurt, that's on me. That motherfucker walkin' into your friends' place, puttin' his dirty fuckin' hands on you, scarin' my daughter, scarin' Tequila's niece...that shit is on me."

"Cain." My voice comes out soft, and I squeeze his neck with my uninjured hand.

He shakes it off. "Not going to hear it, babe. I know you're about to say some shit to try and make me feel like what happened is not my fault, and I appreciate that. My woman has a good heart. I know you got a good heart because of how you protected my girl. You put yourself between my daughter and the son of a bitch who came after her. Then when you got back here to the clubhouse, you hid your pain because you were more worried about Piper and your friend. Now here you are, clearly in pain, your wrist fuckin' broken and you're tryin' to make me feel better. But what you're going to do right now is let me take care of you. Can you give that to me, babe?"

Knowing this is what Cain needs right now, I stop fighting.

"Yeah, honey. I can give that to you."

Fifteen minutes later, we are checking in at the emergency room. A nurse at a reception desk greets us. "Can I help you?"

"I got them, Patty," Teagan says as she approaches. She left the clubhouse a few minutes before us so she could make sure we were seen right away.

"You two can follow me back here." Teagan leads us past the reception desk and down a hall to an empty exam room. "Okay, Promise. Hop up on the bed there, and I'm going to have a nurse come check your vitals and do a workup before we order an x-ray."

As Cain helps me up on the bed, a nurse walks into the room. "Hi, my name is Candace, and I'll be your nurse this evening. I'm going to start by taking your blood pressure, and then I'll ask you some questions."

I nod, and the nurse goes about taking my blood pressure. Satisfied that it's stable, she grabs a tablet from the counter and starts asking a series of questions. She asks the basics, name and my date of birth. Next, she asks, "Since you will be getting an x-ray, I have to ask, are you pregnant?"

"No."

"Are you sure? Can you tell me the date of your last period?"

"Yeah. My last period was..." I stop to mull over the dates in my head when suddenly it hits me. "Oh, my God." I close my eyes as panic starts to creep in.

"I take it pregnancy is a possibility?" the nurse asks.

Instead of answering her, I force myself to look at Cain, even though I'm afraid of what I will see. And when I finally allow my gaze to land on him, I am not prepared for what greets me. Cain is sitting in a chair beside the hospital bed, his face expressionless. I can't read what he's thinking. An uneasy feeling settles in my gut. I start thinking about what Cain has gone through with Piper's mom. How even though his daughter is his world, he may not want another kid. I don't want him to think I did this on purpose. I mean, I'm religious about taking the pill. I never miss a day.

Neither Cain nor I say a word. He stares at me, his face like stone. We're suddenly interrupted by Teagan walking back into the exam room. "Everything okay here? I just got word we can take Promise to x-ray."

"I'm going to suggest we put it off for a few minutes," the nurse tells Teagan. "There is a possibility Miss Bailey is pregnant. I was just about to ask if you wanted to run a test."

Over the next ten minutes, I sit in a daze while my blood is drawn, and the nurse asks a few more questions. The instant we're left alone, Cain is on his feet in front of me. He cups my face with both hands. "I want you to get that look off your face right now, babe."

I close my eyes. "I'm so sorry, Cain." My voice shakes as I speak. "I'm on the pill. I take it every day like clockwork. I don't know how this happened."

"Sugar, open your eyes and look at me."

I don't want to, but I do as he says. I open my eyes.

"Fuckin' love you, Promise."

"Wh...what?" I stutter in shock, his admission catching me off guard.

"I do, babe. I fuckin' love you."

"I love you too, Cain." I sniffle. "I love you so much. This is all so crazy, but I don't care. I know we didn't plan for a baby, but if I am pregnant, I want to keep it. And if this is not something you want, then I understand."

"The fuck, babe?"

"You're not upset?"

His head rears back. "Upset? What the fuck for?"

"Upset that I could be pregnant. Children are not something we have talked about. We're still new."

Cain cuts me off by tilting my head back. "I'm fuckin' thrilled at the thought of you havin' my baby in your belly. I don't care how new we are. You're mine, and I'm yours. End of fuckin' discussion. You hear me?"

"Yeah, honey, I hear you." I take a deep breath and allow some of the tension to leave my body.

"Good. Now give me your mouth."

Without waiting for a reply, Cain claims my lips with his.

I break our kiss when there is a knock on the door. I peer over Cain's shoulder to see Teagan walk in. Cain turns to face her while keeping his hand wrapped around the back of my neck, his thumb softly stroking where my pulse is. He can no doubt feel my heart beating wildly. "Tell me, Doc. Is my woman havin' my baby?"

I reach up, grabbing hold of Cain's forearm, my nails digging into his skin as I wait with bated breath for Teagan's reply. A warm smile spreads across her face. "Congratulations."

"Oh my God," I breathe the same time, Cain growls, "Fuck, yeah, babe."

"I'll give you two a minute," Teagan says. "Once we get your wrist taken care of, I'll have the nurse bring in the ultrasound machine, and we'll take a look at your baby; see how far along you are. I'll also give you the name of a highly recommended OBGYN." Once Teagan steps out of the room, Cain turns back to me.

"I'm going to have a baby," I say aloud to him like he didn't just hear the news himself.

"Fuck yeah, you are."

21

NOVA

Holy fuckin' shit!

For the second time in my life, I'm becoming a dad. My heart is about to bust out of my chest with the amount of emotion sweeping through my body. I become silent for a beat, lost in my thoughts. Piper is everything to me, and now, Promise is giving me another blessing. I love being a part of The Kings of Retribution—a part of a brotherhood, but being a father defines who I am.

Promise twists, facing me. Reaching out, she runs her finger across my brow, and her touch has me closing my eyes. "You okay? You zoned out for a second." Her voice is soft as she sighs. "What a day, huh?"

I bring her palm to my lips, thinking about today's events leading up to this beautiful moment, then kiss her palm. "Aside from the chaos, it's turned into one of the best fuckin' days of my life," I confess, losing myself in the depths of her eyes. What am I saying? I was a goner the very moment I saw her walk into the bar.

Promise's eyes light up. "You're everything I always wanted, Cain."

"I've been waiting for you my entire life, Sugar. Fuck. I'd wait a thousand more lifetimes knowing you would someday be mine."

Promise laughs, with a single tear falling down her cheek. "I'm having a baby." Her eyes widened. "What about Piper?" concern fills her eyes.

"What about her, babe?" I stroke her thigh. "Piper fuckin' adores you," I assure her. "And she'll be over the moon knowin' you're pregnant and that she will have a sibling."

"Yeah?" Promise bites her lip with worry.

"Yeah, babe."

A light knock on the exam room door draws our attention, and Teagan walks in. "Everything good in here?" her eyes dart between Promise and me.

"Never better," I tell her, and Teagan smiles.

"Good." Teagan clutches her clipboard to her chest, her attention focused on Promise. "Okay, let's get you over to radiology for that x-ray. Hopefully, we can have you good to go within a couple more hours."

I help Promise from the exam table, as a nurse appears with a wheelchair.

"Is that necessary?" Promise cradles her wrist.

"For now," Teagan informs her. Sighing, Promise seats herself. Teagan looks over her shoulder as she follows the nurse wheeling my woman out the door. "You can wait here." She informs me when I go to follow her. I give her a look that doesn't faze her. Teagan is in her element. Her brow lifts. "Shouldn't be twenty minutes, thirty at the most."

Fighting every instinct to not let Promise from my sight, I stay put. As Teagan steps into the hall, she reaches to close the exam room door. "Leave it open."

I pace the floor, as I wait. Time slows, and it feels like twenty minutes has passed. Looking at the clock on the wall; I notice it's only been ten. I tell myself she's fine, but with everything that has happened over the past few weeks, my body doesn't want to relax unless Promise is at my side.

Distracting myself, I pull my phone from my pocket, calling my brother. He answers on the second ring.

"What's the word?" he eagerly questions.

I'm bursting at the seams, and want to yell the news at the top of my lungs that my woman is carrying my baby. Instead, I hold it in, reserving it for later. It's not just my news to share. "They took her to x-ray. It looks like her wrist is broken."

"Shit, man. Sorry to hear that." He pauses before saying, "It could have been worse."

"Yeah."

"She's a fighter, Cain." I hear the pride in my brother's voice.

That she is.

"How's Piper holdin' up?"

"She's good, brother. Josie and Payton haven't let her out of their sight. You focus on your woman at the moment. We're holdin' it down here."

Just then, the nurse wheels Promise through the door. "Got to go," I tell Riggs, then quickly disconnect the call, shoving my phone back into my pocket. "What's the verdict?" I ask her.

"Don't know yet," Promise stands, and I help her sit back on the exam table. "Someone should be in soon to let us know." Great. More waiting.

It turns out, we don't have to wait long. An unfamiliar face walks into the room. "Mrs. Bailey?" "Yes?" Promise replies.

"Hi," the doctor extends his hand to my woman. "I'm Dr. Lamer, the Orthopedic surgeon on staff today. His eyes land on me, unfazed by my hard gaze, as he takes in my appearance. "You must be, Mr. Bailey?" His brow quirks.

Accepting his offered hand, I give him a firm handshake. "Mr. Leblanc. She's mine." I don't try to hide my caveman possessiveness.

"You gonna piss on me too?" Promise seems amused by my territorial actions.

Dr. Lamer clears his throat. Walking across the room, he pulls the x-ray image from the manilla folder in his hand, clipping it to the light board on the wall. "You have a scaphoid fracture." He points to a small wrist bone in the image. "The good news is, it's not displaced, which means you won't require surgery to stabilize anything. However, you will require a cast to immobilize movement, which will extend over your thumb to limit mobility." Taking the image down, he places it back in the folder. Pulling a stool over, he sits in front of Promise. Carefully lifting her arm, he examines her wrist.

"Swelling is minimal, so we should be able to hard cast you today."

"How long will I have the cast?" Promise asks.

"Ten to twelve weeks," Dr. Lamer explains. A young nurse walks in, pushing a cart. "While Hayley here gets you casted, I'll get your prescription written." Dr. Lamer stands and sifts through Promise's file. He lifts his head. "I see here you just found out you're expecting—congratulations." My woman's face lights up with the doctor's remark, and I have to say, my insides flop with illation as well. "Mr. Leblanc." Dr. Lamer regards me with another handshake, then turns his attention to Promise once more. "Miss Bailey." Suddenly, I hate hearing him address her by her last name. "I'll see you at the outpatient clinic in a week. Your appointment will be attached to your discharge papers."

"Thank you, doctor." Promise smiles at him and damned if my jealousy doesn't rise again when he flashes his smile back at her.

Once he exits the room, the nurse has her workstation organized, and all the things she needs to fix my woman up. "How long have you two been married?" Hayley asks, sitting beside the bed.

Promise, and I look at each other. "We're not married," Promise tells her.

"Yet," I quickly add. Promise and the nurse share a look. "What?" I ask, looking at the two sharing a giggle.

"He's a bit possessive, but I like that about him." Promise relaxes as Hayley begins to wrap her wrist with a soft cloth.

"I have one just like him at home." Her eyes lift to mine as I hover over my woman. "Okay. What color would you like?" She pulls out the bottom drawer of her cart, exposing a rainbow of wraps.

Promise takes a moment, thinking, and I chuckle. "What?" She looks back at me. "If I have to wear this ugly thing for twelve weeks, I want it to look good." She turns back around. "Purple," she confirms, and Hayley sets the chosen color aside.

A short time later, the nurse has her wrist immobilized, and the cast has hardened. "This cast is waterproof. Just make sure you keep the liner clean and use a blow dryer on the cool setting to dry it after showering." Hayley smiles. "Any questions?"

"Nothing comes to mind," Promise tells her.

The exam room door opens with a tap on the door, and Teagan pokes her head in. "How's it going in here?"

"Done," Nurse Hayley tells her. "She's all set." Then she turns to face us. "It was nice to meet you two."

Teagan opens the door all the way and walks in pushing a sonogram machine, and Nurse Hayley closes the door on her way out. "A sonographer from OB will be here any moment." Teagan peers over her shoulder as she fiddles with the monitor, and types on the keyboard.

Walking across the room, Teagan opens a cabinet, pulling a white folded sheet from inside. "Being that it's early in the pregnancy, they need to do a vaginal ultrasound."

Without hesitation, Promise nods. Leaning back, she lifts her hips, trying to shimmy her panties off from beneath her dress, while Teagan steps out. "A little help?" Promise huffs.

"Lay back, Sugar." Promise leans back against the raised bed, and my palms slide up the sides of her thighs. I feel her skin prickle beneath my touch, and her pupils dilate. Hooking my fingers at the sides of her panties, she lifts her hips off the bed as I slip them off her body. Her face flushes.

"What's the matter, babe?"

"Must everything be sexual with you?" Promise fidgets.

"I'm not doing anything."

"Right." She drapes the sheet across her bottom half. Scooting to the edge of the bed, she places her feet in the stirrups Teagan already readied for her. "Stop looking at me that way—Like you want to devour me."

"I do." I have no shame in saying so.

"You're too good looking. I can't concentrate." Promise closes her eyes. "I can't look at you right now."

I burst with laughter. "I can't help the way I look, babe." Tucking her lace threads in my pocket, I stand at her side, lean down and kiss her lips. "I work with what God gave me. I can't help the way my body reacts around you no more than you can when you are near me."

There's a knock, followed by a new voice. "Ready?" An older woman steps into the room. "My name is Beverly, and I'll be performing the ultrasound today."

I smile down at Promise, who takes hold of my hand.

Beverly takes a seat, placing herself at the end of the exam table. "This will be a bit uncomfortable," she tells Promise.

My woman stares at the ceiling, a small twinge of discomfort appearing on her face as Beverly performs the ultrasound. My gaze shifts to the monitor screen, not knowing what I'm actually staring at.

"There." Beverly breaks the silence that had fallen in the room.

After tapping on the keyboard, she then points to the image in the screen. "I would say you look to be around six weeks." Six weeks?

I think back. That would have been around the night Promise walked into my life. Dropping my head, I look at my woman whose eyes are fixed on the screen, tears falling down her cheeks.

"That little blip is our baby? We created a human," Promise whispers in awe.

Suddenly the room fills with a rhythmic whooshing. "And that is the baby's heartbeat. It's steady and strong." Beverly says.

Everything around me fades, all but my woman, and the sounds of the baby she carries in her womb. I can't take my eyes off Promise as she continues to stare at the first images of the life we made. How did I get so fucking lucky? "I love you," I repeat those three words, finding satisfaction in the way it makes me feel.

Her watery eyes connect with mine. "Thank you."

"Babe." I swallow the lump of emotions stuck in my throat because I know why she said what she said.

"I finally have everything I ever wanted. I love you too, Cain."

Night has fallen by the time Promise is given the all-clear to leave the hospital, and we finally make it back to the clubhouse. As I'm helping her from the truck, she asks, "Did Sadie and London stick around?"

"Yeah, babe. Riggs texted me at the hospital, while I was bringing the truck around. They're both here."

"Good. I think I'll sleep better knowing they are close." Promise falls quiet for a minute as we walk to the entrance, tucked in close to my side. "And the biker?" she waits for my reply.

"You and Piper don't have to worry about him ever again." Opening the door and stepping inside, we find the place quiet, with a few of the guys lingering by the bar.

"It's unusually quiet here," I remark as Promise and I stop by the bar.

"Everyone turned in early. Rough day for a few of them." Riggs lifts his whiskey filled glass taking a sip. "Why don't the two of you join us for a drink? You could use it after the day we've had."

Promise, and I share a look, and my eyes fall to her stomach. "I think we'll call it an early night ourselves." I clasp my brother on the shoulder, before walking away from him and the others. "Catch ya in the mornin'," I call over my shoulder as we climb the stairs to the second floor.

"Can we stop and check on Piper?" Promise whispers just outside her bedroom door.

"Yeah, babe." Turning the handle, we peek inside, finding her asleep in her bed with her earbuds in her ears. I close the door quietly. "Come on." I guide Promise down the hall to my room.

Stripping her of her clothes, I slip one of my shirts over her head. "I have clothes I can go and get, Cain."

"Don't care, Sugar. You're not leavin' my sight. Besides, I like seeing you in my shirt."

"I have to admit, I like the smell of you against my skin." She smells the shirt then slides into bed, yawning.

I strip, slipping into bed beside my woman, pulling her close. Promise drapes her leg over mine, tucking her thigh between my legs, and rests her casted arm on my torso. Almost instantly, her breathing becomes heavy as her exhausted body finally relaxes. As soon as I think about it, I say it. "Marry me."

"What?" her sleep-filled voice asks.

"Marry me." Promise is silent for a moment, and I start to think I've spooked her.

"Okay." I feel her smile against my skin.

My hold on her tightens. "Damn. Where have you been all my life?"

"Waiting for you," Promise's whispers.

A moment later, Promise is softly snoring. It doesn't take long before I'm drifting off to sleep myself.

The following morning I wake to an empty bed and the smells of bacon and something sweet wafting through the air. How the hell did she slip out of bed without waking me? My body feels stiff as I move from the bed. Damn, I roll my shoulders on the way to the bathroom. I don't think I moved a muscle the entire night. Fuck. I rub my neck, then turn the faucet on. I splash cold water on my face to aid in waking my tired ass up. After doing a little grooming and brushing my teeth, I walk to the dresser, grabbing some clean clothes from the drawers. Dressed, I sit on the side of the bed, and lace up my boots, then grab my cut before exiting the bedroom. Heading down the hall, I shrug my cut on and listen to the voices coming from downstairs.

I find everyone gathered around the tables that have been pushed together, and the women carrying platters of food from the kitchen. Promise smiles as she walks toward me, holding a plate stacked with pancakes. "Good morning." She kisses me, and I deepen it.

"You snuck out again," I smirk, gripping her ass, and pulling her closer.

"Only to help cook breakfast. You were sleeping so well. I hated to disturb you."

I press my mouth to her ear, for only her to hear my next words. "Too bad. Because I woke up hungry—for you." Promise's breathing hitches. "As far as I'm concerned, the taste of your sweet pussy is all I need to start my day off right." My mouth lingers against her neck, and I feel her pulse against my lips.

"Jesus, Cain." Promise's airy whisper, as she tilts her head to the side, makes my cock twitch.

"You two lovebirds get your asses over here, I'm fuckin' starvin', and I'd like us to eat together this mornin'!" my brother yells from across the room. Making him wait, I grab the back of my woman's head, and claim her mouth with a deep passionate kiss, while giving Riggs the middle finger.

The room fills with laughter, and Promise's lips lift in a smile at the end of our kiss. "I love your family," she says with her lips still touching mine.

"Your family, babe." I pull back. "And they fuckin' love you too."

"Damn right we do," Kiwi speaks above the others chattering amongst themselves. "I'll love you even more if you bring those pancakes over here." The others laugh at his banter, and I chuckle.

"Come on." I walk with my woman to the tables, joining the family.

"Good morning, Daddy," Piper hugs my neck once I've settled in the chair beside her.

"How you feelin', Bean?" I kiss her temple.

Piper pours syrup over her pancakes, before locking eyes with me. "I'm good, Daddy." Then she drops her voice, low enough so only I can hear what she says. "I know I don't have to worry about that terrible man anymore." My daughter searches my eyes. Without me saying it aloud, she sees the truth behind them. She knows I'll do anything to keep her safe and is not naive to what the club does to make sure it stays that way.

I lovingly smile at my daughter, then pull her to me for a quick side hug. We say nothing more about the subject, letting it die right along with the motherfucker who did her wrong.

As we sit around the table, enjoying food and family, I can't help but be grateful for all that I have. At the head of the table, I watch my brother's interaction with his daughter. Riggs lifts her pink shirt, blowing raspberries on Aria's tummy, causing her to go into a fit of giggles. The way his face lights up with her laughter is contagious, and I find myself smiling too. Luna sits to the side, her face just as bright with happiness as she watches her husband.

I notice Promise watching them as well when I look at her.

Leaning into her, I whisper in her ear. "Should we tell them?" Promise tears her eyes away from my brother.

"You sure?"

"Yeah, babe."

Promise looks past me, watching Piper as she heads toward the kitchen. My woman's eyes are filled with so much love for my daughter. Our daughter, I correct myself. Ours. God, I fuckin love the way that sounds.

Promise tells me, "I'd like Piper to be the first to know."

Just when I thought my heart couldn't be any fuller, my woman proves otherwise. Though I'd like to be there when she tells her, I feel this could be another bonding opportunity for the two. I rub her thigh, where my hand is resting. "Go tell her."

Promise's eyes water. "Me?"

"Yeah, babe. Your mine. That makes Piper yours too." I continue to keep my voice low, not wanting the others to hear our conversation. "Go tell our girl she's going to be a big sister, and that we're getting hitched."

Promise struggles to keep her emotions at bay and lightly brushes my lips with hers before standing. I watch her walk away. Looking around the table, I catch Riggs' gaze fixed on me. He says nothing, but I feel that he knows. It's just a connection we have. Call it twin intuition if you want. Some people don't believe it's a thing, but I'd have no qualms telling anyone they don't know what the fuck they are talking about. The connection exists. It's been there our entire lives.

Just then, Piper burst through the kitchen door. Pushing my chair from the table, I stand, just before she barrels into me, hitting my chest like a linebacker. Her arms wrap around my waist, squeezing with all she has. Her action causes all talking to stop, and the room stills with silence. I don't have to look to know every eye is fixed on us. Tilting her head back, Piper looks at me, tears pooling in her eyes. "Does this mean you're happy?" I grin.

"It's about time," Piper says.

"Well, hell, don't leave the rest of us hanging," Tequila quips.

"Can I tell them?" Piper can hardly contain herself. Looking past her, my eyes land on Promise quietly standing a couple of feet away.

Promise nods, and I look back down at Piper. "Go for it."

"Alright, listen up." Piper makes a production out of it, waving her hands in the air. "I can't believe I'm saying this." She takes a deep breath, her excitement clear. "Promise and Daddy are going to get married, and I'm going to be a big sister!"

When I tell you, the room erupts like a bomb exploded, I'm not exaggerating. Everyone pushes from the table. The women converge upon Promise, and my brothers huddle around me, with words of congratulations.

"I fuckin knew it!" Riggs boasts, pulling me in for a hug. "Goddamn, I am so fuckin' happy for you, brother." It's a brief moment between us, and his words are short and to the point, but they mean the fucking world to me.

22

PROMISE

Sunlight filtering through the window wakes me from sleep, and I snuggle closer to the warm body wrapped around me from behind like a blanket. It's been a couple of weeks since Cain and I discovered I'm pregnant. It's also been the same amount of time since I officially moved in with him and Piper. Although I kind of didn't have much choice in the matter. I came home from a trip to the grocery store last week to find all my belongings unpacked and put away, hanging in the closet, and a few knickknacks and pictures of my mom and me strewn about the house. Mine and my mom's photos sitting on top of the mantle in the living room, amongst pictures of Piper, Cain's brothers, his grandfather, and grandmother, is the first thing I noticed when I walked through the door that day. Cain was in the kitchen standing over the sink, washing his grease-covered hands.

"Uh, honey." I eyed the photos and then Cain.

I was about to question why my photos were out when Cain gave me a look that said he dared me to say anything. Apparently, he took it upon himself to make my stay official without consulting me. And apparently, I had no problem with it because all I did was smile and say, "Okay." We are getting married and having a baby so me moving in was our last step in making everything official.

After getting over the initial shock of being pregnant, I have been riding cloud nine. I have fully embraced the idea of being a mother and can't wait to welcome mine and Cain's baby into the world. On that thought, my mind drifts to thoughts of my mother, and a sense of sadness washes over me. I would give anything in the world to have been able to share this moment with her. To be able to ask her advice and to have her pass along her wisdom on raising a child. But I'll never have that.

"What are you thinkin' about so hard, Sugar?" Cain's sleep filled voice fills the room.

I sigh. "How do you know I'm thinking about anything?"

"I know you, Promise. I felt you tense up about five seconds ago. Now tell me."

Careful of my wrist, I turn to face Cain. His hazel eyes meet mine. The man doesn't miss a thing when it comes to me. "I was thinking about my mom and how much I miss her. Especially now. She would have been the best grandmother," I choke out, and Cain pulls me in closer to him until my head rests against his chest.

"I wish there was something I could do or say to take that hurt from you, babe. But I can say that just because she's not here, doesn't mean she's not with you. She's still going to be our baby's grandmother. Because all the things your mom taught you, you will teach our kid. The wisdom and life lessons your mom passed down to you; you will pass down to our son or daughter. That's how we keep those we have lost alive. That is how their memories live on. Your mom is not with you physically, Promise, but she is with you spiritually. She lives inside you, babe. By us going on with our lives and living, that's the best way we honor our loved ones who are no longer on this earth."

I suck in a deep breath as I raise up on my elbow to look at Cain. He continues. "My grandmother taught me glassblowing. I know with every piece I make, she is with me. For me, that is how I keep her alive." Cain places his hand on my chest over my beating heart. "In here. I keep her here just as you do your mom. Never forget that, babe."

By the time Cain is finished speaking, I'm a blubbering mess. I don't know if it's because of his words or because of my crazy hormones. Maybe it's a little of both. "Thank you for saying that, honey." I lay my head back on his chest and get lost in the rhythm of his heartbeat. "You always know what I need, and I needed that," I whisper.

"Always, Sugar." The last thing I remember before falling back to sleep is Cain stroking my hair.

The next day I'm down at the office with London. A new client of mine just left, and London is gathering her things to go since she has court in an hour.

"Want me to bring you some lunch when I finish with court? Or we can go to Maggie's and see what her special is today."

I look up from my computer, my mouth salivating at the thought of Maggie's gumbo. "Let's hit up Maggie's. I haven't been there in weeks." I smile.

"Great." London slings her bag over her shoulder. "I'm out."

"Knock 'em dead, girl."

Thirty minutes later, I close my laptop and stretch my arm above my head, working out the kinks in my back. I have been working hard on a case involving a young woman whose boss made a pass at her, and when she declined his advance and called him out for inappropriate work behavior, she found herself fired two days later without cause. She came to London and me, asking for help. I'm going to enjoy nailing that jackass's balls to the wall.

A moment later, my tummy lets out a loud rumble. Knowing London won't be back for at least another hour, I decide to have a little snack to tide me over until lunch. Standing from my desk, I make my way to the back of the office to the small break room we have. There is a refrigerator, a kitchenette, and a four-seater table. Opening the fridge, I snag a cup of yogurt and a bottle of water, taking them to the front of the office in the little waiting area where we have a comfortable sofa that sits in front of a large window. The warm sun is shining through, and it feels good on my face. While enjoying my snack, I take the time to admire mine and London's finished office. The waiting area has grey walls that look fantastic with the exposed brick. The room has a sofa, four chairs, and a coffee station equipped with a mini-fridge with bottled water and juice. London and I both wanted a place where our potential clients could feel relaxed. Down the short hallway is where two rooms are located. One is my office—the other London's. The space is not grand, but it is perfect for us.

Remembering the framed artwork in the trunk of my car I bought over the weekend to hang in my office, I stand from the sofa and toss the empty yogurt cup in the trash. Once I grab my car keys from my purse, I make my way outside to the parking lot. Using my key fob, I pop the trunk. Just as I lean over to grab the canvas, I hear a noise behind me. Looking over my shoulder, I'm startled by a large man in a suit with buzzed hair and a menacing scowl on his face. I have no time to react before a burning sensation takes over my entire body, then everything goes black.

I slowly come around sometime later, disoriented. It takes several seconds for my memory to come flooding back to me, and when it does, I panic. Lurching forward into a seated position, the first thing I note is I'm on a bed in a bedroom. My eyes dart around the room. I take in my surroundings. Dark walls with stained molding. The place is enormous. There is a large black oak dresser directly in front of the king-size bed I'm lying on. Hanging on the wall above it is a flat-screen tv. The floor to ceiling window to my right is draped in charcoal grey curtains. On either side of the bed are tables that match the dresser. And directly above me is an extravagant chandelier.

"Good, you're awake," a familiar voice calls out from the bedroom door. I snap my head in that direction and suck in a sharp breath when Leon Velasco strolls in. He steps inside the room, and I take in his usual power suit, slicked-back hair, and dark empty eyes. He takes several steps in my direction, causing me to jerk back. And when I try jumping off the bed, I'm halted by a pair of steel handcuffs around my uninjured wrist. "What am I doing here? Let me go." My voice shakes as a sudden bout of nausea threatens to take over. It's also then I remember being knocked unconscious. My first thought is of the baby. "What did you do to me? Did you give me something?"

"You weren't injected with anything. Harvey only tasered you. The shock was harmless."

"Harmless? Please, you have to let me go," I plead. "I'm pregnant. I have to make sure my baby..." I don't get the chance to finish my sentence because the next thing I know Leon is in my face with his fist in my hair, wrenching my head back.

"You let that piece of shit biker defile you?!" he roars, his face turning red. I cry out in pain as he continues. "You had to make me do this the hard way. You couldn't just accept that you were supposed to belong to me. Instead, you opened your legs to a King. Now, look what's happened. Now I'm forced to get rid of it."

At his words, my stomach sinks, and I swallow down the bile that rises in my throat. He can't mean what I think he means.

"Please," I plead again. "Let me go." I try jerking away from Leon's grasp; only he's too strong.

"You're not going anywhere. First, I'm going to deal with your little mistake. Then I'm going to work on bringing you to heel. It's time you face the fact you belong to me now, Promise."

"You're crazy. When Cain finds me, he's going to kill you." This time when I speak, my tone is steady and confident.

Leon tugs on my hair again, making me wince. "Repeat his name and you will suffer the consequences." He lets me go and makes his way back across the room. Just as he reaches the door, he turns back. "We can do things the easy way or the hard way. I'll give you some time to decide."

Hours have passed, and I'm still alone in the room, cuffed to the bed, my bladder on the verge of exploding. I spent an hour trying to wiggle free of the handcuffs with no avail. All I managed to do was rub the skin around my wrist raw, to the point, it's starting to bleed.

Cain has to know by now I'm missing. I'm sure London suspected something was wrong as soon as she got back to the office. I should have taken Leon's advances over the last few months more seriously.

At first, I thought it was harmless. Creepy, but nothing to be concerned about. I knew from representing him he was a dangerous man, but I never expected he would go as far as to kidnap me. Cain said if Leon were a smart man, he would heed his warning to stay away. Leon has proven he is not very smart. Men like Velasco think they're untouchable.

The problem with thinking you are untouchable is you underestimate certain people. In Leon's case, he underestimated Cain and The Kings.

The click of the lock on the bedroom door causes me to tense. Leon's earlier threat has me sick with fear and on high alert. But it is not Leon who enters the room. It is the man who tasered and kidnapped me. He doesn't speak as he advances toward the bed. I squirm and hug my body as close to the headboard as possible. "What are you going to do?"

'The man doesn't speak as he reaches into his pocket, producing a key. When he grabs my arm, I begin to struggle. "Don't touch me."

The guy's vice-like grip tightens. "Stop," he spits as he uncuffs me from the bed.

"Let's go." The man tugs on the end of the cuffs, and I have no choice but to climb off the bed and follow him. He leads me to the other side of the room to the bathroom. Walking inside, he stops next to the toilet, and he jerks his chin. "Go."

Mortification sets in as I realize he expects me to pee in front of him. He can't be serious.

"I don't need a babysitter."

"You either squat and piss now or hold it until morning. Your choice but I'm not waitin' all day for you to make it. I have better things to do than deal with Leon's latest whore. Now fuckin' go."

"Can you at least turn around?"

When the guy doesn't answer and continues to stare at me, I decide I have to swallow my embarrassment. Or rather, my bladder decides for me.

Swallowing the lump in my throat, I wiggle my pants, along with my underwear down my thighs. I try not to flash the asshole in front of me. By the hungry look on his face and the way he licks his lips, I'd say he's enjoying the view.

"I think I'm going to ask the boss if I can have a little taste. He's had no problems sharing his whores in the past."

The guy's vile comments make my skin crawl. I do my best to ignore him as I finish my business. Once I'm done, he tugs me back over to the bed where he cuffs me to the headboard once again. "Be a good little whore." He gets one last dig in before he exits the room, locking it behind him.

More time passes, and soon I'm no longer able to fight off the sleep that is hell bent on taking me. My last thoughts before darkness takes over are of Cain as I send up a silent prayer hoping he finds me.

Sometime later, I'm jarred awake by the bedroom door bursting open. Leon walks in stone-faced with his lackey trailing behind. "It's time, Promise."

For some reason, those three words out of Leon's mouth sends a chill down my spine. He and his goon advance in my direction. My eyes dart between him and Leon. "What's going on? What are you doing?" I start to panic as Leon's goon grabs hold of me and presses my body into the bed. "Get the hell off me!" I start flailing and kicking my legs.

"This is for the best, Promise. We can't start our new life with you carrying that scum's baby," Leon sneers as he stands back in the shadows.

"You can't do this! You can't take my baby! Please! Please don't do this!" I continue to struggle. My attempts to free myself get me nowhere. And I'm proven right when another zap of liquid heat takes over my body, and I'm forced into darkness once again.

The next time I wake, my body is freezing. My eyes flutter open, and I note I'm no longer in the bedroom. My vision is blurry, and the only thing I can make out are the concrete walls that surround me. I blink my eyes several more times, but no matter how hard I try, I can't seem to focus. I'm cold. Why am I so cold?

"Relax. This will all be over soon."

I blink my eyes again and try to focus on where that voice is coming from. "What's happening?" I try lifting my arm to my face, but it feels like lead. Twisting my neck, I look down at my arm to see an IV in it. Oh, God! My baby!

"Please," my words slur. "Don't take my baby."

23

NOVA

Reloading my gun, I hang another target, then press the button, watching the paper flutter as the track pulls it to the far end of the shooting range. Everything is finally getting back to normal. I had my hearing on the charges I was facing a few days ago. Luckily, I didn't have to do any jail time. The judge reduced my charges, leaving me to pay a heavy fine, which I paid in full before I left the courthouse the same day.

Even though the dust has settled, and the threat of the Punisher's wayward brother is no longer an issue, I still feel a sense of unease. A looming feeling that won't go away. Which is why I'm here, at the range, instead of the bar tending to my usual duties. I know Promise needs to get back to life, and her law practice, but the need to make sure her and Piper stay safe is still strong. So, for several days now, I've stayed close enough to put my mind at ease but far enough to give her space to work.

Sliding my ear covers on, I widen my stance and aim at my target. Before I can pull the trigger, Kiwi's raised voices shouting my name alerts me to something being wrong. The headphone is ripped from my head, and I toss them to the counter in front of me. I take in his expression and my gut wrenches.

"Promise is gone," he tells me.

"What the fuck do you mean gone?"

"Let's talk while you follow me to the security room." Kiwi turns on his heel, and I follow. "London burst through the store doors seconds ago. Said she found the trunk of Promise's car open, her keys laying on the ground, and Promise nowhere to be found." The door to the security room flies open, bouncing off the wall behind it with a loud thud. Tapping feverishly, Kiwi pulls up the feed from outside Promise's building across the street. As he rewinds the history of the footage, my breath catches in my throat.

"Shit." Kiwi's eyes dart to mine, before looking back at the computer screen. We watch the twelve seconds of footage. A giant of a man, wearing a black suit comes up behind my unsuspecting woman. I hone in on what he's holding in his hand but can't quite make it out. That is until he points it at her, and I watch her body convulse before her knees buckle, and she falls to the pavement. The man scoops her in his arms, just as a black sedan rolls into view. I instantly recognize the man the moment his face comes into focus. He's one of Velasco's men. His goon loads her in the backseat, then disappears into the car himself before the vehicle takes off. Everything happens in less than a minute.

My phone is at my ear, calling my brother as I rush toward the front of the store.

"How's it goin'?" Riggs' voice sounds chipper.

My voice cracks. "Promise was taken." Stalking into another room, I punch in a code unlocking a gun safe. Reaching inside, I grab a sawed-off double-barrel shotgun, then load my pockets with shells.

There's a commotion in the background as my brother barks out orders. "Who?"

"Velasco."

"Fuckin' hell." He knows what this means. We are about to go up against a notorious drug kingpin. I also know my club will go to war against anyone. "Kiwi, still with you?"

"At my side," I tell him as Kiwi loads himself with a few extra clips.

"Location?" Riggs asks, and I briefly take my phone from my ear, texting him the details, then press it to my ear again.

"Just sent his address."

"The rest of us will meet you there." He disconnects the call, and I shove my phone in my pocket. "Fuck!" I put my fist through the wall. He took her right out from under my goddamn nose.

For the past two years, Velasco has been one of the leading criminals bringing drugs, and death to our city, Louisiana and the surrounding states. Velasco is not your run of the mill street dealer and has not been much of a problem locally. Up until his recent run-in with the law. Up until now, his bullshit has never been enough to start a war. Today I plan to end it before it begins. "Shit. Where the hell is London?" I remember the moment we hit the front of the store.

"I told her to take her ass to the clubhouse. The girls will let her in."

"Good thinkin'." We bust out the double doors, stepping out into the muggy air, the skies ominous with dark storm clouds. Cain. I hear Promise's voice in my head as I strap the shotgun to the side of my bike. "I'm comin' for you, babe,' ' I say out loud as if she were here as I fire up the engine.

Dread pools in my gut with thoughts of something awful happening to her and the baby. I take off down the road, with Kiwi riding at my side. As we maneuver our bikes through the city streets, I can't help but feel like I've let my woman down. I was supposed to protect her, and that doesn't sit well with me. I should have killed the motherfucker weeks ago. Nerves eat at my insides, knowing two lives are at stake.

Doing my best, I shake those thoughts from my head. Right now, getting to her in time is all that matters to me. Even if that means giving my life to save hers and my unborn child.

Before long, the building Velasco resides in comes into view. So do my other club members who merge with us as we cruise down the road, with Riggs leading the way. Our approach becomes muffled by the sound of thunder overhead, just before heavy sheets of rain begin to fall. Throwing his hand in the air, we roll to a dead stop, keeping out of sight on the side of a vacant warehouse. Riggs signals, warning us of the men posted at each side of the building's front entrance.

We kill our engines, and I reach down, unstrapping my shotgun. Rain-soaked, we seek refuge within the abandoned building. As Riggs goes over how we will execute our following actions, I zone out. My imagination starts fucking with my head. Visions of what my woman could be going through and what we might walk in on consume my every thought. Fear of the unknown takes up all my headspace.

"Cain." My brother's voice cracks the surface, and I look at him.

"Focus." He eyes me for a second until he is confident that I'm paying attention. "Good. Now, listen. We're going in completely blind. So, we have no idea the odds that may be stacked against us. Wick, Fender, take out the two fuckers keeping watch, then I want you both covering all outside exits." Wick and Fender nod, then take off. Riggs finds Everest and Kiwi to his left. "Once Nova and I gain entrance, I want the two of you to start searching the first floor. Take out anyone associated with Velasco." Kiwi and Everest nod.

My brother averts his attention to me, grasping my shoulder with a firm grip. "She's your woman. You take the lead this time. We've got your back."

"Velasco is mine," I say with venom.

"Wouldn't have it any other way," Riggs confirms. "Ready?"

"Let's do this."

From there, everything moves so fast you hardly know it's even happening. We hear the signal to go the moment gunshots ring out. Charging toward the entrance, I notice Velasco's two men, on the ground, unmoving. The rain is still pelting at our backs, but I can make out their faces as the same men Kiwi and I ran into weeks ago. We enter the building guns raised. Riggs fires off a shot, and a man, sitting behind a desk with his weapon aimed at us, hits the wall behind him, then falls to the floor before he gets the chance to pull the trigger.

Following orders, Kiwi and Everest take to the stairs, as Riggs follows me to the only elevator. Pressing the penthouse button, the doors close, and we ascend three floors to the top. The moment the doors open, exposing the hallway leading into the suite, we're met with silence.

Advancing down the short corridor, we approach the door with caution. A suited man, with his gun raised, suddenly appears, and bullets whiz by my head, piercing the wall behind us. Falling back, Riggs and I take cover by jumping back into the elevator.

"Shit." I breathe heavily. "That was too close for comfort, brother."

Riggs tries peering around the opened door, and Velasco's goon fires off several rounds, luckily missing my brother, who wastes no time returning fire. The thud I hear lets me know the man is dead before we step out of the elevator.

Stepping over the man's lifeless body, we pause just outside Velasco's door. Grasping the handle, I give it a turn, finding it unlocked. Dumb fuck. Giving each other a look, my brother and I ready ourselves for what could be waiting for us on the other side.

Bursting through the doors, we rush in, guns raised.

The fuck?

The place appears to be empty. Riggs goes one way, and I the other. We canvas the entire top floor suite, searching every room, only to find each baron. We meet back at the entrance. "No one's here," Riggs states, appearing to be just as frustrated as I am.

No. I'm certain Promise is here. I feel in my bones. "She's in the building. Don't ask me how I know, I just do." Riggs nods, not questioning how I feel.

His phone rings. Taking it from his pocket, he answers, while we take off for the elevator once more. All this running round, cat and mouse shit is wasting time. "Report," he barks. Putting it on speaker, I hear the desperation in Kiwi's voice.

"We found Promise, but we can't get to her." In the background, I listen to what I believe to be muffled screams for help. Every hair on my body stands on end. My eyes fix on Riggs, as the elevator descends, feeling more like a long ride to the gates of hell. "Shit!" Kiwi yells with frustration.

"Location," my brother demands.

"Basement. You can only access it using the stairs. A keypad is the only way into the room. I managed to pry the cover off to attempt an override of the system. I'm cross-connecting wires now."

"Keep at it. We're on our way." Riggs shoves his phone away.

We dart for the stairwell as soon as the elevator doors open. Exactly one flight down, we run into Everest, his gun aimed in our direction. His arm lowers immediately. Behind him, we find Kiwi fumbling with wires in a desperate attempt to disarm the system. On the other side of the metal door—silence. Nothing like the fearful screams heard over the phone just seconds ago. I place my ear to the surface of the door, straining for signs that my woman is okay.

Crying.

I hear Promise crying, followed by pleas—her asking the sorry son of a bitch to let her go.

"I think I've got it," Kiwi says, and my head jerks back, waiting for something to happen. The locking mechanism in the door clicks, and I hold my breath when I push the handle down. In the fraction of a second, the four of us enter the small, dank room, none of us prepared for what we see. Promise is strapped to a table. An older man in a lab coat is looming over her. He's caught off guard by our intrusion and spins around. The slug from my shotgun finds its mark, dropping the guy on the spot.

Promise cries out for me. "Cain," her voice hoarse from screaming.

Before we make another move, Velasco steps from the shadows. He presses the end of a 9mm against the side of Promise's head, and her body physically trembles with terror. My breathing stalls, and I push back the bile, threatening to rise up my throat. "Move one more inch, and I'll kill her."

"You have nowhere left to go, Velasco, and the four to one odd aren't in your favor." The shotgun in my hand feels like an extension of my arm as I keep it aimed at his chest.

"Cain," Promise whimpers, her eyes full of fear. "He was going to kill our baby."

"Shut up," Velasco yells. "Just. Shut. Up. I could have given you anything you ever wanted, and you chose this good for nothing biker trash over me."

A rage I've never felt before makes its way to the surface from the depth of my soul, and my body starts to vibrate. My woman being strapped down to a table with a gun trained on her will forever be ingrained in my memory.

What would have happened had I not made it to her in time?

Shaking those thoughts away, I focus on the here and now—on retribution. "Promise," I call to her, keeping my voice neutral, but firm. "Eyes on me." She listens, locking her eyes with mine. "You trust me, babe?" Without hesitating, she nods.

"Don't fucking talk to him, you cunt." Velasco's eyes become wild, darting from face to face in the room. To my right, something falls, and the already jumpy Velasco swings his weapon in the direction of the noise, shooting off a wild round. His carelessness gives me the opening we need. Riggs fires a shot of his own, right through Velasco's hand. The gun he was holding, slips through his fingers, falling to the floor.

Without missing a beat, I close the few yards between us. Holding his bloody hand, and with nowhere to run, Velasco's back smacks against the concrete wall. I press the sharp end of my sawed-off shotgun into his flesh and blow a hole in his chest the size of Texas. His eyes widen, and he gurgles as blood bubbles from his mouth. Immediately blood seeps from his chest wound in massive quantities, soaking his crisp white shirt in crimson.

I watch the life drain from his eyes before his legs give way, and his body slides to the floor, where he takes his last strangled breath.

Knowing Velasco is dead, I rush to my woman's side, my eyes roaming her body as my brothers unbind the leather straps pinning her to the cold hard table. My hands exam every inch of her looking for injuries. "What the fuck is in the IV bag?" I notice the needle stuck in the flesh of her arm.

"Simple saline fluid." Riggs skillfully removes the needle. "But there's an empty syringe on the table—a mild sedative."

"Cain, I think he gave me something that knocked me out earlier too. Oh my God, Cain. The baby." Promise throws her arms around my neck as I lift her from the table. Pulling her to my chest, I carry her from the room.

"I've got you, babe." I keep moving as my brother, Kiwi and Everest lead us out of the building. Worry settles in my stomach, knowing whatever Velasco injected her with could harm the baby. "Someone get a hold of Teagan," I order to no one in particular. All that matters is that she's waiting at the clubhouse when we get there. The rain has stopped, and the sun beats down on our faces the instant we rush out the door, into the street, where we find Wick and Fender in wait.

"I think I should go to the hospital, Cain."

"No hospital, babe. You saw what just happened back there. They'll ask questions we can't answer. I promise we'll take care of you. You need to trust me," I tell her.

"I trust you," Promise says, and it's all I needed to hear.

Realizing Promise will need to ride on the back of my bike, I carefully set her on her feet once we get back to where we left them. She seems a little wobbly at first but otherwise okay. "Babe, I'm going to need you to hold on as tight as you can. Think you have enough strength to do that?" I brush the hair from her face.

"I won't let go." Her red-rimmed eyes stare back at me.

With weapons stowed away, and Promise huddled against my back, holding me tight, we roll out, headed for our side of town. Finding it hard not to think about our baby, the ride back to the clubhouse house feels longer than usual. I'm not much of a praying man, but I do believe in a higher power. So, I pray, hoping he hears me.

After arriving at the clubhouse, everything is a blur. London is near frantic as I carry Promise upstairs to my room where Teagan examines her. "She seems to be okay, considering all that she's been through, and Riggs was smart enough to bring the syringe found at the scene. They used a mild sedative," Teagan states as she tosses her stethoscope into her bag. "It would take several strong doses of sedatives to cause any concerns when it comes to the baby. To be sure and ease both your minds, I brought a portable ultrasound machine."

There's a light knock at the door, followed by Piper's concerned voice. "Daddy. Is everything okay?" I open the door to find not only Piper but damn near every set of eyes in the clubhouse huddled in the hallway, staring back at me. Piper glances past me at Promise, who is lying in bed.

"Teagan was just about to check the baby. Would you like to come in?"

"Promise won't mind?" She is hesitant to step into the room.

"I don't mind," Promise states, her voice hinting at how exhausted she is. As Piper crosses the room, I go to close the door.

"Wait."

Stopping, I look over my shoulder.

"Leave it open. I want the family to hear it too," Promise adds, and the emotions I've been holding back for so long make themselves known. My eyes become misty as I reopen the door. Everyone squeezes their way into my small room, including her best friend, London.

Piper slides into bed beside Promise, as Teagan rolls the waistband of Promise's jeans down, stopping just shy of her panty line. Teagan warms a small packet of jelly between her hands before peeling it open and squeezing it out onto Promise's abdomen. Promise holds out her hand, and I take it in mine.

I hold my breath, as Teagan moves the doppler around. There's a faint whoosh, and the room falls silent. Reaching over, Teagan turns a small nob, increasing the volume output of the machine.

The room fills with the sound of our baby's heartbeat.

Promise starts to cry, and relief washes over me. Releasing the breath I was holding, I lean down, kissing my woman. "I fuckin' love you so much." Emotions cause my voice to crack. I gather my girls into my arms, thankful for all that I have, and grateful my prayers were answered.

EPILOGUE

Nova

"What the hell you sittin' over here sulkin' about brother?"

Riggs takes a seat next to me at the bar. The whole family is here getting ready to head to Piper's graduation. The women are upstairs fussing over my daughter now, helping her get ready.

"I'm not sulkin'," I grumble.

Riggs calls me out on my lie with a look. He knows better.

"Fine. My baby is growin' up too damn fast. It seems like just yesterday I was walkin' her into school on her first day of kindergarten. Now she's graduating high school. Not only that, she's officially an adult."

It's true. Piper turned eighteen four days ago. This evening after her graduation, the whole family is heading to Pop's to celebrate her finishing high school and her birthday. I asked her a couple of days before her birthday what she wanted, and I wasn't surprised by her answer when she said she wanted to do something with just her family. But that's Piper. To her, family is everything. While most kids her age want to hang out with friends and see what trouble they can get into, my little girl is happy hanging with her old man, Gampy, and her uncles.

"She decide what to do about college?" my brother asks.

"Not really. I've been laying off her about it. Don't want to stress her out or say too much to sway her decision. Piper knows I want her close, but I don't want her feeling like she has to base her decision on what will make me happy."

"My niece likes being around her family too much. I'll bet money she'll stick close to home."

"Fuck, I hope so, brother. But I'll support her either way."

I take a pull of my beer when Riggs asks another question. "Where does Piper stand with her mom?"

"I asked her if she wanted to invite Madison to her graduation, but she said she wasn't ready for that yet. When it comes to her mom, she's not all the way there. Hell, she's not even halfway there, but she's trying. It's going to take time."

Riggs and I are quiet for a minute before he speaks again. "What the fuck is takin' those women so long? Swear to Christ."

I chuckle. "Beats me. Those women have been getting ready since seven o'clock this mornin'. Promise took Piper to Sadie's to get her hair and nails done. Then she informed me they were goin' shoppin' for a new dress and shoes." I shake my head. "Don't see why women need new clothes and shoes for every occasion."

"Beats the hell out of me, man. I stopped tryin' to figure women out a long damn time ago."

The sound of the clubhouse door opening draws mine and Riggs' attention. I turn on my stool to see Kiwi, Fender, and Everest strolling in. Behind them is Wick, Tequila, and Sydney.

"Hey, brother. When did you all get back in town?" I ask Wick as he and Tequila sidle up to the bar. They took Sydney to Nevada to see her mom. They've been gone almost a week.

"Got back last night. You know we wouldn't miss Piper graduating, man."

"Speaking of," Tequila cuts in, "Where is she? Doesn't the ceremony start in an hour?" She looks down at her watch.

"Piper's upstairs with the women gettin' ready." I turn to Sydney, who is standing close to Tequila. "Hey, darlin'. Why don't you go upstairs and see what the ladies are doin'? While you're at it, see if you can rile them up. We need to hit the road."

"Okay." Sydney giggles and takes off up the stairs.

An hour and a half later, all my brothers and I are sitting outside on the bleachers while we wait for Piper's name to be called so she can walk across the makeshift stage on the football field and accept her diploma. Promise is tucked in close to my side with a massive smile on her face. Her friends, London, Sadie, and Ruby, are here too.

"Look." Promise taps my thigh. "Piper is up next. This is so exciting."

I grin at how giddy my woman is for my little girl.

"Piper LeBlanc!" the principal calls out over the loudspeaker. And as my little girl makes her way across the stage, the whole first row of the bleaches stands and cheers. "Fuck, yeah, baby girl!" I cup my hands over my mouth and shout.

"Whoo-hoo!" This comes from beside me, where Promise is jumping up and down.

"That's our girl!" Riggs, Pop, Wick, Kiwi, Everest and Fender all shout in unison. We get a few disgruntled looks from some of the folks in the crowd, but my brothers and I don't give a damn.

I watch my daughter shake the principal's hand and accept her diploma. Piper turns toward her family, wearing a prideful smile on her face. She raises her diploma in the air with one hand, then gives us devil horns, and shouts, "Hell, yeah! I did it, Daddy!" Her show of celebration causes all of us to roar with laughter.

That's my girl.

I have a hard time keeping the smile off my face as I watch Piper exit the stage and make her way back to her seat until I hear the roar of Harley pipes in the distance. I turn and look over my shoulder. That's when I see Crow and Madison riding out of the parking lot of the school.

"Was that...?"

I shove my hands in my front pockets. "Yep."

"Did Piper decide to invite her?"

"No. She wasn't ready. But I'm not surprised she came anyway. As long as she keeps her distance and lets Piper come to her when she's ready, I won't interfere."

Promise wraps her arm around my middle and snuggles closer to me. "It'll all work out. Just give it some time."

"Yeah, sugar, you're right." I lean in and kiss her.

Later in the night, we are sitting around a fire at Pop's place with our bellies full of his kickass catfish and hush puppies.

My brother hands his daughter to Luna, then stands from his seat. "Listen up. I got somethin' I'd like to say." All chatter stops, as everyone's eyes settle on Riggs. He clears his throat. "Piper. It feels like only yesterday when I arrived home on leave from the military and was helpin' your dad change your shitty diapers."

Piper giggles, "Oh my God, Uncle Abe. I'm tryin' to eat here," she says with food in her mouth as chocolate squishes out the sides of her s'more.

Riggs continues. "Or when your Gampy and I came to the rescue, when you were five years old, and sick with fever. The three of us rotated in shifts, and pulled all-nighters for three nights straight until you were feeling better. Your dad was sometimes too proud to ask for help, but we gave it anyway."

Most teenagers would probably cringe with embarrassment by now, but Piper is sitting near the fire, with her legs crossed, with nothing but love in her eyes and a smile on her face as she listens to her uncle speak. "Or the time you started your period on your first day of middle school. You called your dad cryin'," Riggs chuckles. "Your dad had no clue what he should do, so we tackled it like we always did—together. He drove to that school, dried your tears, then took you for ice cream. Wick was in town that week." Riggs looks in Wick's direction, "Do you remember, brother?" Wick throws his head back laughing hard. My brother continues. "I think Wick and I bought out the entire feminine product aisle at the local drugstore and had it all waitin' for you when you got home."

Some of us are holding our stomachs we're laughing so hard, but Riggs keeps going. "Okay. Getting serious for a minute." My brother pulls in a long breath. "Piper. You've been one of the greatest blessings to come into our lives. You've been raised by a bunch of knuckleheaded, Harley-ridin' bikers," Riggs' eyes cut to Pop, "and a hard lovin' cantankerous old man, but you've givin' us so much more than we could have ever givin' you. You've grown into a beautiful, caring young woman—despite all our tumbles along the way. I know I speak for every damn person sittin' here today when I say, I'm so fuckin' proud of you." Without any warning, Piper stands and rushes to Riggs, burying her face in his chest.

"I love you so much, Uncle Abel."

He kisses the top of her head. "I love you too."

I think the reminiscing and the sharing portion of this night is over once Piper returns to her quilt, spread out on the grass, but my brother continues. "Cain." My eyes leave the flames dancing on the fire, and settle on my brother's face. "You're a good father, and the best damn brother and friend a man could ask for. We've had our shares of hard times, been through a lot of changes and growin' throughout our forty-one years, but I've always had you by my side. I couldn't imagine it being any different." Riggs clears his throat again, and I swallow the lump of emotions clogging mine. "Promise." He directs his attention to my woman. "Cain waited a long damn time for the right one to come along. I can tell you now; he didn't realize he was lookin' for the other half of his soul until he found you." His gaze briefly leaves Promise to look at his wife. "I should know. Love has a way of sneakin' up on you when you least expect it."

Promise sniffles, and I rub my hand that I have tucked between her knees against her skin. My brother scans over each of us men before looking back at Promise and me. "I just realized I've never officially said this." He raises the beer in his hand. "Welcome to the family."

The silence around us is broken with cheers. Leaning back, I smile so hard my face hurts. I'm the luckiest fucking man alive. I got my daughter sitting beside me, my woman on my lap, my baby in her belly and my ring on her finger. I'd say life doesn't get any sweeter than this.

Seven month later

"CAIN."

My eyes open when Promise calls my name. I bolt upright in the bed and find her side empty along with a large wet spot on the sheets. I look across the room to see her standing inside the bathroom door, cradling her round belly.

"My water broke."

I blink several times before the situation registers. "Fuck!"

Tossing the blanket aside, I climb out of bed, snagging my jeans off the floor, pulling them on. In a rush, I open the dresser and grab a t-shirt. As I'm making my way to the nightstand to retrieve my wallet and keys, I trip over my boots. My ass tumbles to the floor. "Son of a bitch," I grumble.

Promise giggles. "Cain, are you okay?"

"Fine," I grit as I pick my ass up off the floor, sit on the edge of the bed and pull my boots on.

"Is everything okay in here?" A sleepy-eyed Piper asks from the doorway of the bedroom. "I felt the house shake."

Piper's statement causes Promise to giggle harder. "Your dad tripped and fell."

"Oh. Are you guys going somewhere? It's the middle of the night?"

"Promise's water broke, Bean," I tell her.

Piper suddenly looks more awake. "Oh, my God! Really?"

"Yup. So, if you could get dressed, we can get a move on."

"I'll be ready in two minutes." Piper dashes back down the hall to her room with a squeal of excitement in her tone.

With the three of us ready, I carry Promise's overnight bag in one hand and help her down the porch steps and to the truck with the other. Piper takes the bag from me and climbs into the back seat. Before jumping into the truck herself, Promise faces me and cups my face. "Let's go have a baby."

I rest my forehead against hers and kiss her lips. "Let's go have a baby, Sugar."

Ten hours and seventeen minutes later, Jaxson came into this world, kicking and screaming. He weighed in at nine pounds three ounces. My son has his mother's dark hair and hazel eyes like mine. In other words, he is perfect. So perfect, I can't stop staring at him. Promise and I both agreed to name him after her father who passed away and my grandfather.

"Are you going to hog him all night?"

I look over at Promise, who is lying in bed, glowing with happiness. "Yes," I grin, telling her the truth before leaning in and kissing her.

I peer down at my son then back at my woman. "I'm so fuckin' proud of you, Sugar. You did good, babe."

Her face softens. "Thanks, honey."

The hospital room door opens, and Piper sticks her head in. "Can we come in yet?" You can hear the excitement in her voice. And by we, I know she means the entire family. I called them on the way to the hospital, and they've been patiently waiting to meet our newest member.

"Yeah, Bean. Tell everyone we're ready."

A minute later, the door opens again and leading the pack, the patriarch of LeBlanc men, Pop.

Filing in behind him is Riggs and Luna, who is holding their daughter. Behind them are Wick, Tequila, Sydney, Kiwi, Fender, and Everest. Behind the guys are London, Sadie, Ruby, and Jackson. Even though my woman washed her hands of the toxic relationship she had with her step-father, and Avery, she still has a strong bond with her step-brother.

Once my brothers and family have gathered around the hospital bed, I announce with pride. "Everyone. I'd like you to meet Jaxson Abraham LeBlanc."

Then my eyes drop to tell my son. "Welcome to The Kings family."

www.ingramcontent.com/pod-product-compliance
Lightning Source LLC
Chambersburg PA
CBHW072114300726
48975CB00003B/809